The Power of Blood

LIES THE DEAD TELL: BOOK 2

H.B. LYNE

Published in 2022

Copyright © H. B. Lyne 2022

H.B. Lyne asserts the moral right under the Copyright,
Designs and Patents Act 1988 to be identified as the author
of this work.

1

All Rights reserved. No part of this publication may be
reproduced, stored in a retrieval system, or transmitted, in
any form or by any means without the prior written
consent of the publisher, nor be otherwise circulated in any
form of binding or cover other than that in which it is
published and without a similar condition being imposed
on the subsequent purchaser.

ACKNOWLEDGEMENTS

My awesome Patrons; Andy, Linzy, Monica,
Emé, Faye, and Jay

My editor; Zoë Markham
My cover designer; Olivia Pro Design
My formatter; Julia at Evenstar Books

My writing buddies who encouraged this work; Angeline,
Julia, Shane, Sacha, Meg, Matt, Scott
and many more!

My mentors; Becca and Elli

ARE WE A PERFECT MATCH?

The Power of Blood is dark urban fantasy. In these pages you won't find sparkly vampires or teenage heroines with perfect hair.

This is NOT a romance. There are dark themes and scenes that may be of a distressing nature.

I write dark, gritty, emotionally compelling stories filled with flawed protagonists, anti-heroes and deliciously dark villains.

There will be plot twists that bring out your most colourful language and yes, I write in British English.
If any of these things bother you, turn back now.

If however, darkness is your poison, then read on and lose yourself in the shadows for a while.

CHAPTER ONE

FOR THE FIRST TIME IN MY LIFE, I was relieved when Christmas was over. It just wasn't the same without my parents. Sure, I was in a serious relationship for the first time, but that was complicated. My best friend was hardly speaking to me and was grieving for his mum too. It was all a big mess. We'd all lost people and this veil of sadness hung heavily over everyone I knew.

So, I was looking forward to the New Year's Eve party that Antonio was taking me to, despite it being this big, fancy ball with all of the city's most powerful people and worrying that I wouldn't fit in or have anyone to talk to. It was the kind of thing that I needed to shake me out of the slump that I'd been in.

I looked myself up and down in the floor-length mirror in Antonio's room. I'd bought a new dress for the occasion and hardly recognised myself. The soft, black fabric was velvety and shimmered slightly in the light. It draped across my collarbones and had long sleeves, but plunged loosely at the back, exposing my pale skin. It cascaded to the floor with a mermaid-style skirt. I was barely balancing in my super-high heels and ran my hands down the dress to smooth it out. I'd curled my hair and let it hang over my right shoulder. I was wearing bright red lipstick for the first time in my life.

'You look good enough to eat,' Antonio said from behind me, his Italian accent lightly caressing his lips. I looked over my shoulder at him leaning in the dressing room doorway, fitting his cufflinks without taking his eyes off me.

'Coming from you, that means something extra. You know that, right?'

'I did not choose my words accidentally.' He smiled his stunning lopsided smile. He was wearing a crisp, black tuxedo and white shirt, with a dark red tie and waistcoat. His long, black hair was tied back in a sexy man bun that I found irresistible. He ambled across the plush carpet to me and laid a soft kiss on my neck. I gazed at our reflections in the mirror and was struck by what an incredible couple we made. The huge, low bed was a mess from our marathon love-making session earlier that day. The drapes and blinds were open, revealing a star-studded sky outside.

'Careful now,' I said, smirking. 'No pre-dinner drinks.'

'I wouldn't dream of it,' he murmured against my skin. His lips were cool and there was no rush of breath. Despite what one might think on seeing him so clearly in a mirror, Antonio Vitale was a vampire. I turned to face him and slipped my hands around the back of his neck. I didn't dare kiss him and ruin my lipstick, but I gazed into his eyes.

'Do I really look okay for a ball?'

'You look perfect. You'll fit right in, if that's what you're worried about. But I'm hopelessly biased and think you look stunning in anything.'

'Fit in? So you don't think I'll turn heads, then?' I feigned bruised feelings with a pout. He wasn't falling for it. He held eye contact, unblinking, and held me tight against his body.

'That is not what I meant and you know it. You'll outshine the lot of them. I know you, Eve. I know you don't want to be noticed. I know that you've spent your whole life trying to hide your exceptional gifts. But you don't have to do that any more. You're allowed to stand out.'

'Thank you,' I said, my cheeks burning and the corners of my eyes prickling. I shook my head to clear away the swell of emotion. 'We should get downstairs.'

Antonio released me and checked his watch. He nodded and held out his hand. I took it and scooped up my sequinned clutch from the vanity. We headed out of his huge bedroom and along the landing to the grand, sweeping staircase that led down to the foyer. The chequered floor gleamed in the light from the chandelier that hung over the foot of the stairs.

'Good evening, Signore, Miss.' Antonio's dedicated manservant, Frederick, greeted us at the foot of the stairs with our coats draped over his arm.

'Thank you,' Antonio said with a smile. He took my coat and helped me into it before putting on his own.

'The car is ready,' Frederick said. He strode to the door and opened it for us. I was still uncomfortable with being waited on and gave him an awkward smile as I passed him. The night air was bitterly cold and I pulled my coat tighter around myself. Antonio led me down the front steps to his sleek, black Maserati Ghibli. The back door nearest us stood open and his driver, Nicholas, stood beside it. Light from the entrance of the house spilled down the steps to the car, lighting our way. Beyond the car was an ornate fountain, its flowing water tinkling lightly in the still air.

I slid carefully into the car, pulling my dress with me. Antonio sped to the other side and slid in beside me. We exchanged nervous smiles, mine was nervous, at least. I doubted he was capable of anything resembling nerves.

Nicholas closed my door and we were soon sweeping down the curved driveway towards the tall, iron gates at the edge of the property. They swung open and we pulled onto the wide, tree-lined street. Other huge houses like Antonio's stood back from the road behind their tall gates and high walls.

It was a short drive. The city of Oris wasn't a vast metropolis. It was a small, old city in the north of England. The roads were wide out here on the outskirts, but as the car whisked us into the heart of the city, the roads narrowed and the buildings got older. We passed through an archway of ancient stones that formed part of the old city wall that surrounded the original castle. The tarmac gave way to cobblestones and the car rumbled over them. I watched the lights passing my window. Little old shops in wonky buildings lined the one-way street. Right here in the centre of Oris the roads were barely wide enough for a single car. It was like something from a postcard or fairy tale. But I was used to it, having grown up in the city.

Antonio reached for my hand and gave it a squeeze. I looked at him and smiled. A knot of nervous energy spun madly in my belly, but as long as I was with him, I'd be fine.

The car pulled up in front of the old castle, or what was left of it. A tall tower was mostly intact and dominated the buildings packed in closely around it. A grand arch stood in the base of the tower and the ancient castle walls flanked it, complete with ramparts. A red carpet had been set up leading through the archway and a modest queue of people filed along it accordingly. There was a small pack of press there, their cameras flashing rapidly as they tried to capture the city's finest inhabitants.

'Ready?' Antonio asked.

'As I'll ever be,' I answered.

My door was opened for me and I stepped carefully out onto the smooth cobbles, worn down over the centuries. I was terrified that I would topple over on my ridiculous heels and wished I had worn more practical shoes. But I'd wanted so much to fit in with all of the glamorous people who were sure to be attending this grand function that I'd decided to do my best to cope with the gorgeous shoes I'd picked out. Antonio was at my side before I'd managed to get to my feet completely. I was sure he must have used his super-speed to get to me so quickly, and I glanced anxiously around at the hundreds of people in the vicinity who might have seen him.

'Don't worry,' he whispered. He took my hand and held me steady as I adjusted my weight and straightened out my dress.

'The press?' I couldn't tear my eyes away from the snapping cameras. I wasn't just thinking of him using his powers, I was acutely aware that I was about to have my picture taken a thousand times and may end up appearing on a website or in a magazine. I wasn't built for so much attention. Antonio was right, I'd spent my whole life trying not to be noticed.

'I've got you,' he said, smiling just for me. I knew what was about to happen and I appreciated him giving me that moment of the Antonio that only I knew. I nodded and linked my arm through his. We set off to join the line filing along the red carpet past the press.

Loud voices shouted all at once, so chaotic that I couldn't pick any one out. The crowd's thoughts were as loud to me as their voices and my head swam. I held tight to Antonio and focused on placing my feet carefully in front of one another so as not to tumble over and humiliate myself completely.

'Antonio! Antonio!' I searched the crowd for the sharp, female voice but the flashing cameras obscured the faces behind them. I blinked and wished desperately to get through this as quickly as possible.

'Michelle? Is that you?' Antonio asked, loosening his grip on my arm slightly as he edged towards the rope that separated us from the paparazzi.

'Is that Armani you're wearing tonight?' the faceless voice called out.

'As keen an eye as ever, Michelle,' Antonio replied, stroking his lapel and smiling his dazzling smile. I fought the urge to scowl and pull him closer. I had never felt such fierce jealousy before and it surprised me. I felt the reporter's desire oozing from her, even though I couldn't see her face. This was why I considered my ability a curse, despite Antonio's insistence that it was a gift.

'I know your tastes, as you well know,' she called over the other voices around her.

'Who's your date, Mr Vitale?' Another voice leapt out, taking advantage of Antonio's focus on the press. He looked at me with those deep eyes and I couldn't help but smile. He put his arm around me and steered me away from them without answering. We moved a little further along and he leaned close to me.

'Are you all right?'

'Fine. Thank you for not giving them my name.'

'Of course.' He laid a gentle kiss on my cheek and the clicking of cameras went crazy. They all got what they wanted, the juicy gossip of the night. Antonio Vitale's latest conquest. But they wouldn't identify me so easily. It wouldn't have mattered so much if he was famous for being an actor, or an athlete. But my boyfriend was a notorious gangster. Infamous, rather than famous. I was a nobody, but that was certain to change now that we had appeared together so publicly.

'Who was she?' I whispered, glancing over his shoulder towards the crowd.

'Michelle? Just a journalist.'

'She seemed to know you quite well.'

'Only from a few dozen of these ridiculous functions. Are you jealous?' He grinned at me, disarming me completely. I turned away and tugged him along as the queue ahead of us moved forward. 'Eve?'

'Why would I be jealous? I'm the one up here in the amazing dress with your arm in mine.'

'That's right.' He squeezed me gently.

I focused on the couple ahead of us for the first time as we inched closer to the entrance to the castle. The woman was wearing a slinky, silver gown that brushed the floor. She wore a white fur shrug across her slender shoulders and her hair fell in a silvery blonde sheet of perfection down her back. On her arm was an older man with greying hair. I tried not to make any judgements, but an obvious assumption flitted into my mind before I could help it. I shoved it aside and fought the urge to have a quick scan of their surface thoughts to see if I was right. It was none of my business.

The entrance hall was not quite wide enough for a car and had an arched ceiling. Lights on chains hung from the stone ceiling and I gazed up at them as Antonio led me slowly along the corridor.

The man in front of us turned to see who had joined them and the slightest flinch passed over his pallid face when he saw Antonio. It was gone in an instant and he put on a broad smile.

'Mr Vitale.' He turned and held out a hand, which Antonio took with a smile of his own creeping over his lips.

'Mr Mayor,' Antonio replied. I had never felt so awkward, standing there beside these two men. The pit of my stomach dropped several inches. The mayor's wife turned her head and her smile froze on her fair face, her eyes going hard. 'Mayoress,' Antonio said silkily, his smile not faltering in the slightest. She didn't reply, but her gaze flickered my way and her smile slipped. I looked from her face to Antonio's and understood at once that there was a history between them. Whether it was prior to her marriage to the mayor, or since, was open to speculation. A tight knot had formed in my stomach and I found it impossible to fake a smile. Antonio slid a hand inside my coat and let it rest on the middle of my back against my bare skin. His thumb gently caressed my spine, but I ignored the pleasant sensation, determined not to be distracted.

'Who is this young lady?' the mayor asked, turning his attention to me. He was a large man, his suit straining slightly over the girth of his belly. His light blue eyes danced down my body. I suddenly regretted my choice of dress.

'Eve Rawling, a local business owner. Eve, this is the mayor of Oris, Winslow Shaw.' Antonio's hand pressed a little more firmly against my back.

'Pleased to meet you,' I said, trying to sound genuine.

'Rawling?' The mayor frowned and finally met my eyes. 'Not Jonathan and Sylvia's daughter?'

'That's right,' I said, blinking in surprise. I hadn't expected my parents to know the city mayor.

'I read about what happened in the papers. I'm so sorry for your loss, my dear.'

'Oh, thank you.' Heat rose in my cheeks and I shook his offered hand. I didn't know where to look. I hated the pity in his watery eyes.

'I hope that Mr Vitale is taking good care of you.'

'Oh no,' Antonio replied, a small smile tugging at the corner of his mouth. 'Ms Rawling is quite capable of taking care of herself. In fact, she's even saved my life on occasion.'

The mayor blushed and gave a nervous laugh. I pressed my lips together to hide a smile. The mayor's wife looked me up and down, an expression of shrewd curiosity on her steely face.

'This is my wife, Isabel.' Mayor Shaw seemed to suddenly remember the stunning beauty at his side.

'Charmed,' she said, sounding anything but. She extended a hand and I shook it with a grip firm enough to match hers. She was several inches taller than me, even in my crazy high heels. Of course, she was wearing heels as high as my own. She looked about forty, and wore it well with sophisticated confidence. Despite looking at me with mild disdain, I didn't sense that she was envious of my youth. No, it was just about Antonio. I quickly withdrew my attention from her thoughts, afraid of what I might pick up. There was certainly a history there. It was all over her face. And his, I saw, when I turned my attention to it.

'Isabel,' he said, a slight edge to his voice. 'Good to see you again.'

'Always a pleasure,' she said. She tossed her hair over her shoulder and turned away, moving up to fill the space ahead of her. The mayor smiled jovially and turned away to join her. I gripped Antonio a little more tightly than was strictly necessary. How could two women have me this rattled in just a few minutes? I wished I had Isabel's self-assurance.

The mayor and his wife were moving through the doors and a small crowd of people had built up behind us, but Antonio only had eyes for me. He dragged his attention away from my neck as we stepped up to the open doors, where there was a tall podium and a woman in a dark suit with a clipboard. A server in a white jacket silently took our coats and a shiver ran up my arms at the sudden chill. Antonio's hand quickly returned to the bare skin at the small of my back.

'Welcome, Mr Vitale,' the host said brightly. Beyond her was a vast hall that was open to the starry sky. The roof of the main part of the castle was long gone, lost to age. Warm white fairy lights were strung all around the tall walls, set to a slow fade in and out, casting a ripple of light around the large hall. At the far end was a stage where an orchestra was playing a beautiful and haunting piece. There was a large dance floor in the centre of the hall and around the edges were dozens of large tables laid for a feast with glinting silver cutlery and crystal glasses. 'You're seated at Thyme, over there on the right.' The host indicated a table near the stage.

'Thank you,' Antonio said, smiling at her, his eyes twinkling in the glowing fairy lights behind her.

He took my hand and led me down the steps into the hall. It was packed with people and we negotiated the crowd carefully. I glanced at the little signs on the tables we passed. Rosemary, Sage, and Mint were all filled with people in fine clothes and sparkling jewellery. The mayor and his wife were taking their seats at another table we passed and Antonio inclined his head briefly, his gaze skimming over the mayoress's neckline. I gave his hand a hard squeeze and scowled at him. He looked at me with a puzzled expression.

'What was that for?' he asked.

'You staring at her. It seemed like there was bad blood between you two back there.'

'Pun intended?' He smirked and raised his eyebrows.

'Yes,' I replied. He chuckled but offered no explanation. 'Well? Is there?' I pressed.

'Eve, I can't even begin to answer that here.'

'Speak in code.'

He smiled at someone passing us who greeted him with a friendly nod, and nodded in return. Somebody else called his name and moved in to shake his hand. He pressed a few palms on the way to our table, avoiding answering me. We arrived at the table labelled 'Thyme' and he greeted the five people already seated there. One man stood up and leaned over to shake his hand.

'Antonio, good to see you.'

'And you, Commissioner.' My ears pricked up and I watched the two men carefully. Antonio shook more hands before pulling out a chair for me and then taking his own seat next to the commissioner. 'Eve Rawling, this is Marco

De Luca, he's the Police and Crime Commissioner. Marco, Eve owns Piero's, a stunning Italian restaurant.'

'Hello,' I said, holding out a hand, which De Luca leaned across Antonio to shake. He was a relatively young man, perhaps in his forties, with thick, dark hair. His eyes widened in recognition and he cracked a broad smile, showing his fine set of white teeth.

'Ms Rawling. *Buona sera come stai?*'

'I'm sorry, Signor De Luca, my Italian is somewhat rusty.'

'Apologies,' he said, dropping his accent entirely. 'I just asked how you are this evening.'

'Very well, thank you. And you? It's an election year coming up, isn't it?'

A server had appeared at our table and began pouring wine. The commissioner nodded, unflinching.

'It is. Not many young people pay attention to that.' He nodded again, approvingly.

'Well, I can't help it, with the company I keep these days.' I gave Antonio a playful nudge. He was looking at me shrewdly. 'Are you standing for re-election?'

'I am.'

Antonio cleared his throat and leaned forward to pick up the glass of red wine in front of him, cutting me off from the commissioner.

'No business or politics at the table,' he said, sitting back with his wine.

'What on earth will we talk about all evening?' De Luca said, smirking.

'We shall simply have to get painfully drunk instead,' Antonio replied, before sipping his wine.

'Well, it is New Year's Eve.' De Luca tilted his glass towards Antonio and the two of them clinked glasses in a silent toast, smiling at each other. I picked up my own wine and took a large swig. It was going to be a long evening.

CHAPTER TWO

'BUT HE DIDN'T KNOW?' Antonio asked, a broad grin lighting up his face.

'No. It was all over his face and he just looked up at me like, *What*?' De Luca was laughing his way through his story and Antonio was laughing along with him. I smiled politely and sipped my wine. The table was littered with mostly empty plates and the streamers from inside the party poppers that had been popped before the meal was served. The white linen tablecloth was stained with multiple dark, red rings. Three empty wine bottles stood on our table and the server had just brought a fresh bottle of red.

Another member of the staff followed for the second time that night with a basket for donations. It was piled high with crisp, high value bank notes, and many cheques with multiple big, fat zeroes after round numbers. Antonio and De Luca were too engrossed in their conversation to notice it, but they'd both put their generous donations in earlier in the evening.

'It can be a bit like an old boys' club at these things sometimes.' The cool female voice at my ear caught me by surprise. I looked around to see the mayor's wife standing beside me and looking scornfully at Antonio. 'Walk with me?'

I glanced back at Antonio, but he was deep in conversation and chuckling away. He didn't notice me stand up and leave the table. The tall, slender woman led me between two of the stone pillars that lined the room. Behind them was a quiet area that ran the length of the hall, enclosed with the only remaining roof of the main part of the castle. We walked in silence in the shadows while laughter, music and merriment babbled away under the glowing fairy lights.

'How do you know Antonio?' I asked at last.

'Oh, you know…We have a history.'

'If this is the part where you warn me about how dangerous he is or how he broke your heart, you needn't bother.'

'No. I don't suppose you would pay the slightest bit of attention to me anyway.' She stopped and turned to look at me, her perfect hair falling softly over her shoulder and her white fur.

'Was there something you wanted to talk to me about?' My voice came out a little shorter than I had intended.

'Besides how dangerous your lover is?'

'Besides that.' I held my chin up and resisted the urge to poke around in her thoughts. She smirked at me and crossed her arms. 'Look, I've done the whole bitch fight thing, had the femme fatale rival. Whatever. It's all bullshit and I'm not doing it again. If you have a problem with me either get over it or keep it to yourself. I'm not interested.' I turned and set off walking back to the table, trying to keep my dignity by not wobbling on my heels.

'Eve,' Isabel called out. I stopped and looked over my shoulder.

'I don't do that shit either. I'm just not very good at making friends.' She strode up to me, perfectly stable on her equally high heels. 'I wanted to give you some honest advice about being with a powerful man.'

I raised my eyebrows at her.

'Really?'

'Yes. I'm sorry for being frosty. I'm not jealous of you. I don't want what you have and I'm not especially bitter.' She glanced down at her feet and was smiling when she looked back at me. 'Just a little.' I let out a snort of laughter that was not remotely attractive. She laughed with me.

'Okay. So, what's your advice?' I relaxed a little and allowed myself to smile.

'Make sure you have a little power of your own. He doesn't own you. Don't let him think he does.'

'I don't think he would—' I stalled when she gave me a

wide-eyed glare. 'Okay. Thanks. I'll keep that in mind.'

She nodded, apparently satisfied that she had made her point, then walked away from me towards her own table.

'Eve?' Antonio called from behind me. I turned and saw him walking towards me; his bow tie and top button were undone and he looked devilishly sexy. 'Everything all right?' He snaked an arm around me and kissed my cheek.

'Fine. I was just making a new friend.'

The slightest glimmer of worry crossed his face and I smiled to myself. I would let him keep that worry, for now. My own little bit of power.

'Would you like to dance?' he asked, abruptly changing the subject.

'I can try,' I said, looking down at my aching feet.

'I'll keep you upright.' He grinned and took my arm.

The orchestra was playing something grand and sweeping. The dance floor wasn't exactly crowded but a good number of couples were swaying gracefully around it, so I didn't feel too much like I would be on display when Antonio took a firm hold of my hand and waist and moved me with ease among them. For a few seconds I felt as if everyone was watching us. I was sure that every person at the event knew who Antonio was and that they must be curious about me. I glanced at the seated people around the room as they watched us swirl past. Several people caught my eye and hurriedly looked away again. The other dancing couples seemed to steer out of our path.

I had never danced quite like that before. Antonio led expertly and guided me around the floor with ease. My feet didn't really know what to do, but I barely stumbled. Soon I was lost in his dark eyes and forgot all about the people watching us.

'I'm sorry I neglected you,' he said softly at my ear.

'You didn't.'

'I did. I apologise. I'm all yours now, I swear.'

I smiled up at him.

The music slowed and Antonio brought us to a halt. He pulled me against his body and tucked our clasped hands in against his chest for a slow dance.

'What did you make of Ms Shaw?'

'I'm not sure yet.'

'What did she have to say?'

'Why does it matter?' I looked up at him. He was looking over my head into the mid-distance, his eyes slightly glazed. He glanced down at my question and gripped my back more tightly.

'She and I—'

'I guessed. I don't want to know about it.'

'It's probably not what you think.'

'It's okay, I said I don't want to know.' I pressed my cheek to his shoulder and breathed in the scent of his cologne. It was mostly true. I couldn't help feeling curious and a little bit jealous, but I really didn't want to know the details. The less I knew, the less I would imagine. Or that was my theory, anyway. Ms Rational was tapping her foot at me, but I ignored her.

'Are you having a good time?' he asked, his voice soft.

'I am now,' I said, smiling even though he couldn't really see my face.

'I'm glad.'

'You seem very friendly with the police commissioner.'

'We've known each other a while.'

'He doesn't seem scared of you, like most people are.'

'True.'

'Why is that?'

'I suppose he knows me well enough to overcome my reputation, at least a certain amount.'

'But I guess he doesn't know you well enough to know that your reputation is justified.' I looked up at him. He looked into my eyes, a small, knowing smile forming on his full lips.

'Yes, I suppose.'

'Does he work for you?'

'What a question. No, Eve. He's a democratically elected public servant. He works for the city.'

I raised my eyebrows and he looked down at me with mock innocence on his face. I didn't press it. I nuzzled back against his shoulder and he tightened his hold as we swayed slowly to the music. I felt so safe and warm in his arms. I didn't want to think about his criminal empire or the politicians in his pocket. I just wanted to enjoy the ball.

We danced to another piece of music before the pain in my feet got too much.

'I need to sit down,' I said, staggering slightly when I tried to take a step.

'Of course.' He supported my weight as I walked gingerly back to our seats. Our dining companions had vacated the table, including De Luca. We sat alone and Antonio poured us both some more wine.

'I have to decide what to do about my degree.' I wasn't quite sure where the statement came from and I blinked in surprise at myself. Antonio didn't seem surprised.

'I know.' He leaned back in his chair and took a long drink.

'I want to finish it. I don't like the idea of throwing it away.'

'I agree.'

'You do?'

'Of course.' He looked me in the eye, his jaw tense.

'I don't want to leave you. We talked about you coming with me.'

'I can't leave Oris at the moment.'

'What if I waited until September and restarted my final year? Could you come with me then?'

'If I get all of my ducks in a row, yes.' He nodded.

'What does that actually mean?' I sipped my wine and kept my eyes fixed on his.

'I have certain investments, things that I need to see through. I explained this before.'

'I know, but you were as vague then as you're being now.'

He put down his glass and leaned forward, propping his elbows on his knees, and took hold of my hand. He looked down at the stone floor.

'Eve, you don't want to know the details of my business. Not just because I think it will upset you, but legally speaking. I don't anticipate being arrested any time soon—' I let out a snort of laughter. De Luca was dancing with two women at once just behind Antonio. 'But if things change, if there is a change in leadership in the city, shall we say, it's possible. You don't want to be embroiled.'

'No, that's a fair point.'

He looked up at me, his dark eyes wide and pleading.

'Just let me conclude things and then we can go away together and be free of all of that bad business.'

'Okay.' I leaned forwards and kissed his lips. They were cool but warmed quickly with the heat of my breath. He kissed me back, cupping my face in his hands. My head felt lightened by the wine and it started to spin slightly as the kiss went on. I was lost in him. My passion for him was my weakness, it made me forget to be sensible. Ms Rational, my cynical inner voice, was not impressed with me, but she had a secret soft spot for Antonio herself and right then she was as into the kiss as I was.

'Sorry to interrupt,' De Luca said silkily, breaking our intense kiss. I pulled away from Antonio and wiped my moist lips with the back of my hand. I felt the heat in my cheeks and deliberately looked away. 'It's nearly midnight. Can I steal a dance before the big countdown?' I looked up at him in surprise. Antonio was looking from me to him with shrewd eyes.

'If Eve doesn't mind.' He held out a hand to indicate that it was over to me.

'My feet...'

'Take off your shoes. No one will care,' De Luca said quickly. 'I've seen at least half a dozen pairs of discarded shoes around the place already.' I immediately started looking around for these shoes but couldn't see any. Antonio let out a throaty chuckle.

'Did you seriously just break up our kiss to steal my girlfriend for a dance? Isn't that a bit bold, even for you, Marco?'

'Hey, you owe me.' De Luca grinned wickedly at Antonio and I cleared my throat pointedly.

'I'm not actually property to be traded.'

'Of course,' De Luca said, bowing his head and looking abashed. 'I apologise for that implication. It was a poor joke. But I would truly like to dance with you, if you'll oblige.'

'Okay.' I nudged my shoes off my feet and the relief was instantaneous. I looked at Antonio as I stood up. 'Are you sure you don't mind?'

'I'm sure.' He smiled but the flicker in his eyes gave a different answer. I stooped over him and captured his lips with mine. He returned the kiss hungrily. I pulled my lips from his and leaned close to his ear. 'You're taking me back to your place as soon as is polite and you get to make love to me all night long.' I straightened up and smiled seductively down at him. He was almost blushing as he gazed at me with dark desire in his eyes.

I took De Luca's offered arm and he steered me towards the dance floor. He held me at a slight distance and began to sway to the music. I stifled a giggle at his slightly inept attempt to lead me.

'How did you meet Antonio?' I asked, unable to stop my curiosity from taking control of my mouth.

'I don't really remember,' he replied. 'It was a number of years ago now. I think we were introduced at something like this.' He waved a hand around the castle hall.

'You seem to know each other very well.'

'Oh yes, I think so.' He smiled. He was rather handsome, in an obvious sort of way. He looked a few years older than Antonio, but I knew he was a great deal younger, probably barely twice my age, as opposed to ten times the number. 'How about you? How did you meet him?'

'He came into my restaurant one evening and, well, it was a bit like being struck by lightning. I knew my world would never be the same.' I smiled and glanced over towards Antonio. He was watching us, his arms crossed over his chest, an icy glare on his face.

'How about we talk about something else?'

I looked back at De Luca and his expression had turned serious.

'Sure.'

He tightened his grip on me a little, pressing closer to me. He turned me away from Antonio and steered me into the heart of the dance floor, surrounding us with other couples.

'He's changed recently.'

'I thought you wanted to change the subject.'

'I do. I just get the feeling he's backing out of something important. My career is riding on plans we've had in place for a long time and I have to admit, I'm nervous. Do you know anything about it?'

'No, I don't. He keeps me separate from his business, ironically, so that if the police ever question me I won't implicate myself.' I arched my eyebrows and glared at him pointedly.

'Fair enough.' His lips bulged as he rolled his tongue over his teeth behind them. 'You met Isabel Shaw earlier, didn't you?'

'I did. Interesting woman. How did she end up married to the mayor?'

'In the way most attractive women end up with older

men.' His tone was one of mock indifference, but there was bitterness lurking there.

'How am I supposed to take that?' I pulled loose from his hold and stared at him.

'Not personally,' he said, genuine surprise in his wide eyes. 'I apologise. I didn't mean any offence. I wasn't suggesting that you—'

'Good.' I turned to go but he grabbed my wrist. A shot ran up my arm and my head spun, causing me to stagger sideways. A flash of a memory coursed through my mind, one that didn't belong to me. De Luca was a younger man, not much older than I was. Isabel stood before him, younger still. Her face was flushed and tears streaked down it. They were screaming at one another, their voices a terrible jumble, too incoherent to distinguish what either of them were saying. But the passion and pain could not be plainer.

I felt cool arms around me and when I blinked away the distressing vision, I was face to face with Antonio. He was searching my eyes to find me.

'I'm all right,' I said. He glanced past me towards De Luca, who had released my wrist and stepped away. Couples still danced around us, though I noticed people casting wary glances towards us.

The music came to a halt, the babble in the hall died down and all eyes turned to the stage, where the host who had greeted us on arrival now stood at a microphone.

'Thank you all so much for being here tonight. Your contributions have raised one million, seven hundred thousand, six hundred and forty-two pounds for this year's causes, which include a local hospice, a women's refuge, and a national wildlife charity.' There was a lively ripple of applause, but I was shaking slightly from the unexpected vision and all I could do was cling to Antonio, desperate to remain on my feet. He held me gently and kept casting furtive looks at De Luca, who stood near to us. I looked over my shoulder at him and saw a concerned frown on his brow. He clapped absently along with everyone else but was watching me cautiously.

'Yes, thank you all very much. Now, it's almost time.' The host looked back at the orchestra and checked her watch. A few seconds passed in which everyone waited, the air thick with anticipation. 'Here we go! Ten...' The drummers struck up a soft drum roll, and strings plucked in time to the countdown.

'Nine, eight, seven...' Almost every voice in the hall counted along with bright smiles of excitement. I drew closer still to Antonio and led us a few steps away from De Luca. I couldn't stand the feel of his gaze on me.

'Six, five, four...'

'What's wrong?' Antonio asked.

'Later.'

'Three, two, one! Happy New Year!' several hundred voices cried at once.

Chimes from the nearby minster began to ring, loud and clear across the night. A moment later, there was a whoosh and a bright rocket flew up into the dark sky right overhead. It burst with a loud bang and an explosion of green sparks. Dozens more followed in a bright and loud fireworks display over the castle. The faces of the assembly were lit with bright colours as they smiled and oohed and aahed. People all around us were kissing and hugging and crying out, 'Happy New Year' to one another.

'Do you want to leave?' Antonio asked.

'Yes, please.'

'No problem.' He took my hand and led me back to the table, where my shoes and purse were tucked away out of sight. He stooped to retrieve them and took my hand again. We were halfway to the exit when De Luca caught up with us. He ran up alongside Antonio and took his arm. He instantly released it and looked mortified. Antonio glared at him with dangerous eyes.

'I'm sorry,' De Luca said, flustered and blushing. 'Is she— Eve, are you okay?' He changed approach mid-sentence and addressed me directly, looking past Antonio.

'Fine. Just ready to leave.' I couldn't look him in the eye. Even if I hadn't had a vision, he had offended me and grabbed my arm. I was extremely uncomfortable to be anywhere near him. How much had Antonio seen? I suspected the crowd had not really concealed us at all and that he had seen every moment. I hoped he had.

CHAPTER THREE

WE HURRIED OUT OF THE CASTLE to where the car was parked and waiting for us. Nicholas leapt out of the driver's seat when he saw us coming and rushed around to open the rear passenger door. Antonio was still carrying my shoes, and my feet ached from walking quickly over the cobblestones. I climbed into the car and tucked my feet up onto the seat so I could rub them. Antonio slid in beside me and put his arm around me.

'Do you want to talk about it?' he asked softly.

'What did you see?' I asked as I played for time.

'I saw you dancing.' He tensed up a little, squeezing me tighter. The car slowly pulled out of the parking space and I glanced towards Nicholas. I wasn't sure how much I wanted him to hear. Antonio obviously trusted him completely and I mostly did. But I was wary of discussing my visions. 'He was holding you a little too close for my liking.'

'He's your friend, isn't he?'

'Yes,' he replied. There was a degree of hesitation in

his voice.

'More than colleagues or associates.' I watched his face carefully. It was dark but the glow from the orange street lamps passed over his face in waves. He had a deep frown etched onto his brow.

'Yes.'

'And there is something in the past that ties you and him and *her* together.'

'Yes.' He wouldn't meet my eye. 'What did *you* see?'

'Not much. An argument.'

'Between?'

'Him and her. He was shocked when I blacked out for a second. He obviously doesn't know that much about me.' I kept my voice low, hoping that only Antonio would hear me.

'No. I don't see how he could know. I wouldn't tell anyone.'

'I know.' I smiled at him and to my relief he looked at me and kissed my forehead. 'You caught me.'

'Every time.'

'Don't make promises you can't keep, Antonio.'

'I try not to make a habit of that. I keep my word.'

'But you can't always be there to catch me when I fall.'

'No, but I can always pick you up. I love you, Eve. With all of my heart.'

'I love you too.' Our lips met in a soft and tender kiss. His mouth was cool and breathless. It was still odd to kiss someone who didn't breathe, even though I must have kissed him hundreds of times.

The car pulled onto the driveway to Antonio's house and rumbled over the paving up to the front door. He led me inside. My feet were throbbing painfully and I walked gingerly, my shoes hooked onto my fingers. The house was dark and still. Frederick didn't appear, for once. Antonio locked the front door behind us and scooped me up into his arms. For a split second I wondered where Nicholas went when he wasn't needed. Did he have a home to go to? I pictured him sleeping in the back of the car, or maybe in a room in the garage. I was too tired to ask Antonio. I rested my head on his shoulder as he carried me easily up the stairs.

We entered his bedroom and he laid me down on the bed. There was hunger in his eyes as he crawled up the bed over me.

'You look mouth-watering tonight. I should have expected someone to try to take you from me. I didn't quite imagine it would be a friend.'

'Maybe he was the only one who would dare. He's not as scared of you as everyone else.'

'Maybe he should be. He hurt you.' He took hold of my wrist, the one De Luca had grabbed. It wasn't even slightly bruised. He hadn't grabbed me all that hard.

'I'm fine.'

'You're mine.'

'He knows that. Everyone knows that. He wasn't trying to take me. I think he was trying to find out what I knew about this tangled past between you three.'

Antonio avoided my invitation to expand on this messy business, whatever it was. He dipped his head and kissed my chest as he slid his hands up my thighs, under my dress. I grinned as he made his way up my body, kissing my exposed skin. He tugged my dress up and I wriggled about to help him pull it off over my head. He shrugged his jacket off and tossed it to the floor. His shirt and trousers were quick to follow. His lips were on my neck in an instant, kissing me with hungry moans. I groaned and arched my back. Every inch of me sizzled with burning anticipation. He pressed his weight down on me, pinning me to the silk sheets.

With a growl he made short work of my underwear and his own. I grabbed his shoulders and pulled him back to me, planting my mouth on his and kissing him deeply. I wrapped my legs around him and ground my hips against him. I was as hungry for him as he was for me.

He pressed his forehead to mine, our eyes locked on each other as we made love.

'I need you,' he said.

'I need you too.' I tilted my head so that my neck stretched out before him.

'I can't.'

'You can. Just don't take too much.'

'You don't know what you're offering me.'

'I think I do.'

He looked at me carefully, considering my offer. I thought he was going to be firm and refuse. I was about to turn my head back when he lunged down with a snarl and thrust his teeth into my neck. I cried out and arched my back. The thrusting of his hips became erratic as he lost himself in feeding. A shiver ran right through my body, with every muscle tensing. My climax rushed over me and my ecstatic cries echoed down the hall through the open doorway.

Antonio yanked his head back, my blood on his teeth as his fangs slowly receded back into his gums. He cried out, his body shaking. His long, black hair fell over his shoulder, brushing over my prickling skin. I whimpered as an aftershock rippled through my body. He collapsed on top of me and I stroked his soft hair.

'I'm glad we left early,' I said, smiling broadly.

'As am I.' He lifted his head and smiled at me. 'Thank you.'

'What for?'

'Everything.' He rolled over and lay on his back, staring up at the ceiling. 'I mustn't do that again for a while.'

'Oh.' I pouted and gave him a shove so that he would look at me.

'Just the feeding part. I can do the other thing again in

a few minutes.' He smirked at me.

'Good,' I said, drawing my lower lip between my teeth.

'But seriously, you weren't fully healed from last time. I shouldn't have bitten you again.'

'I'll try not to tempt you.' I laid off the joking and looked at him earnestly. He was right.

'It's not your responsibility. I need to control myself.' He stroked my cheek and I leaned into his touch.

'Okay.' I stared at him, my breathing slowly returning to normal. It had felt like a very long evening. We had rushed away from the ball during the fireworks in the wake of a vision and I realised, there in the stillness, that I could still hear fireworks popping and fizzling somewhere over the city. 'Oh. Happy New Year.' I smiled sleepily.

'Happy New Year. Are you making any resolutions?'

'No, I don't really do them. You?'

'I stopped making them after a few decades.' He smiled sadly.

'What a pair we make.'

He let out a throaty chuckle.

'When you had the vision tonight, do you remember what the argument was about?'

'Not really. Why?' I asked, frowning, though my eyes were dragging themselves closed and I had to fight to keep them open.

'Just curious.'

'Are you worried about something?'

'Not really.' He was lying. I saw right through him, even as my eyes drifted shut. But that was a concern for another day.

CHAPTER FOUR

The night was crisp and stars dotted the black sky. I hugged my coat around myself and watched my breath mist on the air. I leaned on the icy stone and looked out across the river below, rippling gently in the breeze and winding its way through the heart of the city. The city wall on which I stood was a thousand years old but here it was, having endured so much over the centuries. It stood twenty feet above the river below. Where I stood, the wall was a walkway six feet wide between battlements to stop people falling into the river. But further along the wall were long stretches with no battlements or barriers. I always loved those parts of the wall as a kid; they felt dangerous and scary and gave me a thrill as I ran close to the edge, even though the drop onto the grassy slope below was only a foot or two. Beside the river was a busy road, cars zipping past, their lights blurs in the night. The old world and the new, separated by the timeless river.

Peter stood beside me, his hands wedged into the pockets of his jacket. He was my best friend from childhood. We'd grown up together and his parents had taken me under their wing following the death of my own parents. Peter was tall and lean, with sandy hair and kind, blue eyes. He'd filled out a bit since we left school and he'd become a shapeshifter. More often than not, he spent his nights prowling around the city in the form of a fox, and there was something of his animal form in his features now, too.

'It seems an age since we used to walk along here on our lunch break from school.'

'Yeah,' he said, nodding and looking down at the light-coloured stone beneath our feet. 'Why is he late?'

'I don't know.' I didn't want to admit it to Peter, but I was worried. He didn't need to hear that. 'He'll be here any minute.' I was trying to reassure myself more than him.

'How was that ball thing last week?'

'Mixed,' I replied with a shrug. 'I met some interesting people.'

'Oh yeah?'

'The police commissioner for one.'

'The one on the phone?' He looked at me with eyes more alive than I had seen in a while. Peter knew all about the phone call that I'd overheard Antonio make back in the early days of our acquaintance.

'Yeah. He and Antonio go way back.'

'Interesting. Not surprising though.'

'I suppose.' I gave a shrug.

'Remember when it was us investigating him?'

'Of course, but that's not the situation now. We're all on the same side.'

'Are we?'

I looked hard at him, a little shocked. Beyond him a dark figure was approaching, walking quickly, his long coat flapping in his wake.

'He's coming.' I nodded over Peter's shoulder and he gave a shrug of apathy before turning and leaning against the wall. Antonio reached us, his cheeks as pale as ever, not brightened against the cold like mine or Peter's. His breath didn't fog in front of his mouth. He greeted Peter with an uneasy nod and, to his credit, did not inflict a public display of affection toward me on Peter. He was growing.

'Apologies for my lateness.'

'It's okay,' I said.

'What kept you?' Peter asked, a snarl on his lips.

'I was looking into something and it took longer than expected.' Antonio fixed his dark eyes on Peter and his voice was firm, but not unkind.

'Celino and Laguardia?' I asked, my throat tightening as I thought about the vampire who had broken my fingers. I flexed them, though they didn't hurt. A tiny taste of Antonio's vampire blood had healed the broken digits swiftly. But the memory of the pain was like a ghost in my bones.

'I was following a lead, but it was a dead end.'

'Funny.' Peter clucked his tongue, no trace of amusement on it. 'That isn't what you asked us here to talk about.'

'No, it isn't. There's something you need to know. I wasn't sure how to broach this subject before. We had so much to contend with. But you both need to know the whole story of why I was working with your parents, Eve.' He looked pointedly at me. I blinked at him in surprise.

'Okay.'

'It wasn't out of the goodness of your heart, was it?' Peter was glaring at Antonio, with no attempt to conceal his contempt.

'No,' Antonio replied, a small smile tugging at the corner of his mouth. 'I found out that something big was on the horizon, something in the demon world that I couldn't handle alone. I had to enlist their help, and that of all of the shifters. I wanted your kind to be free and able to fight.' He looked directly at Peter, who stared at him, unblinking.

'What sort of something big?' Peter asked.

'There's a demon at work here in Oris, something growing stronger. But I haven't been able to trace it.'

'How do you know about it?' I pressed.

'While I was guarding the veil I noticed an increase in demon activity over the years. I was getting busier and busier. Eventually I delayed killing one of them in order to question it. It admitted that something was drawing the demons into Hepethia and then across the veil into this world. But it couldn't clearly identify it. It was like a distant voice calling to it and it couldn't resist.'

'That sounds like a summoning.' Peter was frowning and staring hard at Antonio.

'It does, rather.'

'A summoning?' I asked, looking from one face to the other.

'Shifters can summon demons to this world. There's a ritual. We can drag demons across the veil against their will, if the ritualist is strong enough. No one here is powerful enough to do anything like that, though. We're all just figuring this stuff out.'

'Quite. And it's been happening since before you were all liberated.' Antonio's voice was as steady as a rock. I wanted him to show some remorse for his role in keeping the shifters subjugated, but there was none.

'What a nice way to put it.' Peter glowered at Antonio.

'Isn't there a chance that someone was doing the summoning despite being under your control?' I asked Antonio, hating having to use the words.

'Yes, of course. It's not like I kept tabs on everyone at all times. In case you've forgotten, an uprising was organised right under my nose.' Antonio smiled playfully at me, but I couldn't return it, not in front of Peter. I glanced at my friend. He was looking away across the river, his jaw was clenched tight and his fists were balled up by his sides. I cleared my throat.

'It's not any of us,' Peter said, his voice low and hard.

'No, I agree,' Antonio said. 'I think it's something else. Another demon, something old and powerful, something that's probably been here for a while. It's amassing forces.'

'What kind of demon?' I asked.

'I don't know.' Antonio shook his head.

'Did my parents know?'

'No. I was going to tell them, but then my sister—' His words died out and none of us could look at one another.

'I don't know enough about this stuff,' Peter said, turning to face Antonio. 'I need to talk to my father.'

'Of course. Yes. I want this shared. I have a bad feeling that time is of the essence.'

'Why are you telling us now? Why not sooner?' I asked, frowning.

'I wanted to have more details to bring you. It all sounds so vague. I have to confess, I'm out of my depth here.' He held out his hands in surrender. I had never seen him so vulnerable and uncertain. I nodded reassuringly before turning to Peter, who was staring at Antonio with narrowed eyes. He scoffed, shrugged, and walked away without another word. 'Peter!'

He kept walking, his hands shoved deep into his pockets, his head bowed against the wind before disappearing through a gap in the wall that led down to the riverbank.

'Eve, leave him.' Antonio scooped me into his arms, cupped my chin in his fingers and turned my head to face him. His dark eyes bored into mine before he drew me into a crushing kiss.

I pulled back and glanced towards Peter's retreating back. I still felt so caught in the middle of their power play. I never wanted this. Peter was being annoyingly childish, but Antonio kept walking right into it. He really ought to know better at his age. I looked back into his face, searching it for some insight.

'Aren't we just like children to you?'

'Sometimes,' he said with a light snort of laughter. 'But you continually surprise me with your wisdom. You have an old soul.' He smiled warmly and kissed me again. I wouldn't be distracted; I pulled away right out of his arms and leaned back against the battlements.

'What do we do about this demon?'

'Figure out how to send it back where it came from.'

'And that's not Hepethia?'

'No,' he said, shaking his head. 'There are many realms. The one you saw the other week, through that tear in the veil, was Muspelheim, the fire realm. A lot of demons come from there. But there are others. Not all demons are the fire and brimstone kind.'

'I see.' A shudder rippled through me that had nothing to do with the icy night air. 'And you haven't been able to work out where this one is from? Or where it is? Or what it wants?'

'No.' His face was hard, his jaw clenched tight. I had touched a nerve. I stepped closer to him and put a hand on his shoulder.

'I'm sorry.'

'It's all right. I'm frustrated with myself. I've been doing this far longer than most shifters ever do. I should be able to figure out such things. I don't know why this one is so elusive.'

'Maybe it's your nemesis?' I suggested, grinning and tugging him closer to me. He scowled at me, not returning my levity. 'Come on. Let's go back to your place. Did you walk all the way or is your car parked somewhere?'

'I walked.'

'Fine. Let's walk back.'

'Are you sure?'

'Hey, who's the fit, young whippersnapper here? Don't you need a Zimmer frame?' I gave him a playful shove.

'Rude.' He chuckled and gently shoved me back. He grasped my hand and we walked along the wall, our joined hands swinging between us.

'Most shifters,' I said, frowning as his words ran back through my mind.

'Hmm?'

'You said you've been doing this longer than most shifters. Does that mean there are some who are as old as you?'

'A few. Very few. Most live short lives due to the nature of what they do. But sometimes they survive the battles and all that mortal peril for many decades. Sometimes centuries.'

'Really?' I looked at him with wide eyes. 'Do they stay young, like you?'

'No, they just age more slowly. Maybe I can introduce you to someone I know in Caerton sometime.' He grinned at me.

'Does that mean that Peter's dad is older than he looks?'

'Yes.'

'That was a quick answer.'

'I've known him nearly his whole life, remember.' He didn't smile. Nor did I.

We walked on in silence for a while. I thought over everything he had said and everything he hadn't. He knew so much about the world, more than I could hope to fathom. If he couldn't find this demon, how would the shifters manage?

CHAPTER FIVE

January took hold in earnest after the events of New Year. The shifters were anxiously trying to follow up on Antonio's revelation, but I wasn't included much. I spent most of my time at Antonio's mansion, which was almost always empty these days. The weather turned colder and snow became a daily occurrence. Some days seemed to barely get light at all; dark clouds filled the sky from morning until night. The darkness suited Antonio and I noticed how much more energy he seemed to have. I saw very little of Dante, Antonio's trusted right-hand man, but Antonio was frequently messaging him and I had to assume that they were also working on the demon problem. I got the impression that everyone was trying to shield me from it. As the shifters organised themselves and formalised their packs and territories, there seemed to be less room for me: the unchanged daughter of two shifters who had passed away. I tried not to harbour any resentment but it still crept through sometimes. I distracted myself with my love life, and Piero's.

The restaurant, however, was quiet, as the inclement weather kept people home. For a few nights we didn't even open because the staff couldn't get there. Kirk assured me that we could cope financially, and I had to trust him. I was trying to run a business for the first time and I really didn't have the experience to draw on. I had to put my faith in Kirk, and Tina, my trusted manager.

I woke one morning in mid-January in Antonio's bed, satiated and still drowsy from a little light blood loss in the night. I smiled, remembering how it felt when he drank from me. A ripple of warmth spread through me, despite the chill in the air. Antonio wasn't there. I sat up to peer into the bathroom, but there was no sign of him there either. I scooped the sheet around me and swung my feet to the floor, scrunching my toes against the plush black and white carpet. I padded softly to the tall door that led onto the landing and pulled it open a crack, straining to hear any sounds of life. It was still and silent. The eeriness of it made me shiver. I closed the door and scurried around the room retrieving my clothes. I dressed hurriedly and again padded barefoot to the door. I stepped out into the hall, onto the thick, red carpet, and tiptoed towards the grand staircase down into the foyer. The huge, round window set above the double doors was filled with thick, dark clouds, so the usually bright foyer was dull. I stepped silently onto the first step and slowly made my way down the sweeping staircase.

Usually Frederick would appear as if he had some sixth sense that alerted him whenever someone stepped into the foyer. But there was no sign of him. A clink of glass broke the silence and startled me. I clapped a hand to my mouth to suppress a mildly hysterical giggle that threatened to burst from it. The noise had come from Antonio's study, and I moved slowly towards the door, which was slightly ajar. He was probably just busily working away. I briefly wondered why I was so on edge. I shook out my head and shoulders and walked more briskly towards the study door.

'Did he?' Antonio's voice stopped me just before I reached the door. I held my breath and waited for a reply. None came. 'Well I can't wait any longer. Make sure he gets the last donation. We need to win this one, at any cost.' Whoever he was speaking to must have replied, but I couldn't hear them. There was a light thump of his phone being tossed onto the wooden desk. I knew he must know I was there so I pushed the door open and stepped into the dark room. Blinds and drapes covered the two windows. A small desk lamp with a green lampshade was the only source of light.

Antonio looked up at me in mild surprise. He tucked a folder underneath some other papers and smiled.

'Morning. You were sleeping so deeply when I got up I didn't like to disturb you.'

'It was too quiet. I was worried.' I padded over to him

and climbed into his lap. I cast a quick glance over the papers on his desk but nothing interesting caught my eye. When my gaze settled on him, Antonio was watching me with a small smirk.

'Sorry to worry you. But it kind of seems like you're sneaking about and trying to find out what I'm working on.' He gave me a playful tickle and I creased over, giggling.

'Maybe I am. What *are* you working on?'

He dug his finger into my ribs again and I balled up in his lap, squealing. I slid to the floor and he was on top of me before I could squirm away. I gave in to him and he made short work of my jeans and t-shirt. Somewhere in the back of my head Ms Rational was saying that he kept using sex to distract me from the difficult questions he wouldn't answer, but the primal part of my brain that enjoyed sex didn't care. By the time we were both spent it was almost lunchtime and my stomach rumbled loudly as we lay there on the floor behind his desk.

'I'd better feed you, hadn't I?' Antonio asked sleepily, stroking my belly with his slender fingers.

I craned my neck towards the open door, suddenly aware that if Frederick had been anywhere near the entrance hall he would have at least heard what we were up to, if not seen a full show. My cheeks blazed and I looked back at Antonio with wide eyes.

'This wasn't terribly private.'

'Frederick's not here. It's his day off.' He grinned at me.

'Huh. I guess I didn't think he ever had days off, but of course he does.' I half laughed and covered my face with my hands. 'No wonder it's so quiet.'

'Come on, I'll get you some food.' Antonio helped me up and again I found myself looking around for clothes.

The lights in the white and chrome kitchen were blinding after the dim light in the study, and I blinked against them. Antonio bustled about, perfectly at home, and I hoisted myself up onto a worktop to watch him preparing a meal for me.

'You look very comfortable in here, despite not needing to cook, like, ever. I mean, was electricity even a thing the last time you needed to eat real food?' I grinned at him and he chuckled.

'I happen to enjoy good food very much, as you well know from our many times dining out.'

'True, but I never imagined you being able to cook.'

'I'm Italian, of course I love to cook.' He looked up at me, his thick, dark hair covering half of his face.

'Well so am I, and I own a restaurant, so I guess that ticks that stereotype box nicely.' He went back to chopping tomatoes. My gaze flickered over to the huge metal door that led to the walk-in freezer where Antonio kept his supply of blood, the only sustenance he genuinely needed. My stomach clenched. I was comfortable with a lot, but I knew where that blood came from and that still didn't sit right with me. I shoved the thought aside and focused on his hands moving swiftly to produce a creamy tomato soup from scratch. He moved skilfully, his bare feet making light noises on the tiled floor.

The kitchen was right in the centre of the mansion and had no windows. I realised that this was no coincidence: Antonio could always get to his blood supply, even in broad daylight. On that thought, the lights hanging above us blinked out. The sound of Antonio's knife chopping celery stopped abruptly.

'Eve?'

'I'm okay. What's going on?' The room was pitch-black. Even the little red light on the keypad next to the freezer door had gone out. Antonio's hands were on me and he lifted me down from the counter, setting my bare feet on the cold, tiled floor.

'I don't know.' He took my hand and led me swiftly to the door. He could either see far better in the dark than I could, or he simply knew his domain so well that he didn't need to see. Slowly, he pulled open the door and put his ear to the crack.

'Is it just a power cut or—' His hand pressed firmly against my lips to silence me. I gripped his hand tighter and pressed myself against him, taking the gesture to mean "no" to the first part of my question.

There was very little light in the hall outside the

kitchen, we were too deep in the house for any light from the windows to reach us. He closed the door and set off again for the other side of the kitchen, pulling me along in his wake. His phone lit up in his hand and he pressed it to his cheek.

'Dante,' he whispered a second later. 'Trouble. Return to the barn as soon as you can.' He hung up the call immediately and I didn't know if he had actually spoken to Dante, or just left a message. Dante wasn't much use over the phone, seeing as he couldn't speak. So it was entirely possible that Antonio had got through to him directly but of course not waited for any kind of response. We reached the opposite side of the large kitchen and again he opened the door ever so slightly to listen for intruders.

'It's still light out,' I whispered as softly as I could. 'How will Dante get here?' He didn't reply. He opened the door fully and slipped out through it, pulling me with him. We dashed across a narrow hall and into the huge ballroom that took up most of the west wing of the property. It had floor to ceiling windows all along the far wall, but they were all covered by the most effective blackout blinds available. No sunlight penetrated them and the room was almost as dark as the kitchen. The polished wooden floor stretched away from our feet and I couldn't think why he had brought us in here. He led me quickly across the dance floor to where a grand piano dominated a slightly raised stage. Comprehension dawned as I remembered what stood on top of the piano. Antonio drew a lighter from his pocket and flicked it to life. He swiftly lit the three tall candles in the candelabra. Soft, warm light emanated out from the gently flickering flames. He hoisted it up and turned around, shining the light around the ballroom. It was perfectly still and empty.

Bang! I gasped and leapt into Antonio's grasp. The candlelight wobbled with the sudden movement but he promptly steadied it. The sound of a door slamming had come from the other side of the large double doors at the other end of the room that connected this one to the foyer.

Rain pattered on the huge windows and my gaze couldn't help but be drawn to the sound. Antonio squeezed my hand and began walking slowly towards the foyer. I held back, tugging on his arm. My feet wouldn't move. He looked over his shoulder at me; his eyes were wide and glistening in the candlelight. He was afraid. I'd never seen him like that. I took a step, the wooden floor cool against my feet. Goosebumps had broken out all over my bare arms. We walked slowly and silently across the ballroom. I wanted to ask him his plan. He couldn't possibly set foot in the foyer with that huge window spilling in the daylight. Even on a heavily overcast day like this. Why did he want to go towards the slammed door, anyway? All I wanted to do was run away from the strange noise and preferably find somewhere to hide until sunset when he could let loose his full power. But we kept moving towards those big double doors. Another door slammed and I winced, tightening my grip on Antonio's hand again.

We reached the door and he pressed his ear against the wood, holding the candelabra away from it. I couldn't hear anything, but I didn't have heightened senses like his. He stepped back and passed the candelabra to me. I shook my head, my eyes wide and pleading, but I took the only source of light and grudgingly allowed him to release my hand. I held the metal candle holder in both hands, shaking slightly and causing the tall candles to wobble. Antonio placed one hand on the door handle and the other on the opposite door. He slowly turned the handle and pulled the door towards him. Dull grey light filled the entrance and a crack of it appeared in the opening doorway. He carefully shielded himself with the door, but the light was weak enough that it didn't burn his skin. I peered over his shoulder through the growing gap. The foyer looked empty. He opened the door wider and took a cautious step forward, his bare toes touching the edge of where the sunlight reached. He squeezed out of the ballroom, sticking to the shadows. I moved into the doorway and peered out into the foyer. The round window above the door was solid, slate grey and speckled with raindrops. The black and white chequered floor normally shone, but it looked dull. I tiptoed to the right and peered around the end of the grand staircase. Antonio's study door was closed. I was sure we'd left it open when we emerged for food.

'Eve,' Antonio whispered from the shadows behind me. 'Careful.' I glanced back at him, holding the candelabra above my head and casting the flickering light over his face. A deep frown creased his brow. I nodded and turned back to the foyer. I took a cautious step towards the end of the stairs and craned my neck to look up over the banister. The air was eerily still. I took another step out into the open, and another. Each step felt like stepping closer to a cliff edge. The candelabra was growing heavy in my hand, and my arm shook. I reached the foot of the stairs and a gust of wind rushed through the foyer, snuffing out the candles and blowing my hair across my face.

A cry rose in my throat. I dropped the candelabra with a clatter. One of the candles fell out and rolled across the floor, a small trace of smoke issuing from the wick. Intangible hands wrapped themselves around my throat and I was yanked up into the air. My cry caught in my throat as I flew up towards the domed ceiling.

CHAPTER SIX

'Eve!' Antonio's voice echoed through the hall. My blood pounded in my ears as my legs thrashed desperately against thin air. Hands I couldn't see gripped my throat so tightly I couldn't breathe. Choking noises just about made it out of my mouth. The pressure on my throat was crushing. I hung there, level with the window, twenty feet above the chequered floor. Antonio kept screaming my name below me, sounding further and further away. My vision blurred and I couldn't fight for my breath any more. My limbs went limp and everything went quiet. All I could hear was a soft rushing sound like a waterfall in the distance.

In the fog there was a tiny spark. Just a flicker of light on the periphery. My eyelids fluttered and I gasped. My throat was still restricted, but some air got through.

Eve, please hear me. Please. Don't leave me. Fight. You can fight the demon. Antonio's voice was desperate, pleading. It was in my mind. As if struck by lightning, I drew another great breath and remembered my abilities.

My body rocked in the air, swinging from the vice-like grasp of the demon that held me. A roar of fire rushed up from my belly and I pushed out from my core, expelling the presence from around me, forcing it away from me.

Breath flooded my lungs as the demon's grip loosened. I pushed again and a great, guttural roar tore from my aching throat as I broke free of its grip. A massive release of pressure freed up my lungs and I laughed before I plummeted towards the floor. My stomach lurched up into my throat and I dropped like a stone. I didn't have time to scream.

My body collided with something less firm than the tiled floor. I was moving in a blur, surrounded by smoke. A door slammed and I tumbled to the floor, rolling away from Antonio, who doubled over onto all fours. His skin was sizzling; smoke snaked up from him into the darkness of his study. His clothes smouldered and were full of holes. He stayed there, shaking like an injured dog. I looked around the room for anything that could help, but I had no idea what he needed. I moved over to him and ducked down low to try and catch his eye. He gingerly lifted his head to meet my gaze.

'Well done,' he croaked.

'You caught me,' I said. My throat burned and my words came out broken. I winced and clutched my neck in both hands.

'I'll always catch you.' He pushed up with his hands

and rocked back to sit on his heels. He cringed in pain. I could see how pink his skin was through the holes in his shirt, but he had at least stopped smoking.

'Is it gone?' I asked in a hoarse whisper.

'I think so. You surprised it. It didn't know you could do that.'

I chuckled and immediately regretted it. I clung more tightly to my neck, as if that would help. I'd surprised myself as much as the demon. Antonio gently pulled me into his arms and we rocked there on our knees for what felt like hours.

Eventually he pulled back from me and I looked over his body. The burns were completely healed. He gently caressed my neck and examined the alabaster skin.

'Is it bruised?' I croaked.

'A little red.' He laid a soft kiss on one side of my neck, and a little shiver went through me. The inside of my throat burned every time I swallowed. I placed a hand on his cheek and pressed my forehead against his.

I can't talk, I thought firmly, pushing the words into his mind.

'It's okay,' he replied out loud. 'I know. I'll look after you.'

A door somewhere nearby blew open and I leapt sideways, a squeal escaping my aching throat. 'It's Dante,' Antonio said, getting to his feet. He strode to the study door and flung it wide. I got to my feet and followed him.

Dante stood in the hallway leading back beside the grand staircase, shrouded in shadow. He dashed over to the shaded study doorway and Antonio welcomed him into the safety of his office. His eyes blazed as he looked from Antonio to me. He was a tall, imposing figure, with dark skin and a bald head. He wore a dark suit and heavy boots. He quickly signed with his thick hands, his fingers moving at an alarming speed. I only knew a little sign language and couldn't follow what he was saying. Antonio was nodding. He took hold of Dante's shoulders to calm his friend.

'It's okay. I think Eve repelled it.' He released Dante and put an arm around me. 'It tried to kill her. I need to know why.'

Dante signed something else. His gaze raked up and down Antonio's body, taking in his burned clothes.

'I'm fine,' Antonio replied calmly. 'I got a little sun, but nothing I couldn't heal. The power went out. I need it restoring.' Dante nodded firmly and spun on his heels. He strode back out into the dimly sunlit hall and down the passage that he had come from behind the stairs. He disappeared through a narrow door that I guessed must lead to the basement. I took a few steps after him, looking cautiously around the large entrance hall. Aside from the dropped candelabra, there was no sign of the encounter with the demon.

'Is that how Dante got here?' I croaked, pointing at the dark doorway he had vanished through.

'Yes,' Antonio replied, not blinking.

All that time sneaking about in the catacombs below Oris and the vampires had access the whole time. I'd known that on some level. After all, Lucia had taken me prisoner and held me in one of the caves underground, but it had been a couple of months since we'd met and Antonio had never told me that he could get into the tunnels from inside his own house. I heaved a sigh and shook my head. Secrets were the bread and butter of our twisted relationship.

Antonio peered at me from the study doorway, his dark eyes narrowed. I moved in and planted a soft kiss on his lips. We parted and he grabbed my hand and dragged me towards the kitchen. I scurried along behind him. The lights flickered to life just as we reached the room.

'Thank you!' Antonio called out. The kitchen was just as we'd left it. He went straight to the freezer, where the keypad light was safely illuminated as it should be. He tapped in the code and yanked open the door. There was a hiss and cold steam billowed out. He glanced around inside and swiftly shut the door again. 'Good,' he said under his breath. He spun around and went back to preparing my soup. 'You need this more than ever.'

I leaned against the counter and watched him without complaint. Dante entered a moment later, a spanner in his hand. He dropped it onto the counter beside me and took hold of my shoulders. He looked intently into my eyes, searching them.

'I'm okay,' I said, my voice scraping painfully. I touched my neck again and swallowed, which hurt just as much as talking.

'The demon tried to choke her,' Antonio said. Dante's eyes blazed and he slammed a hand down on the metal surface beside me. 'At sunset I need you to head out and see what you can find out. I want to know who was behind it. It won't have been acting of its own volition. I'll follow up on that lead on Celino. Eve.' He turned to me, suddenly softer. 'Where do you want to be?'

I grasped his hand and thought of Piero's, busy and full of people I knew and trusted. Peter popped into my head too and I let him wander through my thoughts. Antonio gripped my hand tighter. He'd got the message. He pulled out his phone and started a call, then pressed the phone to his cheek while he stirred my soup.

'What do you want?' I heard Peter's voice dully through the phone. Antonio rolled his eyes.

'I need you to keep Eve company tonight, at the restaurant. Can you handle that?'

'What happened? Why isn't she asking me?'

'She can't talk right now. She's going to be absolutely fine, she has just lost her voice.'

'Eve? Can you hear me?' Peter's voice was louder. Antonio tossed the phone down onto the counter and put it on speaker.

'Yes she can. She's here and so is Dante. Neither of them can speak though, so you'll have to trust me.'

Peter let out a snort.

'Peter,' I croaked, flinching with the pain. 'I'm here.' A tear leaked from my eye and I swatted it away.

'Okay,' Peter replied softly. 'Sorry. When do you need me?'

'Sunset. In fact, could you collect her from my place, please? I'd feel better if she was with you as soon as possible.'

'Sure. Eve, I'll see you in a couple of hours. You'll be okay.'

I leaned forward and blew softly into the microphone to give him a sign that I'd heard and appreciated his words.

'Bye.' He clicked off and Antonio pocketed his phone. He ladled some soup into a bowl and placed it in front of me. I frowned down at it. I was desperately hungry and my stomach confirmed as much with a loud growl. Antonio and Dante both chuckled. I picked up a spoon and girded myself against the coming pain in my throat. It wasn't too bad. The warm soup stung for a second but then felt soothing as it made its way down my tender throat. I nodded appreciatively. Antonio pulled up a stool and I perched on it as I ate.

'Dante,' Antonio said softly. 'Could you check the property, please? Make absolutely sure we're alone.' Dante nodded and swept from the kitchen. Antonio placed a hand on my shoulder and gave it a squeeze. 'I'm so sorry you got hurt. It's my worst nightmare, you know? I couldn't bear it if anything happened to you.'

I placed my hand on top of his and smiled at him. I'd managed to get myself free of the demon's grip. As much pain as I was now in, I actually felt a surge of confidence that I could take care of myself. I'd rarely felt like that. My gift had always been something dirty and complicated before. I was afraid of it and a little ashamed for the longest time. It was only recently that I'd realised I was telekinetic as well as telepathic, and it was very new. But I was excited by it. I could have died, but I'd saved myself. Well, okay, Antonio saved me from the fall, but I got myself free. I grinned at him as I thought it through and he gave me a half smile and a shake of his head.

'Don't get cocky,' he said, a rumble in his chest. He leaned in and kissed me. 'Eat.' He pointed at my bowl and I went back to the soup. It tasted amazing and was really helping my throat.

Thank you, I said in my mind. He glanced at me, nodded, and set about cleaning up. He kept on surprising me. He lived such a life of luxury, but he was showing me a more practical side lately and I liked it. I wasn't sure I would ever really embrace the red carpets and ball gowns, but part of me liked being driven around and having doors opened for me. Then I felt guilty for liking it. So seeing him unafraid to roll his sleeves up and pitch in reassured me that I didn't have a life of idleness ahead of me. A sobering thought intruded then: the life ahead of me with Antonio included me growing old and him staying young. He would have to watch me die someday, be it from some dangerous element I couldn't rescue myself from, or the mundane and predictable old age. Death was an inescapable part of life. Or it was for me. He would never know what it was like to be arthritic and bed-bound, to lose his memory, to need help climbing the stairs. Would he stay with me and be the one to nurse me through those difficult years? Could he do that?

Lucia had warned me that he would grow bored of me and trade me in for a younger model at some point. Was she right? If I was going to stay young and beautiful forever, would I spend my time caring for an elderly lover? I couldn't honestly say that I would. As I watched him and let my thoughts tumble through my mind, another, obvious one occurred. Maybe I had the option to stay young and beautiful with him.

CHAPTER SEVEN

Antonio was restless for the rest of the afternoon. He kept pacing, like a caged animal. Dante returned from checking the property with nothing to report. Frederick arrived late in the afternoon as the sky was growing dark, called in early from his day off. He bustled through the foyer tidying things up.

'I'm glad to see that you're well, Miss,' he told me as our paths crossed.

'Thank you,' I whispered, still protecting my voice. He didn't seem to mind returning to work. His kind face was deeply lined and his grey eyes told me he had lived a long life of servitude that he was content with.

Antonio watched the light in the foyer retreating below the window, leaning forward on his toes, which were now tucked inside polished shoes, finishing off a new suit to replace his ruined clothes. The moment the last ray of sunlight had dipped below the rim of the window and the chequered floor was lit only by lamplight, he was out from the shadow of the staircase. He swept across the hall with an angry glare up at the spot where I had dangled helplessly just a few hours before. I didn't dare look up there and see just how high it was.

Frederick appeared and went to the door. He opened it and Peter was standing with his hand raised to knock. He blinked in surprise and then saw me over Frederick's shoulder. The butler stood aside and Peter dashed over the threshold and scooped me into his arms.

'Jesus, Eve. You had me worried.' I squeezed him back and then patted him, anxious to be set down before an intrusive vision hit me. Mercifully nothing struck me and he put me back on my feet with an apologetic smile.

'I'm fine,' I rasped.

'Thank you for coming for her,' Antonio said, moving closer to us. Peter shot him an uncomfortable look and shoved his hands into the pockets of his jeans, which had a sort of shrinking effect on him. Peter was noticeably taller than Antonio, but his sandy hair and dorky facial features that he hadn't quite grown into yet made him somehow seem smaller than the confident and mature Italian.

'Of course. What happened?' Peter looked quickly from Antonio to me.

'There—' My voice gave up, the pain too much for me to go on. I groaned and clutched my neck again.

'There was a demon,' Antonio finished. 'It attacked Eve here. I'm heading out now to investigate. I was unable to act more quickly.' If Antonio could blush I was sure he would have done in that moment.

'What did it do to you?' Peter asked me, not looking away from my face.

I whimpered impotently and held a hand out to Antonio to beg for his help in communicating.

'It dragged her by the neck and tried to strangle her.' Antonio's teeth were gritted and his voice came out strained. His fists were clenched at his sides.

'Fuck!' Peter rounded on Antonio, grabbed his jacket in both fists and pushed him across the hall to slam him against the wall.

'Stop!' I shouted and instantly regretted it. I ran after them and tugged Peter off Antonio.

'She's supposed to be safe with you. I've been trying to trust you, I honestly have, despite everything you've done to my family! And hers. What the fuck brought a demon into your home to attack her? What did you do now?!'

'Peter!' I pulled him back and, to his credit, he let me. My throat burned like crazy but I was done holding my tongue. 'We have no idea why it was here. Maybe it was just after me! It never went near him. It's almost like it tried to separate us to get me alone in the sunlight where he couldn't go. So stop laying into him.' My last few words barely made it out of my mouth before I started coughing and wheezing. Peter turned to me and his fierce expression instantly died.

Frederick reappeared with a glass of water on a tray. I

gratefully took it and drank deeply. I wondered for a moment if he shared my gift.

'Fine,' Peter snapped. 'Let's get out of here.'

Frederick was there in an instant with my coat. I took it from him rather than letting him help me into it, acutely aware of Peter's judgemental presence. Peter stormed to the door and yanked it open. I pulled Antonio into a hug and kissed his cheek.

'Be careful out there,' I said with a croak.

'You too.' He pulled back from me and looked earnestly into my eyes. 'Call me if anything happens.' I nodded and hurried after Peter. His little blue Honda was parked crookedly at the foot of the steps up to the front door. The sky was heavy with clouds that glowed slightly orange from all the light pollution. We rushed down the steps and climbed into his car. I glanced back up at the house. Antonio stood in the doorway, a grim expression on his chiselled face. I raised my hand as the car began to move. Peter put his foot down and turned the car swiftly, the tyres squealing on the wet paving, and sped away down the drive.

'How did you get away from it?' He asked, his voice light and curious.

'I used my gift.' I winced with the pain of speaking.

'Right.' He glanced at me and slowed for the gates to open and let us out onto the wide, tree-lined road. The trees were completely bare. A few mulched leaves remained in the road, although most of them had blown or washed away by now. There were still piles of grey snow along the sides of the road, packed and frozen hard, taking longer to thaw out than the snowfall that hadn't been shovelled. We drove in silence and I was glad of the break from using my voice. Rush hour was in full swing and once we reached the city, the streets were clogged with traffic. Peter stayed cool and didn't comment on it, but I was anxious to get to the restaurant and found my knee bouncing the longer we sat in traffic going nowhere.

The centre of Oris was over a thousand years old, and many of the old structures had been preserved, with modern elements grafted onto them and roads wedged into what were once narrow lanes built only for horses and carts. Right in the very centre, some of the roads were still cobblestones. The limits of the road system meant that it was often so busy that nothing moved for what felt like hours. I'd always promised never to get a car as long as I lived there. Peter used to say the same. Yet he had caved to the masculine stereotype and bought himself a little motor in the end. As frustrated as I was, I was glad that he had a car, otherwise he wouldn't have been able to collect me.

We eventually got across the city and pulled up near to Piero's. When we got inside it was bustling, and I made a quick beeline for the office, Peter right behind me. Tina emerged from the kitchen just as I reached the office door. She looked at me in surprise.

'Hello. We weren't expecting you in this evening.'

'Yeah, change of plans. I need to keep busy. I just want to do a bit of paperwork, then I'll pitch in.' My voice crackled and gave up towards the end of my sentence. I groaned with the pain and frustration and rolled my head from side to side.

'She's lost her voice,' Peter supplied, patting my shoulder.

'So I see. You don't need to be here if you aren't well.'

'I'm fine,' I croaked and immediately scurried into the office to hide my burning cheeks. There was a little mirror hanging on the wall behind my desk, and I went and checked over my neck. It did look a little bruised. I suddenly wished I had a scarf or something. Peter had followed me into the office and closed the door. He took a seat and hitched his feet up onto the desk. I plonked myself down in my chair and leaned back. 'What a mess.'

'I'm glad you're okay. I think it was a good call to not be alone. I wish I knew more about the demon. We could figure out what it wants. What did it look like?'

I grabbed some paper and a pen and wrote down that it was invisible. He looked over my words and nodded. 'Right. Well that tells us something. Demons always have traits that match what creates them and what they feed on. So anything invisible is going to be to do with secrecy, fear, hidden things, stuff like that. So maybe its job was to hide a secret?'

I frowned at him, then scribbled on my pad, *By killing me?* He read the reply and rocked back and forth on his chair, looking up at the ceiling, deep in thought. *Am I close to revealing a secret?* I wrote, my hand shaking slightly. Peter looked back at my writing and stopped fidgeting. He stared at me, eyes wide.

'Are you?'

I shrugged in response. We sat looking at each other. Neither one of us sure what to make of that idea.

I'm sure I didn't get rid of it for good. I just repelled it. If I'm a threat, it'll be back. Right?

'That's why we're making sure you have protection. And before you object, I know you can take care of yourself, and you proved yourself capable of that earlier, but backup is probably still smart.'

I nodded, swallowing hard against my aching throat. I didn't really object to anything he'd said. If the demon's aspect was something around secrecy, then it was reasonable to assume that it wouldn't strike again in the middle of a busy restaurant. But Piero's wasn't open all the time. What was I meant to do the rest of the time? I didn't really want to impose upon Peter, or any of the other shifters. As if reading my thoughts, which was distinctly not one of his gifts, Peter leaned across the desk and caught my eye.

'It's not a problem. I know things have been tense between us, but I care about you as much as ever, and I know the others are still really grateful for what you did to help us. We all want to protect you.'

I shoved my chair back from the desk and slammed my hands down on the wooden surface. I glared at him.

'I shouldn't need protection,' I said, regretting it at once. My throat burned again. 'Goddammit!' I stood up and kicked the bin over, sending it rolling away under the desk and spilling its contents on the floor. I rolled my eyes and stooped to pick it up. Peter dropped to the floor and helped.

'I get it, I do. It's fucked up, but we'll figure it out. Maybe Antonio already has it in hand.'

I looked at him. He was avoiding my gaze, and his cheeks were pink. It meant a lot that he would say that.

'Thanks,' I said softly. We finished tidying up and got to our feet.

'What do I do with myself?' I winced and swallowed. 'I can't just wait.'

'No, me neither.' He moved around the desk and drew me into his arms. He tucked my head in under his chin and stroked my hair. My head filled with a whooshing sound and I felt as though I was falling through a fog-filled tunnel. The fog cleared and I was looking out through Peter's eyes. He was galloping through the night as a fox, something skimming over the cobblestones ahead of him that was inky black and indistinct. Suddenly his quarry stopped dead and Peter ran straight into it. The darkness engulfed him and slithered down his throat, consuming him from inside. He howled and roared, shifting into his gigantic beast form, and tore at his own flesh with his huge claws. Blood poured from the gashes in his arms and chest, but it came out black and smoking, burning away the skin around the open wounds. His howls of agony ripped at my eardrums.

I was rushing back into the present. Peter still had tight hold of me, but he gently moved me to arm's length and dropped his head to be level with mine.

'Are you okay? What did you see?'

I shook my head, unable to speak. I felt dizzy and sick. He guided me into the chair behind me and crouched in front of me. I held my head in my hands, trying to sort through what I'd seen. I didn't want to believe that anything like this could be happening again so soon. I moaned and fought the wave of nausea moving through me. Was it too much to ask for just a quiet life? What did I expect when I'd got into a relationship with a vampire who ran a criminal empire? Although I hadn't asked for Peter to be a shifter and to get embroiled in all of their conflicts. I'd always just wanted a mundane life. My gift was quite enough excitement and drama for me to handle. I really didn't want more people to die. I felt as though I was responsible for everything. I burst into tears and my shoulders shook.

'Hey,' Peter said, rubbing my shoulder. 'It's going to

be all right. We'll figure it out and make sure everyone gets out of this. I promise.'

'You can't promise that,' I said between sobs.

'I suppose not, but I can promise to do everything I can to help. How's that?' I nodded and sniffed. He passed me a box of tissues from the desk and I took one to clean up my face. 'Let's not worry about what you saw. It'll either be important later, or it won't. We can't do anything about it right now. Let's go and keep busy and take our minds off it. Okay?'

'Sure,' I croaked. I finished wiping my face and took a deep breath that only shook a little bit. We left the office, rolled up our sleeves and got to work. The evening passed quickly as the restaurant steadily filled to capacity. Even as it emptied again we kept busy with cleaning up, and time seemed to rush by in fast forward. Before I knew it, we were saying goodbye to the last customers and I was locking the door. The sudden quiet struck me and I looked around anxiously at the remaining staff members. Peter and I exchanged worried glances but we had to keep our game faces on. We helped finish cleaning up and I tried to join in with the friendly banter in the kitchen.

'We should go,' Peter whispered to me as he piled the last stack of plates into the dishwasher. I frowned at him. 'It's pretty quiet here now. I'd prefer it if we were away from the last couple of people. You know?' I nodded and finished taking the clean glasses through to the bar and stacking them on the shelf behind it.

'Tina, are you okay to finish up here?' I asked. My throat was mostly back to normal after a steady supply of water throughout the evening.

'Yeah, of course.'

Peter and I headed out into the street, me fastening my coat against the cold. He just wedged his hands into the pockets of his hoodie. The street was dark and quiet with just the occasional car sweeping past. I checked my phone but had no messages or missed calls. I wondered what Antonio was doing and if he was safe. I hurriedly tapped out a message asking if he was all right. I pocketed my phone as the two of us set off walking towards Peter's house. The night was a dark cloak wrapped around us, the air close despite being bitterly cold. Peter walked briskly half a pace ahead of me, his head constantly tilting side to side like a dog twitching its ears. I kept glancing over my shoulder, a creeping sensation following me, but I was certain it was just in my head... almost.

As we approached the end of Peter's street my stomach tightened with the memory of being snatched from the dark back road that ran between the back of his house and the river. Rushing water babbled close by now and I made up the slight distance between us to grab his hand. We walked right past the end of his street, heading instead for my house.

'We're meeting some other people,' he whispered

before I could ask. 'We don't know who sent that thing after you. If it was one of the vamps then you aren't safe at my house.' I nodded meekly. We had avoided talking about what had happened at his place when Lucia persuaded Peter's mum to let her and her minions in. If Celino and Laguardia were still after me then they had been invited into Peter's home and could return in future.

We got to my house and I hurriedly unlocked the door. Once we were safely in the hall I was able to breathe a little easier. Peter strode up the hall and into the kitchen. I rushed after him, not needing to ask what he was doing. He flung open the door under the stairs and lifted the hatch into the basement. It hooked back against the wall and he jogged down the steep steps into the pitch-black. I flicked the light on before following him more carefully. When I got down there he was already hoisting open the hidden trapdoor in the floor that led down into the secret catacombs beneath the city. I hadn't been down there since the big fight in which I sent Lucia to hell.

That nervous knot was back in my stomach, but I dutifully followed him down into the cave below my house. A strip light blinked to life, illuminating the sandstone cave. It felt alien after the darkness of the night above ground. The cave was still stacked with boxes that my parents had hidden down there. Mostly they were filled with out-of-date canned goods, but there were also weapons and cans of fuel, clothes and survival supplies.

Everything someone might need for a quick getaway. Before they died, they'd been helping shifters in and out of the city in secret. This was their supply room. Peter didn't hang around. He set off along an unlit passage away from the house, and I scurried after him, lighting my phone on the way. His eyesight was extremely good in the dark, mine wasn't.

'Peter,' I called in a muted voice. 'Where does the protection around my house extend to? If the vamps came at the place from down here, how far could they get without an invitation?'

He slowed down a touch and glanced over his shoulder at me.

'I'm not entirely sure. I think probably as far as the cave. It depends what you consider to be part of your property, really. There's no door. So maybe the trapdoor into the basement? I'm the wrong person to ask.' There was a sharpness to his tone. He was referring to Antonio. Peter would never approve of our relationship. I knew that he loved me and wanted me for himself, so he would probably never approve of anyone I was with. I'd managed to push away my only real friend and I hated that.

The passage led steadily down and the air grew slightly warmer as we descended. Finally we came to the opening into the large cavern at the heart of the catacombs. It was lit with flaming torches in brackets high on the walls. I faintly wondered how they stayed alight, but we were soon joined by three other shifters and my musing was cut short. A tall man with a big axe strapped to his back led the pack, followed by a slender woman who was covered in intricate tattoos, and an older woman with wispy white hair and a lined face. We'd met before when we fought Lucia, but she was in another pack. The young woman with the tattoos grinned at me and waved.

'Hi Crystal,' I said, returning her smile. The guy with the axe was Strikes-Twice. He and Peter greeted each other with brotherly hugs.

'What's happening?' Strikes-Twice asked, looking over us both.

'Walker said we needed ritual help. That's why we invited Water-Over-Stones here.' Crystal nodded her head towards the older shifter. It was the first time I'd caught her name. I gave her a nod and small smile. Walker was Peter's shifter name, and it still felt alien to hear it.

'Eve was attacked by a demon,' Peter replied. 'It tried to kill her. I think it was something to do with secrecy, or something. We need to make sure she's protected and also find out what it was and what it wants.' The others nodded along. I was going to have to recount what had happened and I didn't want to go into the details.

'Where did it happen?' Crystal asked.

'At Antonio's house,' I replied, not knowing where to look. My palms were sweating and I wiped them on my coat. There was the faintest flicker of something unpleasant on Strikes-Twice's face, but he didn't say anything. 'It cut the power and waited until I stepped into the natural light, then it grabbed me and tried to strangle me. It was invisible; I didn't see what it looked like.'

'Right. We can work with that.' Crystal gave me a reassuring smile. 'Shall I try to summon something that can help?' She looked expectantly at Peter.

'We need answers,' he replied.

'Wait, what?' I asked, looking from face to face. 'Why would you deliberately summon anything here? Isn't that dangerous?'

'It's okay,' Crystal said, smiling. 'It's what we do.' She swung a small pack from her back and fished around in it for a minute, then pulled out a small pouch. The others formed a loose circle while she walked around them, sprinkling blue sand in a circle at their feet. She was muttering something under her breath that I couldn't make out. She passed behind me and glanced up from the floor to flash me another smile. I tried to return it but my cheeks wouldn't cooperate. The demons that I'd encountered so far had been big, dangerous, and frightening, to say the least. I didn't like this plan at all and my nerves tingled with apprehension.

Crystal took her place in the circle and raised her hands over her head. The other shifters mirrored her. I followed suit and looked from face to face. They were all so calm. I had to trust that they knew what they were doing.

'Artemis watch and protect this circle,' Crystal said, her voice echoing around the cave. 'We call upon the energy of darkness and secrets. We seek truth and to uncover what is hidden. We ask that our allies come forth.'

My insides churned like crazy. I was half convinced that they were about to summon the very demon who had attacked me. If that did happen, at least I was surrounded by four shifters who could deal with it. Not that I was helpless myself. I took a steadying breath and steeled myself for whatever was about to cross the veil between the worlds. Crystal was still speaking, but her voice had faded away, as if she were on the other side of a tank of water.

The air in the circle rippled and grew cooler. I watched as a shadow emerged, as if peeling itself from around a corner. It was only about four feet tall, but it was like smoke, curling around and over itself. Glowing, red eyes blinked out from between tendrils of black mist. The air around it stilled and Crystal's voice became clear again.

'Greetings, Mist-of-Secrets, thank you for answering our call.'

'Pleasure,' the demon whispered. It didn't appear to be the one that had attacked me, and I was able to relax a little.

'What can you tell us about any powerful new players in Oris? Namely, anyone that would wish to hurt our companion here.' Crystal indicated me and I widened my eyes, not expecting to have the demon's focus drawn straight to me like that. It twisted on the spot, its smokey tendrils rippling around itself, until it was facing me. Its eyes blinked.

'Nothing,' it hissed.

'Now, now, it's truth time.' Crystal crossed her arms over her chest and scowled at it.

'Is it?' the demon replied. 'I don't think you quite understand how secrets and concealment work.'

'What do you want in return for the truth?' Peter asked. The demon slowly rotated to face him.

'A secret, obviously.'

Peter glanced at me, clucked his tongue and then looked at each of the other shifters.

'What kind of secret?' Crystal asked.

'Well, what you want to know is a bit above my pay grade,' the demon said silkily. 'It'll need to be good in order for me to part with this.'

Crystal looked across the circle at Peter; their eyes locked onto each other and I got the distinct impression that they were communicating telepathically. He shook his head ever so slightly, a deep frown on his brow. She raised her eyebrows and then rolled her eyes. 'Well?' the demon prompted, losing a little of its mistiness.

'Right,' Peter said, placing his hands on his narrow hips. 'I have something.' He drew a breath to go on but the demon slithered over to him and planted a smokey tendril against his temple. Peter's mouth popped open in surprise before his eyes rolled back in his sockets and his head lolled to one side.

'What's happening?' I asked, desperate to go to him. Crystal held up a hand and I stayed in my place in the circle, itching to move but not wanting to disrupt things.

'Nice,' the demon said, drawing out the hiss at the end of the word. It seemed to swell and grow more dense as it retreated from Peter. I leaned back a bit, repulsed by the pleasure it seemed to take in learning the secret. Peter's head rolled upright and his eyes were back to normal. He shook his head as if clearing it, and a shudder ran right down his body.

'That was unpleasant,' he said quietly. A smile tugged at the corner of Crystal's mouth, and it was contagious, with the rest of us almost bursting into giggles.

'I would like to tell you everything you wish to know,' the demon said, killing the bubbling laughter. 'However, I believe I only have one piece of the puzzle. And what a puzzle it is.' It turned to face me and leaned closer. I tried not to grimace as its insubstantial smoke wafted towards me. 'You, my dear, are dangerous. You are spoiling somebody's plans. I can smell it all over you. Whose plans and what they are I cannot say, as I do not know.'

'That isn't exactly new information.' Peter folded his arms and scowled.

'You have only just begun to understand my kind. All of you. The bargains that lie ahead of you would make your hair curl. There are layers of power and influence. The depths that you'll sink to in order to get what you think you want would shock you if you knew now how it will unfold.'

'Are you saying that you can see the future?' I asked, daring to be bold. That was part of my gift. I knew all too well how nebulous it was.

'No,' the demon said, purring and turning to me again. 'I can't, but I know how this plays out from experience. You've made a deal with me tonight for information. You've given me a secret in exchange for another. This is just the start.'

'You haven't given us anything we hadn't figured out for ourselves,' Peter said, snapping with impatience.

'Haven't I? Let me speak more plainly then. I cannot see who is controlling this situation because it is beyond the scope of my influence. Whoever it is, is masterful at obfuscation. Layers upon layers of lies and half-truths and power and pawns. They are moving their pieces into place. If they can take the queen, the king will be in check.' It flickered a tendril of smoke in my direction, and my cheeks burned. 'Could you have figured this out without me?'

Before anyone could respond, the demon shimmered across the veil and the cavern grew still and quiet.

'Could we?' I asked, a croak in my voice. No one had a reply for me, but for a few dark looks. Something cold and dark settled at the base of my spine and a shiver ran up it.

CHAPTER EIGHT

I LEFT THE CAVE AND RETURNED TO MY KITCHEN feeling more vulnerable than I had when I entered. How I could feel both closer to the truth and further from it, I didn't understand, but that was the situation. It was well past midnight and I was exhausted, but I desperately needed some sort of resolution, or progress at least. Peter sat in the kitchen and cradled his head in his hands.

'I need to see Antonio.' I pulled out my phone and called him. Peter glanced up at me and dropped his forehead against the table with a heavy thunk. I ignored him and turned away, not wanting to look at him if I got to speak to Antonio. The phone rang for a long time before he answered. The dull sound of an engine hummed in the background.

'Everything okay?' he asked, a snap in his voice.

'Yes. Fine. Sort of. I need to see you. Are you driving?'

'I am. I'm on my way home. What happened?' His voice was raised and the background noise was almost as loud, so he must have been on speaker.

'I'd rather tell you in person. It's nothing awful. No new attacks or anything.'

'Shall I pick you up?'

'If it's not out of your way.' I chanced a glance at Peter, whose head was still planted on the table.

'No, it's fine. I'll see you in a few minutes.' He ended the call without waiting for a reply.

'I'll be going then,' Peter said, getting to his feet.

'Peter,' I said, catching his arm and pulling him into a hug. It was normally him doing that to me. I hated how awkward things were between us. He hugged me back, holding me close.

'I hate it,' he whispered, his breath ruffling my hair.

'What do you hate?'

'You being with him.'

I heaved a sigh and pulled slowly out of his embrace.

'I know. I'm sorry. I love him.' I clutched my own arms over my chest and he nodded glumly, shoving his hands into his pockets.

'I'm trying to accept that. It's just going to take time.'

'I appreciate it. You're still my best friend and I don't want to lose that. I hate how awkward it's been between us lately. I wish it could go back to the way it was before.'

'Me too.' He moved past me into the hall and I followed him to the door. 'Please don't be alone. There's still a demon after you.'

'I know.' I gave him a reassuring smile. I understood

why he was being protective, but I could already tell how stifling I was going to find this. He opened the door and stepped out into the ice cold night. Antonio's car pulled up at the kerb at the same time and Peter rolled his eyes in my direction. 'Be nice,' I pleaded. He pulled me into a one-armed hug and I patted his back. He released me and set off walking without looking at Antonio, who was stepping out of his car.

'Peter,' Antonio said in greeting to Peter's retreating back. Peter held up a hand briefly by way of reciprocation, but he didn't look back or say anything. I would never understand boys. I watched him go as Antonio approached my door. He slipped a hand around my waist and kissed my cheek. 'Everything all right?'

'Yeah. Kind of. Give me two seconds.' I went inside and he followed me into the hall. I dashed up the stairs and grabbed a few things for staying with him overnight. I was back in the hall in under two minutes. Like a perfect gentlemen, he led me to the car and opened the passenger door for me. 'No Nicholas tonight?'

'No, he's doing something else for me. I had to take care of something myself.' We both got into the car and he set off, driving swiftly through the empty streets. 'What happened?'

'We found out that someone wants me out of the way. I'm the queen, or something.' I couldn't look at him. I felt so stupid and self-conscious.

'The queen?' I glanced at him to see him fighting a smirk.

'Like in chess. If I get taken off the board then this thing is free to check the king.'

'And who's the king?'

'You?' I looked at him properly. He didn't say anything, but his jaw twitched.

'I doubt that,' he said at last.

'Why?'

'I don't wish to offend you.'

'What's that supposed to mean?' I turned in my seat, frowning, a little impatience swelling under my skin.

'There is nothing in this world that would need to go through you to get to me.'

'Maybe I'm more important than you think.' I twisted back in my seat and glared out of the window at the city rushing by.

'Eve,' he said, a touch impatiently. 'This is why I didn't want to say. I'm sorry. I didn't mean it like that. You are extremely important, both to me and to others. What I should have said was that you're obviously posing a threat to this thing and it needs you out of its way so that it can carry out its intentions.' He reached out and took my hand. I let him. He raised it to his lips and kissed the palm. I melted a little and allowed myself to relax. Antonio kept hold of my hand for the rest of the drive.

We pulled up in front of his house and made our way

inside and up to his room. The house was still and dark. I shivered slightly being back in the place where I had been so viciously attacked. He seemed to pick up on my trepidation and wrapped his arm around me. He led me to the bed and kissed my neck.

'It'll be dawn soon,' I said, feeling my resistance dissipating rapidly as his lips explored my skin.

'Yes it will. But we have enough time to do something wicked that the night can cloak first.' He peeled my clothes off me and goosebumps prickled all over my body. His fingers were gentle and thorough in caressing each sensitive spot on my body and I quivered in anticipation. Despite everything that had happened, or perhaps because of it, I was more than willing to lose myself in him. I had come so close to death and I was desperate to feel alive. He treated me to some of the best sex I had ever experienced that night, his own yearning for that feeling of being alive evident in the attention he paid to me.

As the room slowly faded from black to steel grey I drifted to sleep at last, utterly spent and ready to sleep forever.

When I woke the room was dark and my stomach gave an impatient growl. I looked around, finding myself alone again. The blackout blinds and drapes were all closed, so I wasn't sure if it was still daylight or not. I slowly eased my aching body from the bed and tiptoed to the dark bathroom for a shower. I was towelling myself dry when the bedroom door opened and Antonio entered, dressed in his typical suit, his long hair neatly tied back. He was carrying a tray of bacon sandwiches and orange juice. I chuckled as I wrapped the towel around me and joined him in the bedroom.

'Did you sleep okay?' he asked, placing the tray on the dressing table.

'Like the dead, thank you.' I pressed myself against him and kissed his lips. He groaned and reluctantly pulled away.

'Much as I would like to repeat last night's activity, I'm actually about to have a meeting downstairs. Do you want to stay or head elsewhere? I don't mind. My marginal preference is for you to stay exactly as you are and wait for me to finish so that I come back and make love to you again, and again, and again.' He laid a trail of gentle kisses across my chest. I whimpered and closed my eyes. His lips were so soft.

'That would be bliss, but I can't just sit around here while you have your meeting.' He lifted his head from my chest and stroked my arms gently, nodding in understanding. 'What time is it, anyway?'

'Eight.'

'In the evening?' I jerked back from him and glared at him. He nodded, smirking. 'You let me sleep all day?'

'You were exhausted. On which note, eat.' He pointed at the food and swept away from me to open the curtains and blinds. I perched on the chair in front of the dresser and picked up a sandwich. I ate hurriedly, anxious to ease the rumbling in my stomach. 'I need to get back downstairs. Will you be all right?'

'Yes,' I said thickly through a mouthful of food. I winced at my own rudeness, but he just chuckled at me and caressed my cheek.

'I'll make sure Frederick knows you'll be coming downstairs soon. He'll call Nicholas to take you home.'

'Thank you.' I had swallowed my food. I stood up and pressed myself against him. My towel came loose and I blinked innocently at him as it dropped to the floor. He groaned again and wrapped his arms around my naked body. He dipped his head and captured my lips in a deep kiss. I returned the kiss hungrily, desperate for a repeat performance but he slowly pulled back and held me at arm's length. His gaze raked down over my pale skin, hunger in his dark eyes.

'As soon as my business concludes I'm coming to find you.'

I giggled, a flutter of anticipation in my belly.

'That sounds good. Are you going to give me the same lecture as Peter about not being alone?' I stooped to retrieve my towel and re-wrapped it around myself.

'You're a grown woman, Eve. I would prefer it if you were with someone else, for backup, but I trust you to take care of yourself if need be. I understand if you don't want to be alone, and if you'd rather be with Peter or one of the others then so be it.' He gently kissed my cheek and a half smile flitted over my face.

'Thank you.' He strode to the door and looked back at me for a final appreciative look at my body before leaving. I giggled again and resumed eating.

Half an hour later I was dressed and made-up and tiptoeing down the thickly carpeted stairs. Voices rumbled from the room down the hall behind the staircase, Antonio's boardroom. Rapid chatter in Italian echoed dully down the hall and I stood at the foot of the stairs to listen, but I couldn't make it out. I picked out Antonio's voice, followed by De Luca, I thought.

'Are you ready to leave us, Miss?' Frederick's voice caught me by surprise and I startled a little, then laughed at myself. He crossed the hall towards me with my coat over his arm and a polite smile on his wrinkled face.

'Yes, thank you.' I took my coat and swung it on, reluctantly following him towards the double doors. He opened one of them and I stepped out into the cold, dark evening. Antonio's black estate car sat idling at the foot of the steps, his driver, Nicholas, waiting by the rear door for me. My phone began to ring and I fished it out of my jeans pocket. I didn't know the number and answered it cautiously.

'Hello?'

'Eve? It's Isabel.' Her voice was bright and overly

friendly.

'Erm, hi. How are you?'

'Fine, thank you. Could you meet me in the morning, please?' My eyes widened in surprise at the odd request.

'I suppose, yes. Where?'

'By the river, where the boats go from.' I knew where she meant.

'Okay. Is it business or social?'

'A bit of both, perhaps?' I could hear the smile in her voice. I approached the car and climbed inside.

'What time?'

'Is eight too early?' I held back a groan. I had no idea what I was going to do about my body clock.

'Fine. I'll see you then.'

'Great, looking forward to it.' Isabel ended the call and I stared at my phone in mild surprise. Nicholas had taken his seat and pulled the car around to set off away from the mansion. I glanced back at it, wishing I was staying. I turned back and watched the back of Nicholas's head, mulling over the odd phone call.

'Nicholas, what do you know about Isabel Shaw?'

'Not a great deal, Miss.'

'Please call me Eve. I hate all that formality.' He nodded and our eyes met briefly in the rear-view mirror. 'I'm sure you must hear things while you're driving people around.'

'If that were the case, Eve, I would have the good

sense of preservation to be extremely discreet about it.'

'Of course, yes. I'm sorry.'

'No problem. May I suggest something?'

'Sure.'

'Be cautious. Cornered animals can lash out.' Our eyes met in the mirror again and his meaning couldn't be more plain.

CHAPTER NINE

IT WAS ONE OF THOSE BRIGHT, CRISP WINTER DAYS. It had been late before I'd managed to get back to sleep again, so I was starting the day in a fog of sleep deprivation. Heavy frost lined the ground and there was a distinct crunch underfoot. I had dressed in black jeans, about four layers on my top half, and my thick winter boots. I had purple, fingerless gloves on that matched my hat and scarf, so I looked surprisingly well coordinated for me. I made for the park just out of the city centre where Antonio and I had once watched *Nosferatu* on the giant projector screen. Memories from that night surfaced as I made my way down the path to the river. So much had happened and changed since then, and yet so much was the same. I was in peril, I didn't quite know who to trust, and I kept feeling as though I was all on my own against the world.

The path curved right at the foot of the hill and I followed it to the bank of the river, which wound slowly through Oris. The banks here were bricked up and a concrete path ran along the edge where tour boats were tied and gently bobbing up and down. It was too early in the morning for the boats to be running, and they were infrequent at this time of year anyway. I looked out over the water as I made my way towards where the path curved back away from the river and under the cover of trees. Benches lined the path, and up ahead I saw a familiar figure sitting cross-legged on one of them. Her long, silvery-blonde hair fell silkily down her back over a thick, white coat. Her impossibly long legs were clad in burgundy jeans and knee-high stiletto-heeled boots. Isabel turned in my direction and saw me. Her eyes brightened. I heaved a sigh and fixed my game face on as I approached her.

'Hi,' she said with a bright smile. She didn't stand up to greet me. I sat down beside her. 'Thanks for meeting me.'

'No problem. How did you get my number?'

'You know who my connections are, Eve.' She flashed a toothy grin my way and I rolled my eyes. That's how it was now. I moved in circles that meant people I hardly knew could find out my phone number and never have to justify the invasion of privacy.

'What did you want to talk about?' I asked, staring out at the water babbling past.

'You don't like small talk, do you?'

'Life's way too short.' We exchanged smiles.

'Fine. I wanted to know if you know what Antonio is doing with De Luca.'

'Okay. I wasn't expecting that.' I frowned and looked out over the gently flowing river. 'Why are you asking me?'

'Because I'm trying to figure something out myself and I would value your input.'

'That's so vague, Isabel. You're married to the mayor. You have that whole thing going on for you. Why does it matter to you?'

'I have an interest in unpicking a messy situation and, quite frankly, I also like you. I admire you, actually. I wanted to try and impress upon you what you're getting into here.' She flicked her hair back over her shoulder and shook it out. I stared at her, completely taken aback. I drew a long breath and exhaled slowly.

'He doesn't tell me anything,' I said softly, staring back out across the water. A family was walking their dog on the opposite bank. I watched the little girl throw a ball and the dog happily bound after it. That was so normal. While I was sitting here with the mayor's wife, discussing my vampire boyfriend's criminal empire. It was ridiculous.

'Has he said he wants to give you plausible deniability?' She smirked and looked sideways at me. I nodded mutely. 'Clever. But you've still seen and heard things, right?'

'I don't know. Maybe. With all due respect, I hardly know you. Why should I share anything like that?'

'Good girl. You're right to be careful about who you trust. I wish I'd been more prudent in my youth.'

I gaped at her. I didn't know how old she might be, but she didn't strike me as someone particularly worldly. I supposed she might have been about forty, but she still looked youthful to me.

'Maybe if you told me something, it might help to break the ice a bit more, build trust, you know? Why are you so invested in my relationship with Antonio?' I didn't want to know that they had once been lovers. My stomach clenched at the possibility. I had no control now over what information she gave me.

'It's probably not what you think, Eve,' she said, gazing across the water. She uncrossed her legs and crossed them the other way—towards me, a gesture of trust and intimacy. She cleared her throat and shook her silvery hair again. 'I had a relationship with De Luca, years and years ago. It was a passion of youth.'

I couldn't hide my surprise and blinked at her with wide eyes. The revelation gave the vision I'd had of them arguing some more context, however. 'I know some things about him that he doesn't want people to know about now that he's the Police Commissioner. So my marriage was arranged on the premise that a little security and influence would keep me quiet.'

'I see. And Antonio helped make that happen, didn't he? For his friend?'

'You're quick.'

'Thanks.' We exchanged glances and smiles again.

'And now you want some insider information on what's going on with them so that you have your own leverage.'

'Nothing's lost on you.' She didn't look at me this time. 'My husband isn't a bad man, really, in the grand scheme of things. He takes good care of me. The poor old fool loves me, I believe. I just don't like other people having power over me.' She kept her gaze on the river and her expression was serene, but there was an edge to her voice that was unmistakable.

'I don't know if I can help you. I mean, I really don't know anything anyway, but I love Antonio. My loyalty is to him. I hope you understand that.'

'I do,' she said, sighing.

What I still wasn't sure about was how much she already knew about Antonio. I was fairly sure that she didn't know about his dietary requirements, but I didn't know how much she knew about his business. I liked her and wanted to help her out of a difficult situation, but what could I possibly say that wouldn't incriminate anyone? There wasn't anything. My mind rushed over all of the things I couldn't say. There was something that Antonio was involved in, however, that twisted my conscience and that I'd do just about anything to prevent. If Isabel could use that knowledge to make a difference, then maybe it would kill two birds with one stone.

'Look, I do know that De Luca has Antonio's support for the election. Like, serious loyalty there.' I caught her eye and gave her a meaningful look. She raised an eyebrow and nodded appraisingly.

'I see. He's quite the political puppeteer, your lover. Did you know that he gets me to influence my husband too?'

'No, I didn't.' I looked at her and she slowly turned her gaze back to me so that we made eye contact.

'Are you shocked?'

'Not really,' I said, shrugging and looking away. I wasn't really shocked by much any more. I knew what Antonio was and that he had his fingers in many pies. 'What sort of things does he get you to do?'

'Give him suggestions for policies to propose and support, or oppose. He likes to get my opinion on things, my husband; he likes to think that he has his finger on the pulse of the city through me.'

'Why do you go along with it? Does Antonio have something on you too?'

She clucked her tongue and shook her head.

'Why are you so sharp? I'm not going to answer that today. I think I've said enough. You have the measure of the man, and of me, it seems. Why do you stay with him? A nice, honest young woman like you should be off having a normal life with a musician or artist boyfriend, surely. One closer to your own age.'

I thought that was a bit rich, considering she was married to a much older man herself. Granted, the mayor wasn't two hundred years older than her, but as far as I could tell, she didn't know just how big the age gap was between myself and Antonio.

'It's complicated,' was all I could think of to say.

'Isn't it always? Is it real between you, or are you as trapped as I am?'

She was glaring at me, but her eyes were wide and enquiring, not narrow and accusing.

'It's certainly real on my part. I hope it is for him too. It seems to be.' Did I really have his heart? Couldn't he be manipulating me just as much as he manipulated everyone else? I heaved a sigh and straightened my coat. 'I don't know anything about how they're doing it, but they're going to make damn sure De Luca wins. Okay? That's all I have. Please don't ask me for anything else.' I stood up, making my intentions clear.

'No, that's very helpful. You didn't have to tell me anything, so I appreciate you saying that much.' She stood up and straightened her gloves. 'Thank you.'

'Just be careful. I really do know how powerful these people are. Are you sure you do?' I asked, catching her eye. 'Don't go making waves and getting hurt.'

'I'll be fine, Eve, don't worry. And I won't allow my knowledge to be traced back to you.' She gave me a wry smile. I wished I could say that I hadn't even been thinking about that, but I couldn't lie. What would happen if Antonio asked me about this meeting, or anything relating to Isabel? I had a terrible track record of trying to lie to him. He could see right through me.

'Well, I appreciate that. Take care.' I set off along the path. Isabel's ridiculous heels clacked rapidly on the path behind me and she caught me up. I looked at her but kept walking.

'Eve, listen. If you get in any trouble, you can call me.' I nodded once.

'Likewise.'

'Remember what I told you at New Year's?'

'To make sure I have my own power? That's not a problem for me.' I laughed lightly, but she fixed me with a stern glare.

'Real power is the ability to walk away. Would he let you do that?' I kept my gaze on the path ahead and tried not to let my face betray me.

'Of course he would. We've talked about me leaving Oris, actually. I was only meant to be back here temporarily. I want to go back to Caerton.'

'But you're still here.'

'For now.'

'Have you asked him to do anything for you? Anything big?' I didn't answer. There was no way she knew what I'd asked him. 'Your silence speaks volumes, Eve. He hasn't done it, has he?'

'You're fishing.'

'No, I have experience. You're young and optimistic.

You probably asked him to give up his life of crime for you because you're a sensible and law-abiding person.'

'Are you sure? You don't really know me, Isabel. As a matter of fact, I have asked him for things and he has given them to me. He changed one of his more dubious business practises for me when we first got together. He gave my friend's dad a big pay rise when I asked him to as well.'

'Well, I didn't know about that, obviously, but has anything really changed?'

I didn't reply. We had reached the top of the hill, and the rumbling of traffic on the main road beyond the park gates drew my attention away from her perfect hair. I hated that she was right.

'I'm not going to make excuses for him. Yes, his business bothers me; yes I have asked him to give it up, but I knew what he was when I got involved with him, and I love him for all that he is. Either he'll go straight or he won't. I make no claim to being able to change him. We'll just have to see what happens.'

'That sounds very mature.' She nodded sagely. 'I had another thing I wanted to ask you about, actually. What happened to Lucia? I haven't seen her in weeks. I get the impression she left town.'

I swallowed and fixed a bright smile onto my face.

'She went home,' I said sweetly.

'To Naples?' Isabel asked, surprise in her wide eyes. I nodded. There was no way I was going to tell Isabel that I sent Antonio's sister to a hell realm. 'I see. Well, I bet that simplifies things a bit for you both.' She smiled sweetly and turned on her heel to stalk out of the park onto the street. I watched her go before following slowly enough to not catch her up. Why did she have to be so right about so much?

CHAPTER TEN

My conversation with Isabel stayed with me all day. I tried to work at Piero's, but my head was still firmly in the park. I had been wanting to believe that everything Antonio had promised me would eventually come to pass. He had been so quick in the early days to make changes to accommodate me. He wasn't feeding on the shifters any more, and he had helped to oust his evil sister. That was big. It was all stuff I couldn't say to Isabel though, and she had got inside my head and made me doubt him.

I shrugged it off eventually and made a commitment to myself to trust him, but I couldn't help that worry gnawing inside me over what Isabel would do with the information about the election. Much as I wanted Antonio to go straight, I didn't want to cause problems or for him to end up getting hurt. I suspected she would just use the information to benefit herself privately. I couldn't see her going public with it. There was no evidence to support my claim anyway.

Needless to say, while all of this was churning inside

my head, I didn't get much work done. Not that there was a great deal I needed to do now that Tina was in charge. She was doing a good job, as far as I could tell. The restaurant was almost always busy. The staff seemed happy and on the ball too. It felt like the best decision I could have made. Of course, it helped that the restaurant was no longer syphoning off twenty percent of its revenue to pay its protection money to the Camorra. That had been the very first deal I'd made with Antonio. That had to have made a big difference to the success of the business.

As sunset approached, I left the restaurant in Tina's capable hands and walked through the bustling rush-hour city. I was utterly exhausted from being up so early on just a couple of hours' sleep. Cars filled the narrow roads and pedestrians packed the pavements on their way to or from work. The city operated on two main shifts – the daytime retail and offices, and the night-time bars, clubs, and theatres. It was a city of two halves, and I had always loved that about Oris, but now I was trying to function in both worlds and it was killing me, slowly and painfully.

I took a detour through a small park, enjoying the fresh air and the last flare of sunlight on the horizon. There was a little wooden bridge across the river, and I spent a minute standing on it and watching the water flow beneath me. The gentle babble across the rocks at the banks was soothing. There were still piles of old snow along the riverbank and at the edges of the path through the park from the previous week's snowstorm. The air was still and quiet. I had almost forgotten that there was a demon after me. I had been unaccompanied all day and felt practically normal. As I approached the gap in the hedge that led out to the road that ran along the back of Peter's house, the shadows seemed to deepen. My heartbeat cranked up a notch and it pounded in my throat. I glanced over my shoulder at the empty park behind me. *It's just the sunset*, I told myself. I walked cautiously towards my exit and peered through it. There was no sign of anything being amiss, and my pulse settled a little. I drew a breath and stepped through the gap. The back road was deserted and still. I stepped onto the road and set off walking more briskly for home. I hated this street. It was where Lucia had had me snatched. It always set me on edge. I had hardly set foot here since that night. I turned the corner onto a lighter and busier road where I could breathe a little easier. I was only a few minutes from home and I practically ran the rest of the way. The sun dropped below the horizon and the sky grew steadily darker. I thought about what Peter and Antonio would make of my going off on my own and hated to admit that they'd be furious. The independent and rebellious part of me was screaming against their efforts to protect me.

I turned onto my street and dashed for my house, drawing out my keys as I approached. A car's headlights swept into the road ahead, and it crawled towards me. It wasn't Antonio's Maserati, or Peter's Honda. I kept my head down and rushed forward. The sleek, silver Audi pulled level with me and slowed to a halt. I was determined not to look. My door was almost within reach.

'Eve?' I came to a halt and looked over my shoulder with a resigned sigh. Marco De Luca was looking at me from the open window of the car. I fixed a smile to my face and took a step towards his car.

'Hi. What are you doing in this neighbourhood?' I found it hard to believe that it was the coincidence his expression was trying to indicate.

'Do you have a minute?' What was going on? First Isabel, now the police commissioner. Why was I suddenly so popular?

'I suppose.' I looked longingly at my front door. I didn't want to get into his car. I equally didn't want to invite him into my little house. 'I don't have long. I have a date.' I hoped that would get me out of it. De Luca smiled broadly and pulled his car up to the kerb a short distance from my house. I waited for him and, sure enough, he got out of his car and ambled over to me, his hands deep in the pockets of his long, black coat.

'How are you?'

'Fine. You?'

'I'm well, thank you. Although, I am slightly concerned about something. Do you think we could talk inside?'

I looked at my door again, and then into his dark eyes.

His immaculate hair and suit gave the impression of someone who cared a great deal about appearances, but I knew that still waters often run deep. There was a lot to this man that I didn't know. There was whatever Isabel had on him. Not to mention how aggressive he had got at the ball. I wasn't at all comfortable with him.

'I don't think so, sorry. If we can't talk out here then perhaps it had better be left unsaid.' I drew myself up to my full height.

'I just wanted to apologise for what happened at New Year. And to check that you were okay.'

'That was weeks ago,' I said, raising an eyebrow.

'I know. I'm sorry for not doing this sooner.'

'Sure.' I crossed my arms over my chest and watched him closely. 'Was that all?'

'Do you need anything? Is there something I can do to make up for my actions?' He took a step towards me. I reached into my coat pocket and wrapped my fingers around a large coin that rested there. I rubbed my thumb over it as I thought about what to say to buy time.

'I think I have all my needs met, thank you.' Was I missing an opportunity to extort a favour from the Police and Crime Commissioner? Was I really even thinking that? I lifted the coin from my pocket and drew it up to my mouth. 'Between myself, Antonio, and Peter,' I emphasised the last name and pressed my lips against the coin, hoping I didn't look too odd, 'I think I have it all covered.'

De Luca tilted his head to one side and looked at me quizzically. One question burned strongly through his mind, strong enough for me to hear it without him saying it out loud: *Who's Peter?*

'Are you sure there's nothing I can do for you?' he asked instead. He took another step towards me and I took a step back towards my door.

'I'm good, really. I'm puzzled as to why you looked up my address and came to see me today. You could have called me sooner.'

He clucked his tongue and shook his head.

'It took a while for me to clear my calendar. It's a busy time for me.'

'Right. Well, if that's everything, I'll be going.'

Pounding footsteps on the pavement turned my head. Peter was sprinting towards us. I breathed a sigh of relief and raised a hand to wave at him. De Luca looked from me to Peter as he slowed to a halt and gasped for breath.

'Hi.' He draped an arm around me and looked De Luca up and down.

'You're late. Bless you for running,' I said, fixing him with what I hoped was a meaningful look. 'Peter, this is Marco De Luca, the Police Commissioner.' Peter's eyes grew wide and he looked at De Luca in surprise.

'Wow. Erm... Nice to meet you.' He extended a hand, which De Luca took. They gripped each other's hands tightly and shook once. De Luca looked at me briefly, confusion flickering across his face.

'Likewise. Are you a friend, or colleague, or...?' De Luca's implied suggestion hung silently on the still air.

'Friend,' Peter and I said together. We glanced at each other and a small laugh escaped my lips.

'I see. Well, it was good catching up with you, Eve. Give me a call if you have any more thoughts on that matter we discussed.'

'I don't think I will, but thank you.' I pocketed my talisman again and gave him a rigid smile. He backed away towards his car, then turned and left without another word or backwards glance.

'What the fuck was that about?' Peter asked. I led him to the door, unlocked it and took him inside.

'I don't really know. He showed up and feigned an apology for his behaviour at New Year.' I immediately regretted saying anything.

'What behaviour?' Peter asked, his voice sharp.

'Oh, it was no big deal. We danced and I got a vision. He sort of grabbed my arm, but it was an accident.' We had made our way to the kitchen and I went about putting the kettle on, out of sheer force of habit.

'Don't excuse it, Eve,' he said, scowling.

'I'm not. It was a bit confusing, that's all.'

'Then why did he feel the need to apologise?'

'He didn't. That's what I mean. It wasn't a genuine apology. It was an excuse to see me. I think he was trying to offer me a bribe to keep quiet about other stuff. Not the ball, but the election.'

'Oh, wow.' Peter dropped into a chair at the kitchen table. 'Why did you call me?'

'Because I felt really uncomfortable. He was pushing to come inside and I wasn't sure where the conversation was going. I got nervous. I hope you don't mind. I didn't pull you away from anything important, did I?'

'No, it's fine. I was patrolling and wondering who was with you.' He looked awkwardly down at his hands splayed on the table. He looked up at me then with narrowed eyes. 'You were alone.'

'I was, and I was fine.'

'You had to call for my help.'

'I didn't have to. I chose to. For backup. I was handling De Luca.'

'Okay, seriously. How fucked up is your life right now? A few months ago would you have ever thought you'd be on speaking terms with politicians, and crime lords?' He let out a bark of laughter.

'It's really messed up!' I started laughing too, a stitch forming in my side, but still I couldn't stop. It was almost as though the tension of the last few weeks had burst completely. The mild hysteria rushed from us both and it felt so good to be laughing with my best friend again. My phone rang, echoing loudly over our laughter. I sobered quickly and looked at the screen. 'It's Antonio.' Peter's face tightened and he looked away. I answered my phone and pressed it to my ear.

'Hi.'

'Are you all right?'

'Yes. Why do you ask?'

'I just had a bad feeling. Did something happen?'

'De Luca paid me a visit. He said he wanted to apologise for what happened at the ball, but I'm pretty sure he was really trying to buy my silence.'

'On what?'

'I don't know. His behaviour that night? On what I saw? Could he know about that?'

'I don't see how.'

'Antonio, how well do you really know him? I know that you're friends and business partners, or whatever, but do you trust him?'

'Eve, I hardly trust anyone. I'd have thought you knew that by now.'

'Do you trust me?' I asked softly, turning away from Peter, suddenly painfully aware that he'd be able to hear every word Antonio said with that super-hearing of his.

'Of course I do, *cerbiatta*. You're one of the few.'

'Okay. Then trust me when I say you need to be very careful with him. Whatever business you still have with him, it would be wise to try to conclude it, I think. I get the feeling that whole situation is going to flare up and I'd really rather neither of us were involved in it.'

'I understand. I will look into it. Carefully.'

'Please, just keep your promise to me, the one you made before Christmas.'

'I am doing, Eve. I'm taking it all apart. It's just going to take some time to do it right. But I promise it is happening. We shouldn't be having this conversation over the phone though. We'll talk more later.'

'Sure.'

'Are you with someone?'

'Peter.' I glanced at him and he looked back at me at the sound of his name. I gave him a half smile.

'Okay. I'm glad you aren't alone. Will you both meet me in an hour?'

'Okay. Where?'

'Hungate Bridge.'

'Sure. Peter?' I asked, turning slightly away from my phone to speak directly to him. He nodded. 'Yes,' I said to Antonio. 'That's fine. One hour?'

'Yes, please. Be careful until then. Something is still out there.'

'I know. I will. See you soon.' I hung up the phone and looked down at the black screen, dully wondering where my laughter went.

'What do you think he wants to talk to us about?' Peter asked, not making eye contact.

'I guess we'll find out.'

CHAPTER ELEVEN

WE LEFT TO MEET ANTONIO. The tension made my muscles ache. I was desperate for some sort of break, that was for sure. We walked quickly, night folding tight around us. The cold went straight to my chest and I clutched my coat and scarf around me. I longed for sunlight and warmth. I suddenly resented how nocturnal I had become since Antonio Vitale entered my life.

Peter led me down a side street and into a dark alley between tall buildings. The alley opened up into a dark courtyard with cobblestones. One of the buildings was the back of a pub which I knew pretty well. Barrels were stacked up by the back door. Attached to the pub was what used to be a stable block back when it was an inn. It stretched out in front of us with its stable-like doors at intervals, and at the far end was a huge arch that led out onto the street beyond. Peter took a few steps towards the arch, and I followed, glancing warily at the long shadows on either side of us.

A breeze lifted my long hair, and Peter came to an

abrupt halt in front of me. He held out a hand to stop me and cocked his head to one side. The breeze lifted again and a whistle carried on the air.

'What is it?' I whispered, clinging close to his side. He gave a single shake of his head.

A shadow moved to my left and my head snapped to face it. It peeled out from between the barrels piled up by the back door of the pub and began to slither across the cobblestones towards my feet. I took a few steps back and Peter turned to see what was happening. Peter placed himself between me and the creeping shadow. It peeled up from the ground and took form in front of us. It was almost pitch-black and seemed to be both without depth and also infinitely deep. It was like gazing into a hole in the world.

'You have no place in this world,' Peter said, his voice strong and commanding. 'If you don't return across the veil of your own accord, I will make you.'

The demon undulated and moved closer to us. I took a step back and glanced over my shoulder towards the archway and the lit street beyond.

'I have no interest in you, dog. I'm here for her.' Something like a long arm slithered out from the centre of the blackness and reached towards me. My vision from before flickered to the front of my mind and I again saw Peter being consumed by a demon like this one. The situation was different, this wasn't the fulfilment of prophecy, but the panic that surged up in my chest was as real as if it were the moment from my vision.

'Never going to happen.' Peter shimmered and shifted in front of me. His whole body erupted in thick fur and he grew a foot taller. His powerful legs thickened and his hands ended in sharp talons. His face morphed into a long muzzle with pointed teeth. A growl rumbled up from his chest and out of his throat. I had seen his Agrius beast before, I had even seen it from his eyes in a vision, so I wasn't afraid of him, but it was still strange to see my childhood friend turn into a monster.

The demon halted and flickered slightly, then it darted sideways and slipped past Peter and towards me. I scurried away towards the arch with my heart pounding hard and my breath quickening. Peter leapt into its path and there was a horrible ripping sound as he tore into the demon. I wasn't sure how something so intangible could tear, but Peter's supernatural strength managed to do something to it as it yowled in pain. It oozed away from him with a chunk hanging off itself, like a partially severed limb, and limped sideways where it bumped into the stone wall of one of the buildings surrounding us.

Peter lunged at it to strike again, but the demon slithered out of his reach and slipped across the cobblestones towards me again. It got past Peter, ducking under his clumsy arms as he lunged. The demon raced towards me and I flung out my arms and pushed with all of the mental energy I could summon to stop it in its tracks.

It stopped and hung there in the air, suspended off the ground. A shadow not attached to any surface. I didn't dare lower my arms. I held them out, shaking with the effort, my jaw tight and my shoulders squeezed back towards my spine. Peter spun around and barrelled into the demon. He managed to wrap himself around it and tumbled to the ground with it.

'Don't kill it!' I dropped my arms and ran to his side. 'We have to find out who sent it.'

'I will not betray my master.'

'Yes you will,' Peter said, snarling as he strained to contain the demon. I crouched down beside them and pulled off my glove. I reached my hand towards the strange, formless darkness, unsure what I would feel. It was like dipping my fingers into thick liquid, like tar, but it was ice cold. A shiver ran up my arm and a familiar rushing sensation flooded my head. I tipped over backwards and collapsed on the cobblestones.

A demon similar to the one in Peter's arms, but more tangible, filled my field of vision. It was inky black and liquid-like, with many tendrils flowing out from its gigantic face. It loomed over Oris with its tendrils connecting to many hundreds of people, who were the size of ants beneath it. The vastness of this thing was horrifying. It cloaked the city in its darkness and was like a puppeteer controlling its many marionettes below with something like glee on its face.

There was a snarl nearby and my mind returned to the dark courtyard. I sat up gingerly just as Peter tore the demon apart with his clawed hands. The thing scattered into pieces and disappeared, absorbed into the shadows of the courtyard.

'Are you okay?' I asked, getting to my feet. Peter had shifted form and was getting to his feet too.

'Fine. Annoyed, but fine. You?' He strode over to me and looked into my eyes before grabbing me by the shoulders and pulling me into a hug.

'I'm okay. I got a vision.'

'I guessed. That's why I thought it was safe to end the thing. What did you see?'

'This is big, Peter. So much worse than we thought. When Antonio said it was too much for him to handle alone, he wasn't joking.' I kept my voice low. A number of lights had flicked on in windows around us.

'Let's get out of here.' Peter led me swiftly towards the arch and we broke into a run when we hit the street. We didn't stop until we had crossed the road and turned a corner. I grabbed hold of a wall to lean against to catch my breath. Peter, of course, wasn't breathless at all.

'It's controlling the whole city,' I said in a trembling whisper. 'It's everywhere.' We both looked around anxiously. 'I think the vision was partly symbolic, but the meaning was pretty clear. It's controlling lots of people, lots of things. I don't know how on earth we'll figure out who or what, or what this thing is really doing. I don't know where to start.'

'Did you see any distinct faces?' Peter asked, his eyes fixed firmly on mine. I shook my head but stopped, frowning, as my mind's eye raced over the scene I had witnessed. That wasn't true. There had been faces, I just hadn't stopped to focus on any of them. I closed my eyes and eased myself into the memory. The people were so small. I squeezed my eyes tight in concentration and tried to zoom in on the figures below the demon. It was like sifting through a photo of a large crowd, looking for a familiar face. I scanned the memory, allowing it to move slowly so that one row of people moved aside to reveal new figures behind them.

There was someone casting a vote, I didn't know their face but behind them was one I did know: Marco De Luca. I gasped and kept looking. Beyond him, closer still to the demon, a little larger than the other figures, in his long black coat with his hair loose and slightly concealing his face, was Antonio. My eyes popped open and I stared at Peter. He must have recognised my expression because he nodded in understanding.

'It's controlling De Luca,' I said, a croak in my voice. Peter didn't look surprised. 'And Antonio.' Peter ran his hands through his hair and closed his eyes.

'Right. Eve, you know what this means?'

'We can't trust him. I know. But we have to help him.'

'Eve,' he said, not hiding his exasperation.

'He probably doesn't even know. Whatever this thing is, it's hidden. It probably hasn't revealed itself to anyone. It looked like a sort of puppeteer in my vision. We need to cut the strings.'

'All right. Let's get off the street. We need to tell the others.' He turned to go and I grabbed his arm, wheeling him back to face me.

'No, Peter! We don't know who else it's controlling. We have to be really careful with this information. If we tip it off that we know this much someone could get hurt.'

'I guess,' he said, not looking sure at all.

'Is there anything you can do, a ritual or something that will help identify who's been corrupted and who's clear?'

'There might be. I don't know. Maybe you could ask Weaver?'

'That's a good idea. We might need outside help to deal with this.'

'If it comes to it, but let's at least try to tackle it ourselves first. Just ask about a ritual. Okay?' I nodded and the pair of us set off for our meeting with Antonio, although I had no idea now what we would be able to say. How was I going to be alone with him now? Was it even safe? If the demon wanted me dead, then maybe it would have Antonio do the deed now that two of its minions had failed.

CHAPTER TWELVE

Peter and I made our way swiftly through the city, avoiding the unlit shortcuts and sticking to the main roads. It was the tail end of rush hour and the city buzzed with nightlife. Cars chugged past on the too-narrow roads; people rushed past us with their shopping bags, phones in front of their faces. Peter had hold of my hand and didn't relinquish it the rest of the way to Hungate Bridge. I was still too scared and shocked to object. We left the city centre and took the riverside walk, which was bustling with people on their way home from work. Cyclists sped past us frequently, their wheels splashing up the muddy slush left over from the snow. The narrow footbridge stood ahead as the foot traffic on the path lightened after several exits into streets beside the river. A lone figure stood on the centre of the bridge, silhouetted against the orange street light that hung from the post on the far side. His hair hung loose about his shoulders and his long coat flapped slightly in the stiff breeze.

Peter filed onto the narrow bridge ahead of me and I

slid my hand free, suddenly acutely aware of how the gesture might appear to Antonio.

'What's wrong?' Antonio asked as we approached. He tugged his hands from his coat pockets and took hold of my shoulders, reading every inch of my flustered face.

'We were attacked,' Peter answered, drawing Antonio's scrutiny away from me. His dark eyes flashed dangerously in Peter's direction.

'What?' he hissed as a couple passed us on the bridge.

'Maybe we should head somewhere else?' I suggested, watching the couple walk away. 'Why did you ask us to meet you here anyway?'

'I have a lead on Celino,' Antonio said quietly, glancing over his shoulder. 'He's been seen near here. But that can wait. I need to know what happened to you two.' I took his hand and marched across the bridge. Peter followed us with a deep frown on his brow and his wary eyes on Antonio. I led us onto the footpath on the opposite side of the river to the way Peter and I had walked. It was much quieter and the path led away from the river between a small field and the end of a row of houses. It was quiet and somewhat private. I stopped and looked both ways to check that we were alone.

'We were on our way here when a demon came at us out of the shadows,' I said in a low voice, still glancing both ways up and down the alley.

'In public?' Antonio asked sharply, shock in his wide

eyes.

'No, it was in a courtyard away from the road,' Peter answered. 'I killed it. We weren't followed here.'

Peter and I exchanged silent, cautious glances, an unspoken agreement to keep the specifics out of the conversation.

'Were you hurt?' Antonio asked, looking me carefully up and down.

'No, I'm fine,' I replied.

'So am I,' Peter put in with a scowl. Antonio threw a filthy look his way and I stepped between them.

'It was an opportunistic sneak attack. That's all. It might not have even been anything to do with what happened at your house.' Antonio fixed his gaze on me, his eyes narrowed slightly and an objection on his tongue. 'Although it probably was connected,' I added quickly. 'But no real harm was done. Peter got rid of it and we're both fine.'

'I don't like this at all,' he said, not meeting my eye. 'We need to know why you're being targeted.'

'Well for now, we just all have to be careful,' I said, looking quickly from him to Peter, who stood scowling silently beside us, chewing his thumbnail.

'Agreed,' Antonio said with a firm nod.

'Yeah,' Peter said, his thumb wedged between his teeth.

'Okay, so I asked you to meet me here because, as you

know, I've been trying to track down Lucia's allies since they ran off. They need to feed, so I've been following up leads on missing people, one or two bodies. They were never very good at covering their tracks, so I thought it would be easy to find them, but it seems they've learned caution at last. They didn't care about human authorities tracking them down before under Lucia's protection, but they care about me finding them.' A sneer crept onto Antonio's face that sent an unpleasant twist through my insides, but I hated Celino and Laguardia and welcomed whatever wrath Antonio visited on them when he found them. They had abducted me, and Celino tortured me at Lucia's command.

'So what did you find?' I asked, glancing anxiously around. We were still alone.

'One of my contacts told me that a young man was arrested here two nights ago for selling drugs. He goes by Davey and has been in and out of police custody regularly for years. They never hold him for long. He was turned out again quickly after giving the police information on seeing someone dumping a body into the river just there.' He pointed towards the bank beside the bridge. 'He described someone who looked remarkably like our old friend.' My stomach clenched.

'Did they find the body?'

'They're not looking, obviously.' He nodded back towards the river. He was right. The area would be taped off and floodlit if they were searching. Even if they'd found the body already there would still be signs of the search. I rolled my eyes.

'De Luca.'

'He's useful.'

Peter let out a derisive snort. Antonio and I looked his way and he held a hand up in apology.

'I don't want police all over this, Eve. It's above their pay grade. You know better than anyone that people could get hurt if they go poking around into Celino's business.' He put a hand on my shoulder and I tried to hide the revulsion from my face. I didn't entirely succeed though, and Antonio withdrew his hand with a concerned frown.

'Have you searched the area for him already?' Peter asked, stepping closer.

'I have, and I haven't found anything. But, Eve, I thought you might be able to pick something up with your gift.' He caught my gaze and gently touched my chin. I clenched my teeth and shook my head slightly to break the contact. I hadn't been afraid of Antonio like this for a long time. I'd gotten so comfortable around him, and even though I never forgot what he was, I trusted him. Now, after seeing that vision, the trust was shattered. I couldn't know for sure that he didn't know about the demon. Maybe he was fully in league with it and doing its bidding. I didn't really believe that; after all, he had told us about the demon in the first place. Even if he was completely unaware, everything he said and did was under question. Could the demon step in and take control of him at will? Was it monitoring everything Antonio did?

'It doesn't work like that,' I said at last, aware I'd been silent for too long, lost in my thoughts. 'I need to touch a person.' I wasn't entirely sure that was still the case after getting a vision from the demon who attacked us, but it had still been a creature. I didn't think I could get a reading off inanimate objects.

'Maybe, but your powers are growing. Maybe it's worth a try?' Antonio urged.

'You don't have to do anything you're not comfortable with, Eve,' Peter said, gently taking my elbow and pulling me away from Antonio.

'Of course she doesn't,' Antonio snapped, glaring at Peter. 'I'm not going to make you do anything, *cerbiatta*,' he added more softly to me. His pet name for me meant fawn. That was how he saw me. A deer in headlights.

'I'll try,' I said, pulling away from both of them. I moved over to the riverbank and ran my hand down the metal post at the end of the bridge. I squatted down at the edge of the gravel path that ran away from the river, and pressed the fingers of my other hand into the wet dirt beside the path, still holding onto the bridge. There was no fence between the path and the river; it was badly lit and not overlooked, the perfect place to dump a body into the river. That was, provided you didn't get seen by a drug dealer. I closed my eyes and took a deep breath, searching through my mind for something that wasn't a thought of my own.

A flicker of an image of a body rolling down the steep bank into the black water below surfaced, but that could just have been my imagination based on what Antonio had told me. I kept searching, waiting for a surge of intruding vision, like I normally experienced. Nothing came.

I tugged my fingers free of the sticky mud and wiped them on the metal bridge.

'Nothing?' Antonio asked.

'No, sorry. I don't normally get visions off objects, let alone the ground.' I kept wiping the mud off my fingers, resorting to using my coat. 'Maybe if you introduced me to the drug dealer I'd get something?' I was mostly joking and a snort of laughter escaped as I looked up from my dirty hand to Antonio's face. He blanched and avoided my gaze. 'What?' I asked.

'He's disappeared.'

'Why am I not surprised?' Peter asked, making a circle with his head in a huge exaggeration of an eye-roll.

'Damnit, Tony.' I smacked the side of the bridge in frustration, and the bridge smacked back with a vision. A rush of energy surged through me and I was standing on the other side of the bridge, about to step onto it, before I saw Celino rolling a deathly pale body of a woman into the river. She was weighted with what looked like a sack of sand tied to her legs. I staggered backwards and ran quickly and quietly away the way Peter and I had walked to meet Antonio. With a gasp I returned to the present and my own body. Peter had an arm around me and Antonio was looking at me with wide eyes, a sickly shade to his skin.

'What did you see?' Peter asked softly at my ear.

'Nothing we don't already know,' I said, leaning against him, thankful for his support.

'Why did you call me that?' Antonio asked. His voice was dark but fractured, and the look on his face was haunting.

'I'm sorry?' I asked, half of me still replaying the vision.

'You called me Tony. You never call me that.' He looked like he was about to be sick, which I didn't think was possible for a vampire.

'I don't know. It just came out.' Confusion made it difficult to form sentences. Peter gave me a gentle squeeze and tried to lead me onto the bridge, but I stood fast and stared at Antonio, realisation dawning on me. 'I'm sorry,' I whispered.

'Why are you apologising to him?' Peter asked, exasperation evident in his tone.

'It's what his sister used to call him,' I said quietly out of the corner of my mouth.

Antonio's nostrils flared slightly and his jaw shifted

from side to side a few times. He clenched his fists and let out a guttural sound from his throat. I found it difficult to summon any more sympathy for him at that moment, when he showed so little regard for my state after the vision struck.

I leaned against Peter and closed my eyes, allowing the vision to replay in my mind. I skipped it back to the start like rewinding a tape. I watched the body drop into the river again. It was a woman in a skimpy, black dress. She was almost translucent, drained of blood. I ran it back again and made myself look away. I could see up the dark alley we were standing at the end of. Red lights shone, slightly out of focus and further away, as the poor witness had been on the other side of the river. There was a car there, its boot wide open.

'Celino moved the body here in a car,' I said, gasping for breath. 'He parked up there.' I pointed past Antonio to the far end of the alley.

'He's got the use of a car?' Peter asked. 'Well that's good, right? If it's stolen then there might be a record of it.'

'I'll check,' Antonio said, his voice slow and far away. 'It might be one of my cars.'

Peter let out another snort. 'Must be nice to just not even miss a whole car.'

Antonio ignored the dig. He focused back on me, suddenly snapping back to the present moment. I hoped he'd stopped seeing Lucia in my place, and a small tug of remorse stirred in my chest. I didn't want to hurt him. I wanted to help him, if I could.

'Yes! If they're still using my car then I can track it!' He swept towards me, his face alight with optimism. Peter tightened his grip on me but allowed Antonio to clasp my face between his cool hands. 'Thank you. I apologise for putting you through that and reacting so poorly. You shocked me, but that's no excuse.'

'It's okay. She was your sister. No matter what she did, you're bound to be reminded of her sometimes.' I managed a sheepish smile.

'Shall I take you home? Both of you. I could drop you off somewhere, Peter.' He released my face and looked into Peter's eyes. I watched the exchange cautiously.

'Sure. Eve? Where do you want to be?'

'My house. I need to sleep.'

'Let's go.' Antonio took my hand and gently pulled me out of Peter's grasp. He grudgingly let me slip away and followed a step behind as Antonio led us down the alley to where I'd seen the parked car in my vision. His black Maserati was parked just around the corner and we all got into it, me sitting in the front passenger seat and Peter folding his long legs into the back seat. A curtain twitched in the downstairs window of the house we were outside of and I hid a smile at the thought of people wondering what a car like that was doing parked outside. I knew what I would have thought a few months ago—I'd have been peeking out at it too.

Antonio pulled away from the kerb and sped us across the city to my house. Peter and I both got out of the car, as he only lived around the corner. Antonio got out too and walked around to the pavement, an excited smile lighting up his face. I couldn't share his enthusiasm, given how my evening had gone.

'I hope you get some rest,' he said, wrapping his arms around me. I hugged him back, sadness tugging at the corners of my eyes. 'I'll see you tomorrow night, won't I?'

'I expect so. I hope the lead pans out. Let me know if you find them.'

'I will.' He released me and turned his attention to Peter. 'Thank you for your assistance, Peter. I appreciate it. I'm glad Eve has you around as well.'

'No problem,' Peter replied stiffly, his hands wedged into the pockets of his jeans.

'Good night,' Antonio said and leaned in for a kiss. I let him kiss my lips softly, not wanting to send him any red flags, but my heart wasn't in it and I was relieved that it was just a brief kiss. We watched him get back in his car and drive away.

'Well?' Peter said, his eyes still on the tail lights as they turned the corner. 'What are you thinking?'

'I feel sick,' I said, rather too honestly.

'Do you want me to come in with you?'

'Yeah. Can you keep me company?' He nodded and we

filed inside. I was exhausted and just needed to sleep. I locked the door and leaned back against it, my eyes closed. 'I'm going straight to bed, Peter. I hate to ask, but can you just hang out here for a bit so I'm not alone?'

'Of course, whatever you need,' he said softly. Guilt gnawed at me. I was taking advantage of his feelings for me, I knew that. It wasn't fair, but it felt necessary. As I trudged up the stairs I made a silent promise to myself to change things and simplify the relationships in my life.

CHAPTER THIRTEEN

I SLEPT BADLY, tossing and turning for several hours and gave up just before dawn. I checked the house and found that Peter had left in the night. A hastily scribbled note sat on the kitchen table saying he had pack business to see to and to text him when I was up. I made a coffee and returned to the sanctuary of my bedroom. I had gradually transformed it from my parents' room to reflect my own tastes. It had new, blackout curtains for Antonio, colourful bedding and soft furnishings, and although I still had my parents' pine furniture, I'd given it a new, darker finish. I felt safe and warm in that room and rarely used much of the rest of the little house.

Guilt and mistrust clawed at my insides like something living trying to get out. It was awful. I had to find a way to do something and knew that I needed to speak to Weaver. Shifters rarely kept normal hours, but it was almost a sociable hour at 7.30 am, so I called her.

I paced my bedroom restlessly, the shrill ringtone at the other end of the line dragging out for long seconds.

Eventually it went to Weaver's voicemail.

'Hi. It's Eve. Can you call me back when you get this, please?' I hung up the phone and tossed it onto the bed. I needed an answer, a solution to this mess. I really hoped she could help. Weaver was a powerful shifter from Caerton who had helped us beat Lucia and free the shifters from the vampires. She was a trusted friend and always seemed to have answers. I had rarely needed something so much.

The phone rang and I lunged for it, scooping it up and answering it in one movement.

'Hey, Weaver. Thanks for calling me back so quickly.'

'No problem,' she said. 'How can I help?'

'We have a situation here and need to know if there is some sort of ritual we can use to check whether a shifter, or a person, has been corrupted by a demon.'

'I see. That sounds serious. Are you all right?'

'I'm worried for my friends, but I'm okay myself. Sort of. I mean it sent minions after me a couple of times. One of them nearly killed me.' A hysterical laugh bubbled out of my mouth and I clamped a hand over my lips to stop it.

'That really does sound serious. What kind of demon is it?'

'A corruption demon, I think. I probably shouldn't be saying this over the phone.' I looked around the room warily, suddenly wondering whether I was actually alone or not. I really didn't know the extent of this thing's powers.

'No, perhaps not, but it's the best we can do right now. At least there won't be a record of the conversation, unlike if we were to email or text. There are constructs that can retrieve that kind of information. I think your best bet for detecting the demon's influence will be a construct that can check someone's digital footprint for any suspicious activity. Or another demon that can detect demonic activity.'

A shiver ran up my spine. I thought of the secrecy demon that Peter's pack had made a deal with. I didn't like the idea of being more in debt to those sorts of creatures. As if she could read my thoughts, Weaver let out a throaty chuckle. 'Don't worry, those deals do mount up over time. It's part and parcel of this life. Often, demons can make strong allies. As long as you're careful with your wording on any deals.'

'Okay, I guess. It just feels wrong.'

'I know what you mean, but your friends will understand. They know how to do this.'

'But they're all still so new to making bargains.'

'I was once, too. You learn fast how to navigate that. Trust them.'

'I'll try. Weaver, I used my ability on one of its minions. I touched it and got a vision. Is that normal?'

'I don't see why not. My ability works a little differently to yours, but I'd say there is no real reason why your power wouldn't work as well on demons, fae, and constructs as it does on people.'

'It doesn't work that well on vampires. I thought that was maybe because they don't have a pulse, or breath, or something. Like those things are somehow currents that the visions get carried on. It works better on Antonio now, as we've grown closer, but at first it didn't work at all. Demons are not like anything living in this realm. It's weird that it worked. I also tested it on a location last night and I did get something, just from touching a bridge.'

'Interesting. Remember, your ability is a gift from Artemis, who is herself a powerful fae. I like to think it's a little piece of herself that she grants to us. If she can use this ability, then why should it not work on beings like her?'

'I hadn't thought of it like that.' I sat down on the bed, suddenly feeling as heavy as lead. The nervous energy that had kept me pacing throughout our conversation ebbed out of me in an instant.

'Don't question it, just relax and accept the growth of your powers, Eve. It's a blessing.'

'Thank you.' I allowed myself to smile.

'Now, if you've had a near-death experience, I need to know if you're really all right. Be honest with me.'

'I'm not all right,' I said, my voice barely above a whisper. Tears started to fall and a vocal sob burst from my trembling lips. 'I'm not all right at all. One of its minions tried to strangle me and I nearly died and now I'm terrified all of the time. I can hardly sleep and I can't concentrate on anything at all. It's awful, Weaver. Please help me!'

'Eve, it's all right. I'm right here. Oh I wish I was there with you and could give you a big hug.' I flopped back on the bed and squeezed my eyes closed.

'It's so fucked up.'

'Yes it is. Look, do you want to come here to get away from all of this?'

My sob died on my lips and I slowly pushed myself up to sitting. I sniffed hard and wiped my cheeks on my sleeve.

'Really? That would be cool, but I don't think I can up and leave in the middle of this crisis.'

'I understand that. Maybe when it calms down?'

'Yeah. I don't know when that will be though.'

'Make sure you take some time for yourself soon. You've been through a huge ordeal and you need to give yourself a chance to heal from it. Never mind any physical healing you may still need to do.'

'I will. You're right. If this was a normal life then I'd be taking sick leave from work or whatever, and getting trauma therapy and who knows what else, but I don't get to have a normal life.' Fresh tears tumbled down my cheeks.

'I don't know what to say, Eve. I'm sorry. I wish you

could have been spared this. Being one of the Chosen of Artemis has always been a gift to me, but to be involved and not change must seem very unfair.'

'I wouldn't want to change now. If it happens I'll probably be even more pissed off. I just want a normal, human life. I don't want powers or anything. I just want to be normal.'

Weaver heaved a sigh and I braced myself for whatever she had to say on the matter.

'I can completely understand why you would say that, Eve. I'm sorry that you've had to endure all of this and that it shows no sign of abating any time soon. But it will. I promise you, these things come in waves. There are periods of upheaval and massive change, and then there are extended periods of relative stillness. We all go through that. You will too. You will have something like a normal life if that is your choice. You just have to hold on tight and get through this challenging time first.'

I took a shaking breath and nodded mutely, tears still pouring down my cheeks.

'Thank you,' I said, gasping for breath.

'These are big things to deal with. Let's take it one day at a time, shall we?'

'Yeah.' I rolled my shoulders to loosen them and gave my head a shake. 'You're right. So, about the matter of figuring out who has been corrupted. What we really need is something like those metal detectors that they use at airport security. A way to sort of scan people to see if they're being influenced or not.'

'You know, there might be a construct that can do that. It's all a matter of interpretation at the end of the day. Have Crystal try to summon something, and be specific in the summoning wording to try and get the right thing. Let me know if you need any more help. Okay?'

'Sure. That's really useful. Thanks.' A smile tugged at the corner of my mouth.

'Any time. Take care of yourself, and call me again if you need to talk.'

'I will, thank you.' I hung up the call and stared at my phone, numb from the outpouring of so much emotion.

Day broke outside my bedroom window, and eventually I got to my feet and went to open the curtains. I half expected to see someone watching the house, but the street was quiet and there was nothing suspicious out there. I stood watching the occasional car slowly making its way up the road. A neighbour set off for work. I felt as if I was existing in slow motion, watching the world moving along without me.

Seemingly out of nowhere, a sudden burst of energy flooded my body. I darted away from the window and bolted down the stairs. I couldn't sit idle any more. It was time for action. I tapped out a message to Peter and Crystal on my phone as I grabbed some food from the kitchen, asking them to meet me in the cavern to share what I had learned from Weaver.

Twenty minutes later I had battled my anxiety about navigating the dark tunnels and was waiting in the cavern for the shifters. They arrived together, eager expressions on their faces.

'Have you filled her in?' I asked Peter, nodding in Crystal's direction.

'I have. What did Weaver have to say?' Peter asked.

I quickly told them and looked expectantly at Crystal.

'Okay,' she said, nodding. 'I can do that. Or I think I can. I might need some help. Summoning can be challenging if it's a powerful entity. It's easier with multiple ritualists. You sort of pool energy.'

'Okay, that makes sense,' I replied. 'Who can help? We'll have to trust them until they can be scanned.'

'We will. It'll be all right, Eve. We'll figure this all out. Don't worry.' She gave me a reassuring smile and Peter patted my shoulder. I nodded and managed to rustle up a smile of my own.

'Let's save the city, shall we?'

CHAPTER FOURTEEN

FIRE CRACKLED BEHIND ME and its light danced over the cavern walls. A blue dome surrounded the little cluster of shifters and myself. Crystal stood in the centre of the circle with her face upturned and her eyes closed. She swayed slightly on the spot, the others humming a deep rhythm like a pulse: Peter; his dad, Kirk; Strikes Twice, and Water-Over-Stones surrounded Crystal. Each of us was holding a piece of smokey quartz.

The shadows cast by the fire seemed to deepen as they stretched out across the ground towards the circle. The dome stopped anything unwanted getting in and disrupting the ritual, but Crystal was trying to summon something specific and she explained that the crystals channelled the shifters' energy to draw the intended target into the circle. I watched, part of the circle but not really involved, aside from holding a piece of quartz. I'd been dragged in to help with their ritual magic before but I wasn't sure how much help I was, really.

Dust began to lift up from the ground around the feet

of the shifters. I squinted, unsure if it was real or my imagination. Their humming increased in volume and the ground vibrated beneath my feet. The grains of sandy dust floating up from the cavern floor were rising higher now and more sand was bouncing low to the ground with the vibrations.

Shadows slithered across the bouncing sand into the centre of the circle and swirled at Crystal's feet. Her body began to tremble as the shadow snaked its way up her bare legs. I took a step forward but Peter's hand darted out across my chest and stopped me. I glared at him; he gave a single shake of his head without breaking off from the low hum he was still making.

Crystal's tattooed body became completely black as the shadow engulfed her. Her mouth dropped open and her eyes turned milky white. Every part of her convulsed and the shadow rushed up her body and into her mouth.

'Peter!' I shouted. I shoved his arm aside and rushed over to Crystal. I didn't know what to do, so I just stared at her as she trembled and jerked about on the spot. She went completely still and then slowly rose up from the ground, her head right back so that her strange eyes were turned to the ceiling. Her hands were splayed out at her sides. A warm breeze wrapped itself around the pair of us. The others had stopped humming and I glanced around at them. They all stood transfixed, staring at Crystal. Peter's brow was furrowed in concern, but he did nothing.

'Crystal?' I asked, my voice a quiet croak.

A long rasping breath gushed out of her open mouth. The sound sent a shudder up my spine.

'She is in here with us.' The voice oozed out of Crystal's mouth without moving it at all. I clamped a hand over my mouth to stifle the shocked cry that burst out.

'Wraith-of-Decay,' Kirk said, his voice far more steady than I felt was warranted. 'Thank you for joining our circle.'

'As if I had a choice. Thank you for this vessel.'

Peter twitched, so did Strikes Twice, and I noticed that at some point he had unsheathed his axe and was tightly gripping the handle.

'Do you need to inhabit her in order to communicate with us?' Kirk asked, still cool and calm.

'Ahhh,' the demon replied in a sickeningly satisfied way. I flinched away from it. 'I choose this method.' I could hear the smile in its voice.

'We summoned you here to make a deal,' Kirk said, steering things back on track.

'I surmised as much. What do you want?'

'We need to know if anyone in this circle has been corrupted by the powerful demon that is controlling things in Oris. It's been working here for some time and some may be unknowingly under its influence. Can you tell us this?'

'I can sense such corruption, yes, but why would I help

you?'

'Because we know that you feed off such corruption,' Kirk said, smiling. 'If you remove it from people, you grow stronger.'

'I don't need to remove it to feed. Why kill the cow when I can drink the milk?'

I grimaced and took another step back. I was livid that this monster was inhabiting my sweet friend.

'If you don't do as we say, we'll banish you back to where you came from and you'll have no food at all.' Peter had taken a step towards Crystal, and spoke through clenched teeth.

'Ahhh, the cub speaks. You lack the courage of your convictions.'

'You are on our territory and we will do our duty with no hesitation.'

'Right now, the only way to get rid of me is to kill your friend.' That thing in Crystal sounded alight with glee. A shudder ran through me. Strikes Twice twisted his axe in his hands; the leather grip creaked.

'If that's what it takes,' Peter snarled. I looked at him in alarm, my eyes wide and my jaw clenched tight. I turned away from the demon, afraid that my expression would betray us. There was no way that Peter was serious. Peter gave me the tiniest nod, barely anything, but I understood completely: *Get ready.* His voice was as clear as a bell inside my head; I was caught by surprise but there was no chance to ask how he had projected his thought. Crystal began to convulse again. The others moved in closer, each of them turning their black crystals over in their hands. I copied them, no idea what it would accomplish.

Crystal's limbs suddenly shot out dead straight, starfishing her in the air. A rancid smell issued from her mouth; the darkness oozed out of it and trickled back down her body. The shadow burst out from Crystal's body and sprayed all of us with dark sparks. They were ice cold and stung. I winced but held my ground. None of the others reacted. The little specks of shadow bounced off us and quickly skidded across the ground, all drawn back together under Crystal's prone and hovering form.

'You are all clean,' hissed the demon. Crystal dropped to the ground and collapsed in a heap. I ran to her and lifted her head. Her whole body was limp and her eyes were closed.

'Crystal?' I gave her a gentle shake.

'Wraith-of-Decay!' Kirk shouted, real anger audible in his voice. 'We have not released you. Stay in this circle.'

There was a loud hiss and the pool of darkness on the ground shimmered. Kirk hoisted a larger piece of smokey quartz out in front of him and held it flat in his palm.

'You will reside in this piece of crystal and test anyone we hold it over for signs of corruption from the demon we seek. We will feed you plenty until our work is done, at which point we will release you back into the realm from which you originate.'

The demon hissed again and rose slowly, circling up to the quartz in Kirk's hand. It slithered into the crystal, its smokey form gradually disappearing. Kirk turned it over in his hands and I watched, transfixed. The quartz had darkened to almost solid black.

'How will we know if someone is corrupted?' I asked.

'The demon will use its power through the quartz,' Kirk replied. 'We'll see sparks. We'll have to be careful about when and where we use it.'

Crystal stirred in my arms, her eyelids flickering open. The milkiness was gone and they were her normal, startling blue.

'Hey, you okay?' I asked. She groaned and nodded. Her pale face was clammy and she suddenly rolled away from me and vomited dark slime.

'We aren't doing that again,' Peter said, pacing back and forth. Kirk came to squat beside Crystal and passed her a bottle of water. She took it with a shaking hand and took a careful sip.

'I'm all right. I expected something like that would happen.'

'That's news to me,' Peter snapped, coming to a halt behind his father.

'Sorry,' Crystal said sheepishly.

'Don't apologise,' Kirk said, placing a hand on her shoulder. 'Were you conscious the whole time?'

'Yes.' She looked down and drank more water.

'Okay,' Kirk said, nodding. 'So we're all in the clear. We just have to carefully check the others.'

'What about Antonio?' I asked. 'Shouldn't we verify my vision?'

'Eve,' Kirk said in a pleading tone. 'It's pretty clear.'

'We don't actually know that.'

'Well, to put it another way,' Peter said, 'which would you prefer? That he is being manipulated by the demon, or that he's doing everything of his own volition?'

I swallowed a hard lump in my throat and held my tongue. That wasn't a question I wanted to contemplate, quite frankly.

'Come on, let's close the circle and get out of here,' Kirk said, getting to his feet. He held out a hand for Crystal, which she took as she got gingerly up from the ground. I stood up too and brushed the dirt off my jeans.

We all emerged in my kitchen a short while later, the whole group subdued. My phone buzzed with a message. I looked at the timestamp and saw it was about an hour old, but it had only just come through now that I was above ground and had a signal again. It was from Antonio.

"Please can you come here? I miss you. I need you." I felt shaken from the ordeal in the catacombs and didn't really want to go anywhere, but the part of me that loved Antonio, no matter what, needed to be with him. I needed to try and get a read of him and figure out how much he was conscious of. I hurriedly replied that I would be right there.

'I have to go do something,' I said, finding my voice at last. 'Crystal, are you all right?'

'I'll be fine. I need something to eat and a hot shower.' She gave a shudder.

'I'll get you home,' Kirk said, patting her shoulder.

The shifters filed out of the front door, Peter bringing up the rear.

'Eve,' he said, stopping on the doorstep and turning to face me. 'Don't do anything reckless.'

'What do you mean?' I asked in surprise.

'Just, promise me you'll be careful. You are still in danger.'

'I know. I'll be careful. Hey, how did you do that thing down there? Push your thought into my mind?'

'It wasn't me,' he said, smiling slightly. 'I felt your mind reach in and grab it.'

'I didn't do that.' I shook my head.

'Yes, you did.' His smile broadened into a grin. 'You're getting more powerful again.'

'Oh.' I frowned. He shook his head in amusement and stalked away, his hands shoved into the pockets of his jeans. I watched him go, still frowning to myself. How could I be activating my powers without realising it? I didn't wait around to analyse it. I stepped outside, locked my door and set off for Antonio's. Dusk was fast approaching and the sky was a dull, slate grey. I was barely at the end of my street when his car pulled up beside me. I peered into the driver's window and saw Nicholas behind the wheel. I climbed into the back seat.

'Mr Vitale sends his apologies for sending me, but he felt that it was important you weren't crossing the city alone.'

'It's fine. Thank you.' I was anxious to get to him and glad of the ride. I was mentally and physically exhausted. Seeing Crystal like that had terrified me and my heart was still racing. Nicholas set off and sped me across Oris to Antonio's mansion. My palms were sweating and I couldn't stop my thoughts from racing over everything that had happened. Tears streaked down my cheeks and I just let them fall. All the crying was exhausting, but there was no stopping the tears. I didn't have the energy to fight them. We pulled up in front of the mansion and I let myself out of the car before Nicholas had even opened his door. I sprinted up the steps and burst in through the front door without knocking. I dashed into the foyer and found Antonio stepping off the stairs onto the chequered floor. He looked at me in mild surprise, then crossed the foyer in a blur of motion to reappear in front of me.

I leapt into Antonio's arms and our mouths collided in a passionate kiss. Tears still clung to my cheeks, but now that I was reunited with him I no longer cared. He kicked the door closed behind me without breaking our kiss. My hands were entwined in his long hair, while his cupped my backside. He hoisted me up and I eagerly wrapped my legs around him. Antonio carried me across the chequered floor and deposited me on the carpeted stairs. His mouth continued to ravish mine, and my breathing grew frantic as I clumsily tugged off his jacket and unbuttoned his shirt. I kicked my boots off and they thumped to the floor. Antonio's nimble fingers made short work of the zip on my jeans and he broke the kiss just long enough to peel them down my legs and toss them aside. The rest of our clothes were soon scattered around us, and he hovered above me, pausing for a moment to look into my eyes.

'I need you so much,' he said, his voice deep and rough. I responded by pulling his face back into a kiss and thrust my tongue into his mouth. What happened next wasn't the sensual love-making that I was accustomed to. It was rough and wild. I cried out, my voice echoing all around the foyer. I didn't care if anyone heard me. I was lost to pleasure. His muscular body was flush with mine, every contour fitting together perfectly.

His dark eyes roved up to the vein on my neck. I turned my head and screamed out while I still could. His teeth were shifting, fangs easing out from the gums, and he bared those bright white teeth with eyes like a starving tiger. He dived down and thrust his fangs into my neck. My scream became a gasp and a sigh. My whole body shuddered. Each erratic thrust of his hips was accompanied by a tug from his mouth as he drew my blood into it. My fingers dug into his back again and my legs gripped him like a vice. He groaned in satisfaction as he sucked eagerly on my neck.

My vision began to blur and I felt as though I was sinking into the stairs beneath me. All I could hear was my pulse echoing inside my head and Antonio gulping my blood down.

'Stop,' I whimpered. I kept sinking into a foggy dullness. *Glug, glug, glug.* 'Stop.' I wasn't even sure I was speaking out loud. He wasn't going to stop. I was going to die right there on the stairs. I couldn't summon the strength to be afraid or to fight for my life. I was almost glad to go out like that. My limbs went limp and my eyes closed completely. Darkness engulfed me. My pulse slowed and silence filled my mind.

'Let me change you,' he whispered, his low, husky voice distant in my fog-filled head. 'Be young and beautiful with me forever. We can do this every day for the next thousand years.'

It was a tempting offer. If I'd had the ability, I would have agreed. Maybe that should have scared me, but in that moment I was dying and I was in utter bliss. This was definitely the way I wanted to go. I had stopped sinking. I was suspended as if hanging by a thread. All was dark but for a pinprick of light above me. Warmth and peace supported me.

I felt the contact between our bodies break. Cold air rushed over my skin. I drew a shuddering breath and began rushing towards the light. Dizziness consumed me and pain shot through my neck. I winced and was suddenly aware of lying awkwardly on the stairs. Antonio's hands rested gently on my face, his lips on mine, kissing me tenderly. My whole body twitched and shuddered. I tugged free of his kiss and rolled away from him, half crawling, half dragging myself out of his reach.

'You nearly killed me,' I snarled.

'Eve,' he said, pain in his voice. 'No, I swear I didn't.' I knew what it was like to lose too much blood to him, how weak it left me, but my strength was rapidly returning to me and I turned back to face him. I sat on the step I had crawled to and wrapped my arms around my knees. Antonio was at my side in the blink of an eye, his arm around my shoulders. 'I know what I'm doing. I know exactly when to stop.' I was shaking.

'I thought I was dying. It was...' I didn't want to finish the sentence.

'You fell over the cliff,' he said, a slight chuckle in his voice. 'It happens sometimes. You come so hard that you sort of break and drift off.'

'Have you done that to many women?'

'No,' he said earnestly. He cupped my chin and tilted my head so he could look into my eyes. 'In my two hundred years I've experienced it once myself, and three times in a partner, including you just now.'

I believed him, but a tiny part of me disliked hearing that he'd been with other women, although of course I knew he had been.

'Did you offer to change me? Or did I imagine that?'

He shifted his weight and loosened his hold on me.

'I was swept up in the moment. I apologise. I didn't mean to say that.' I rested my head on his shoulder and took a few deep breaths. I was alive. I ached all over and swore silently that I would never have sex on stairs again. I wasn't dying any time soon, I decided. I wanted more sex like that; well, maybe not quite as dramatic, but the fact remained that there were now several reasons why I couldn't really trust Antonio.

My head spun as I fell backwards down into the vision. Confusion flooded my thoughts. What was I seeing? Long, blonde hair in a tangled mess around a bruised, swollen face and neck. Isabel's perfect, porcelain skin was purple and blue, her lip was split and crusted with blood. Bile rose in my throat and I was desperate to look away. Her cold eyes stared, unseeing. I was seeing her through someone else's eyes, and they looked up into the bitter, twisted face of Marco De Luca.

'What did you do?' Antonio's voice asked.

'She was going to ruin everything,' De Luca spat. 'I had to act quickly.'

'She was harmless. You've put us all at risk.'

'Well, it's done now and we can discuss the merits and flaws of my actions another time. Will you help me get rid of the body, or not?'

'I don't have much choice, do I?'

I was spinning back into my own head, flying away from that nightmare. I gasped for breath and sat bolt upright. Antonio was sitting beside me, butt naked, on the stairs.

'Eve? Are you all right?'

'What did you do?' I turned to look into his dark eyes, unconsciously echoing his words from the memory. My pulse raced and I suddenly felt more vulnerable than I ever had before. I covered my naked body as best as I could with my arms.

'What do you mean?' He frowned and reached out to brush my bedraggled hair from my face. I flinched and jerked away from his cool fingers. He dropped his gaze and would have sighed if he could. His shoulders lifted and then dropped again. 'You saw something.'

'I don't know what I saw. Explain it to me!'

'Would you like to give me somewhere to start? Or do I have to guess my way through two hundred years of atrocities?'

I started collecting my clothes and hastily dressing myself. My heart thumped wildly and I fumbled with my buttons and zips. He sat there watching me, his jaw clenched.

'Isabel, Antonio. Isabel beaten to death.' My cheeks burned and I snapped my gaze to his face. He grew, if possible, a shade paler. He covered his face with his hands and propped his elbows on his knees.

'*Cazzo*, Eve.' He shook his head. 'You knew before you met me that I am not a good man. I made no secret of that. I've done things in my time that I'm not proud of and that can never be forgiven. You know all of this about me.' He uncovered his face and looked at me with wide, pleading eyes. 'But I did not harm Isabel.'

'You hid the body, though. Right?' I snapped, my arms folded tightly across my chest.

'I had to.'

'No, actually, you didn't. You could have turned in De Luca!' I stooped and grabbed my nearest boot then wheeled about looking for the other one.

'And how do you think that would have gone?!' Antonio raised his voice and leapt to his feet. 'Everyone knows what I do, Eve. Everyone! How receptive do you really think his subordinates would be to a known criminal accusing the Police Commissioner of murdering the mayor's wife? Not one person would take me seriously, and even if they did, what are they really going to do about it? Go after their own boss? Put him in a cell? The world doesn't work that way, and you should know better.'

'You're a monster.' I stood there holding my boots and shaking to my core.

'Maybe, but I'm a loyal friend. He needed my help and I provided it. I may not have raised a hand to Isabel, but my hands are hardly clean. There are things that could have been exposed if her body was found.'

'I know. I know all about the past between the three of you and all of the backhanded little deals you had going on.' Realisation settled over me like a ray of sunlight. It was the demon. How long had it had its claws into Antonio? Could it have been manipulating him for centuries? I closed my eyes and drew a shaking breath. I couldn't say anything about what I had thought in case the demon was present. I gave a shudder at the thought of it watching us before the vision had hit me.

'I don't think you know as much as you think you do,' Antonio said. He stood there, totally naked and unashamed. It was just flesh to him.

'I should go.' I marched to the door, still holding my boots. I didn't want to suffer the indignity of trying to hop my way into them and probably losing my balance.

'I hate fighting with you,' he said softly.

'Me too,' I said, pausing at the door. 'You know how to fix it, Antonio. You know what I need. What you promised me before Christmas. I know you haven't been a good man, but you can choose to be one now.' I yanked open the door, stepped out into the night and slammed the door behind me.

CHAPTER FIFTEEN

'ARE YOU SURE?' PETER ASKED, HIS FACE PALE AND DRAWN. Cars swept past us and the river rushed under the bridge beneath our feet. He looked orange under the glare of the street light nearby. We'd met on the bridge that connected the original part of the city inside the wall to the wider city beyond it.

'Certain. I had a vision, and then he confirmed it when I confronted him. De Luca killed her and Antonio helped to hide the body.'

'When?'

'I'm not sure, but it was only a few days ago that we met in the park. She must have gone straight to De Luca to try to use her knowledge against him and he killed her for it.' A shudder ran up my spine. Peter released his hands and pulled me into a hug.

'I'm sorry you had to see that.'

'Thanks.' A sob welled up in my throat. 'Peter, I think it's my fault. I told her about the election. I gave her that information.'

'You couldn't have known what she would try to do with it though, or what De Luca would do.'

'Couldn't I? I knew what they were both like. I knew she was looking for a way to break out of her situation and I knew he could be violent, or I'd glimpsed that side of him anyway. I didn't have to get involved. I could have stayed out of it and then maybe she'd still be alive.'

'You can't second guess yourself, Eve. You did what you felt was best at the time. You were trying to help her. It honestly isn't your fault that it backfired like that. I promise.'

'I feel responsible, though. I can't just decide not to feel that way.' He was still holding me close against his chest and my tears soaked into his t-shirt.

'I know. I'm sorry. I wasn't trying to get you to switch off your feelings. You feel everything so strongly. How could you not, with your gift? You have all of your own feelings and then all of the feelings of others around you too. I don't know how you function, I really don't have a clue. I wish there was something I could do to ease your burden. I wish I could carry some of those feelings for you.'

'Thank you.' I trembled and squeezed him tighter. No visions came to me now. 'I don't know what I'd do without you. I'm glad we're okay again now. It was awful before.'

'I know. I'm sorry. I needed some time, but I was always going to be fine with you again eventually. I'm here for you now. Whatever you need.'

I thought about his declaration of love for me back before Christmas, before his mother died. I stiffened a little in his arms. Was I leading him on? I still only thought of him as a friend.

'You're my best friend, Peter. I never want that to change.' I kept my voice calm and steady, even though my pulse was racing. I hoped he would take my meaning. He gave me another squeeze before releasing me and looking into my watery eyes.

'Same here.' We both nodded, understanding passing between us. There were things we simply weren't going to talk about any more and that was fine. We were better off as friends, nothing more. I hoped his recovery from his feelings for me would be swift and smooth.

'So what do we do about this? *Is* there anything we can do?' I asked, wiping my cheeks on the sleeve of my coat.

'Could we intervene in some way?' he asked, gazing over my shoulder at the rushing river.

'What do you mean?'

'Well, like you said, if this demon has been controlling him for such a long time, he may not be aware of it, and we could potentially do something to get it to remove its claws from him.'

'Are you offering to help Antonio? For me?'

'For you, not him, yes. I hate to see you like this. And the fact remains that we have to deal with this threat and we have to protect the city. We can't have anyone doing these things, killing people, rigging elections, all of it. We have to stop anything else from happening. The best way to do that is probably to separate Antonio from the demon.'

'Yeah, that makes sense.' I gave my head a little shake to clear the emotional fog that was clouding it. 'How do we do it?'

'We need to catch him unaware and get a quick shield up around him to keep the demon out so it can't hear what we're talking about. We need to reason with him. You know, like when people stage an intervention for someone who's an addict or something? That's sort of what we're dealing with here. He's addicted to power.'

I nodded. That was exactly how it felt. I cleared my throat, not wanting to voice the million thoughts that started tumbling into my head, but I had to start somewhere.

'He's possibly not going to be easily persuaded. He thinks he's doing the right thing.'

'I know, but if we can be sure that the demon isn't around when we confront him, then he should be in his own right mind. If the demon is really controlling his behaviour, then that gives us the best chance of success.'

'Okay. Who do we take? Where do we do it?'

'My pack. We keep it small. He can't feel threatened, or under attack. You have to be the one to talk to him. The rest of us are just there to cast the circle and be on hand in case anything gets in or...' Peter stalled. I didn't need to read his mind to know what he had stopped himself from saying.

'Or Antonio loses his temper. I know. I get it.' I wished I could honestly say that he wouldn't hurt me, but that wasn't entirely true. I leaned heavily against the cold, metal barrier of the bridge and dropped my head onto my hands. Why was this my life? How had I gone from the somewhat sensible girl who wouldn't say boo to a goose, to this smitten fool who wanted to protect a dangerous criminal? I remembered how intoxicating it had been when I met him and couldn't read his mind. How refreshing it was to be held in someone's arms without being overwhelmed by a crushing vision of something I didn't want to see. That was no longer always the case with Antonio. My powers did work with him now, some of the time. And I had to see dead bodies. I stood up straight and smacked my hands hard on the metal.

'You all right?' Peter asked. I looked up at him and nodded silently. I wasn't, obviously, but it was what it was and I had to live with my choices. 'We don't have to do this. You could just leave him and never see him again. We could try another way to fix the city and get rid of the demon.'

'No,' I said with a heavy sigh. 'No, we have to do this. It's the best, cleanest way. We don't want to end up working against Antonio as well. That could be terrible.' I didn't want to leave him, either. I wanted, if at all possible, to save him. What was wrong with me? Was it some sort of hero complex? I didn't know if there was any way to redeem the man behind the monster, but I had to try.

Peter took me home and I bid him goodnight. It was midnight before I got into bed and the utter exhaustion of the day swallowed me up, drawing me into a heavy sleep.

The following day I met with Peter's pack and we made our plan to try and save Antonio. A stirring of hope fluttered in my heart after having had a good night's sleep. We could do this and it would work. Antonio would see reason.

CHAPTER SIXTEEN

'WHAT IF IT DOESN'T WORK?' Peter asked, his face fixed in a frown. He placed his hands on the kitchen table and spread his fingers out. Kirk was leaning against the sink behind him, his arms crossed over his chest. He hadn't shaved in a few days and his jaw was covered in grey stubble.

'It has to.' I needed it to be true. I had to convince myself.

'But it might not, Eve. What's the plan if it doesn't?' Kirk asked, not quite meeting my eye.

'Don't panic. That's all I have so far.' I couldn't look at him. I knew how worried he was. I felt sick to my stomach about it. I had everything to lose here. I couldn't contemplate what it might mean if we couldn't break Antonio free of the demon's influence.

'Let's go and get the job done, then,' Peter said, getting to his feet. 'The others will be waiting.'

We filed out of Peter's house and stepped out in the fresh daylight. We walked quickly to my house and made our way into the basement and then down the steep steps into the catacombs. My pulse raced as we descended underground. I hated going down there now. It was never exactly an enjoyable experience before Lucia captured and tortured me down there. I pushed the memory aside and followed Peter and Kirk down the tunnel that led away from my house.

'Does Antonio know about this tunnel we're using?' Peter asked.

'Yes, but he's never used it to get to my house, as far as I know. Maybe he's being polite. Or maybe he stays out of the catacombs because he knows you guys use them.' He had once mentioned to me that he and Lucia used the tunnels that ran under Oris when they arrived in the city, but that they had stopped. I never really knew why. Surely they were a valuable resource for the vampires? Now wasn't the time to question it. I didn't want to think about what Lucia used to use them for.

Peter and Kirk could see pretty well in the dark, but I lit up the torch on my phone to light my way. The shadows cast by the light bobbed and danced all over the sandstone walls of the tunnel. We hurried over the smooth stone beneath our feet, the shifters at a brisk walk and me almost running to keep up. The tunnel opened up into a vast cavern with a high ceiling, where we found Crystal and Strikes Twice waiting for us. The four shifters greeted each other warmly, and Crystal gave me a broad smile. Strikes

Twice remained stoic with me, as usual. I was learning not to take it personally. Mostly.

'Are we ready to do this?' Kirk asked the pack. They all murmured their agreement.

'What if he perceives it as an attack?' Crystal asked.

'I'll be up front. Everyone keep calm and cool and we'll be fine,' I said, nodding firmly.

'And there's four of us and only one of him,' Strikes Twice said gruffly. He wasn't counting me. I scowled at him but held my tongue.

We set off again, Kirk leading the way. There were many passages leading away from the cavern. We took the one opposite where Kirk, Peter and I had emerged, the passage that led north towards Antonio's home.

The walk felt like it took hours. No one spoke. Our footsteps echoed dully around us and my phone was the only source of light. The tunnel pressed close around me and it was surprisingly warm. The air was so still, with no hint of a breeze. I was beginning to gasp for air, desperate to get above ground.

Finally, the narrow passage began to slope upwards. Kirk was still at the front, the rest of us following close behind. The slope became steeper and then there were steps. I was tired and aching, but made myself keep pace with the others. The steps turned a corner and we filed around it; it quickly turned again and we found ourselves in a tight spiral staircase. The stone was inlaid with wooden slats. A light breeze reached my face, even though Kirk and Peter were both ahead of me in the tight passage. They came to an abrupt halt and I nearly bumped right into Peter. Crystal stopped behind me and patted my back to let me know she was close.

'What's happening?' I whispered.

'There's a door,' Kirk replied softly. 'It's locked.'

'You'll have to force it, Dad.' Peter shifted his weight on his big feet right in front of me. I wasn't keen on the idea, but Peter was right. There was no point in doing this if we weren't going to see it through. A crunch of wood echoed down from above, followed by splintering, and warm air rushed into the stairwell. Kirk and Peter moved forwards and I quickly followed them. My chest was tight and I needed to get out of the confined space as soon as possible. I stepped into a dark basement and staggered forwards. Peter caught hold of me and set me on my feet. Crystal and Strikes Twice were just a moment behind me. I shone my torchlight around the dusty room. The door was hanging on one of its hinges and part of the frame lay on the ground. There were stairs up in the far corner and a door with a small shaft of light shining under it. The basement looked normal enough and we all looked at one another expectantly.

'I hope we're in the right place,' Crystal whispered. 'Otherwise someone we don't know is about to get a rude shock.'

Strikes Twice let out a small, gruff chuckle. I couldn't laugh. I was wound too tight.

'Come on,' I said, brushing past Kirk and setting off up the stairs. I pressed my hands against the door and took a deep breath. This was going to go one of two ways. Either Antonio would think he was under attack and would strike out against us, or we would find him alone and resting, as planned, and manage to have a calm conversation. I glanced behind me and could just make out Crystal moving in the dark below. She was casting the circle. Blue light began to emanate from the powdered crystal she had sprinkled on the ground. The light began to rise, like a thin wall of coloured glass, but rather than forming a dome, like I had seen before, this light rose straight up and then suddenly spread out in a bright burst. It flooded up through the ceiling and a rush of cool air passed over my skin as the light rushed past us. Peter gave me a gentle nudge.

I opened the door and stepped into the hall. The door came out near the kitchen, right where Dante had emerged the day I was attacked. It was definitely the right place. I ran quickly for the sunlit foyer. Kirk and Peter were right behind me. Blue light shimmered up through the floor and slithered up the walls before disappearing through them. The protective dome that Crystal was creating was expanding to encompass the whole mansion. If any demons were in there with us, they would be expelled, and nothing would be able to get in. Strikes Twice remained in the basement with her to protect her during the casting.

Frederick burst out of the small room that seemed to be his little domain. Confusion covered his ageing features. He looked at me with recognition, but his frown quickly returned as he took in my company.

'Miss Eve?'

'Frederick. Please don't worry. We're here to help Antonio. He's in trouble.'

'I see,' he replied, not looking entirely convinced.

'Where is he?' Peter asked. I glanced at him and took in his clenched fists.

Movement up on the balcony landing above the foyer caught my eye; just a blur of motion in the shadows, but I knew it was him.

'Eve?' Antonio's voice echoed down from above.

'We need to talk to you.'

'Very well. But why the entourage and what was that blue light?' He stepped into view. He was topless and barefoot. His hair cascaded down over his shoulders. He crossed his arms and a deep scowl creased his brow.

'This is an intervention,' Peter said, a slight snarl in his voice. I put a hand on his shoulder and pleaded him with my eyes not to escalate this situation. Antonio cocked an eyebrow. I walked cautiously to the stairs and began to climb them. The sunlight reached almost to the top, where they curved around to the right and a wall blocked the light from the window. I came to a halt level with where the demon had dangled me, but kept my eyes on Antonio. I hoped he wouldn't hurt me, but I didn't want him to feel threatened.

'What on earth is going on, Eve?' He had lost patience now and he dropped his arms to his sides and glowered down at me.

'The demon has been controlling you. We know what it is now. It's a corruption demon. It's been influencing you. The protective circle is to keep it and its minions out while we talk to you about this. It's probably been listening to and watching everything here for months.'

'There are shifters in my basement,' he said through clenched teeth.

'Yes, they're just here to protect the space.'

'Frederick?' Antonio called out, perfectly calmly.

'Yes, Signor?' the butler replied, stepping into the hall so that Antonio could see him.

'Are you all right?'

'Perfectly, thank you.'

'We aren't here to hurt anyone,' Kirk said calmly, his hands raised.

'I'm not convinced your son feels the same,' Antonio said, his lip curling.

'Peter just wants to make sure I'm all right,' I said, glancing meaningfully down at Peter. He shrugged, but didn't unclench his fists. 'Do you believe me about the demon?'

'I believe you are sincere. But I don't agree that there is anything to be concerned about.'

I took another few steps towards him. He flinched. He had never flinched away from me before and it made my chest ache.

'It's manipulative. It might have presented itself to you as a friend. It's really sneaky.'

'Eve, you have broken into my home with a pack of—' I could tell he was biting back an insult. 'Shifters, in the middle of the day. You have surrounded us with some sort of magic and accused me of being in league with some monstrous entity. Do you not see how this could be taken as an act of aggression?'

'Of course I do. That's why I'm up here talking to you calmly and they're down there. It's only my intention to help. I don't want a demon controlling you, or anyone that I care about.'

'No one is controlling me. Frederick, have you witnessed anything untoward or different around here lately?'

'Well, no, Signor,' Frederick replied. I looked back to see that he had moved onto the stairs. Kirk was watching him warily. 'Except that, of course, things have changed a great deal with Miss Lucia's unfortunate departure and I haven't seen you so enamoured with a lady companion in some time.'

My cheeks burned and I tried not to look at him.

'Fine,' Antonio snapped. 'Some things have changed.' The corner of his mouth twitched as if he was fighting a smile. 'But as someone with some expertise in this arena, I think I would notice if anyone was coercing me.'

I swallowed a painful lump in my throat. I hated to be reminded of his past and the things he had done to get where he was now.

'Well, you obviously don't see it, but can you please take my concerns seriously?'

'I do, of course I do,' he said, softening his tone and expression. He took a tentative step towards me but was at the edge of the shadow provided by the wall between him and the window. I wanted to leap up into his arms, but the tension in the hall was palpable and I wasn't entirely sure that I wasn't in danger.

'Antonio, please trust me. I wouldn't have gone to such lengths without good reason.'

'I trust you, Eve. But how do you know that you aren't the one who has been manipulated by this thing?'

'I—' I wanted to give him some sort of justification, but he had me stumped. Wraith-of-Decay had found us all clean, but what if that itself had been a deception? Antonio could be right. How did I know that my vision was genuine? Could the demon have shown it to me deliberately? 'Well something wants me dead,' I said at last. 'The only believable reason would be that it either can't control me, or feels that I'm too big of a threat to its plans. Why would I be a threat? Unless I was distracting you from what it wants you to do?'

It was the first time I had really worked it through for myself, and I felt the cogs click into place as I said it out loud. Antonio's eyes narrowed and he rolled his tongue over his teeth under his lips.

'Do you know the name of the demon? Names have power.'

'Not yet,' Kirk replied from the foot of the stairs. I looked down at him and saw that Frederick was now halfway up the stairs to where I was standing. Peter was still in the middle of the foyer, his jaw clenched tight. He was spring-loaded and ready to pounce. 'We're working on finding out more about it, but we have to go carefully. If it knows we're onto it, well, things could go south very quickly.'

Antonio shook his head slowly, his gaze still fixed on me. Waves of anger rolled off him and made me want to recoil from him. Every fibre of my being warned me that I was in danger. Was what I had done so bad?

'Antonio,' I whispered, pleading for him to trust me. His eyes sharpened and blazed with even more fury. I took a few steps back. I didn't think the sunlight would stop him if he really decided to strike out. 'Sorry. Please, please listen to us. We're trying to do the right thing here.'

'Get out of my house,' he said, his voice low and

dangerous. 'Frederick, please escort Eve and her companions out.'

Frederick's hand was on my arm the moment Antonio had stopped talking. I turned and tugged my arm free as I passed the butler and headed down the stairs. Kirk was at my side and we joined Peter in the sunlit foyer. I thought of the others in the basement and at that moment the blue light of the protective circle rushed through the foyer, contracting back down. I glanced at Peter, who had a stern look of concentration on his face. I knew he must have been communicating telepathically with his pack mates. I was a little envious of how clearly that worked for them when I had to make such a strenuous effort to communicate my thoughts to anyone. I needed touch and great focus.

There was a click of a door closing just beyond the staircase, signalling the hasty exit of Crystal and Strikes Twice.

'Can we talk about this later?' I called as I craned my neck to get a glimpse of Antonio at the top of the curved stairs.

'We'll have to, I suppose,' he said before disappearing from view. Frederick bustled us towards the door, far more pushy than his usual manner. We stepped out into the crisp, winter sun and Frederick closed the door without seeing us off the property.

'Well that didn't go as planned.' Kirk folded his arms

and gazed up at the window above the door.

'What do we do now, Eve?' Peter asked.

'We reconvene with the others and figure that out. We can't give up. There's too much riding on this.'

CHAPTER SEVENTEEN

'HE JUST WOULDN'T ACCEPT IT. Even when Eve pointed out the reasoning behind the attacks on her.' Peter was getting more and more fired up and his voice echoed off the cavern walls and high ceiling. Not only were his pack with us, but several other shifters had gathered for the update. A softly glowing blue dome surrounded us all. I sat on the ground fiddling with a loose thread on the cuff of my sweatshirt.

'What do we do?' Crystal asked. I looked up and shrugged. Everyone expected me to have the answers but I was too hurt to think clearly. I had never felt such resentment from Antonio; it hurt that he wouldn't put his trust in me when I had trusted him with my life every day since we met. It was my plan and it had failed. I had promised that I would think of the next step if that happened, but now my mind just raced with his cold words and narrowed eyes.

In hindsight, what could little old Frederick really have done to two shifters and myself if we'd resisted? But would a fight have been worth it? I didn't want him or anyone else to get hurt. There had already been enough bloodshed. The shifters were talking, but it was all just dull background noise to me.

A shadow fell across me and I looked up to see Crystal standing over me. She dropped to the ground, crossing her legs as she sat in one fluid movement.

'Hey,' she said, smiling. 'Penny for your thoughts.'

'You should have seen his face. He was so betrayed.'

'No, you were trying to help him. It's not on you if he took it badly.'

'I guess. How do I unpick this mess?' I dropped my gaze to the sandy ground.

'I don't know. There really aren't any easy answers. We'll figure it out together. We're all trying to come up with something. It isn't all on your shoulders.'

'Thanks,' I said softly, glancing up to meet her gaze. She smiled sweetly at me. A few months ago I would have made a snap judgement about Crystal based on her many tattoos and the piercings all over her face. That judgement would have been horribly wrong. She was one of the sweetest and kindest people I'd met. I made a promise to myself not to assume things about people based on their appearance.

'Moon Caller has something I think we should all hear,' Strikes Twice said loudly, drawing all of the other chatter to a halt. I looked up and saw Kirk. Moon Caller was his shifter name. It was still odd to me to hear it, but I was gradually getting used to it. Crystal twisted around to look at her Alpha. Kirk cleared his throat.

'Vitale wasn't receptive to our help, but there are other things we can do to thwart this demon. It feeds on corruption, so there is a very real chance that it is orchestrating this plan to rig the election. So what if we work to compromise that plan and ensure the election goes ahead fairly?'

'We'd be depriving the demon of its food source,' Strikes Twice added, nodding firmly.

'It might not be enough to hurt it,' Peter said, 'but if it helps to weaken what's left of the Camorra, then that's generally good for Oris anyway.'

'How do we do that though? We can hardly go to the police when it's the police commissioner trying to steal the election.' I looked around to see who had spoken, but it was one of the shifters I didn't really know. I scrambled to my feet, quickly followed by Crystal.

'De Luca killed the mayor's wife,' I said loudly. Every eye turned to face me. 'I can't prove it, but I know it's true. I had a vision. We have to be able to use that. Tip off the mayor? Go to an honest police officer and get them to investigate?'

'As soon as De Luca gets wind of it he'll shut down the investigation.' That was Peter. He wasn't wrong.

'Isn't there something you can do with your alliances and whatnot?' I asked hopefully. 'Is there such a thing as a fae of honesty, or something? Something equally as powerful as the demon?'

The shifters exchanged glances and troubled frowns.

'Maybe,' Crystal said softly. 'The demons tend to be the more powerful things. They have more ample sources of food.' It struck me how bleak that was. Silence hung heavily between the gathered shifters.

'We can probably use our allies for small acts that undermine the corruption demon, though,' Peter said, his tone rising. He was almost smiling. A few people nodded.

'Yeah,' Crystal said, moving towards him. 'If we can find out who else it's controlling, then we can make small adjustments and quietly take out branches of its influence. Just little things here and there so as not to get noticed. We have the talisman to check who's clean and slowly bring in more people. We have to go carefully, of course, but we have time.'

'Do we?' I asked, looking at her all-too-optimistic face.

'Yeah, if this is all leading to the election in May.'

'If we can destabilise the demon enough, it may voluntarily withdraw from Oris,' Kirk said, rubbing the bristles on his chin with his fingers.

'We can hope for that, but I think we need to be ready to fight it once it's weakened. And if we can stop the election from being rigged somehow, then we have to try that.' Strikes Twice rarely strung more than a few words together and it was odd to hear him speak like that.

Everyone turned to look at him. He looked mildly surprised at the attention and shifted his weight awkwardly. Peter began to laugh; others quickly followed. I allowed a small smile to creep onto my face, but had no laughter in me. I still felt crushed by Antonio's reaction.

How had it come to this? I had been so independent for so long and was so determined when I met him not to be taken in by his charm and his supernatural abilities that allowed him to control others. I had been so sure that I was resisting him, even as I fell in love with him. The fear that I had felt at first had slipped away and I was completely taken in by him. I had almost forgotten his true nature, despite the fact that he had physically assaulted me back when I revealed to him that I knew what he was, and despite his feeding on me. I had come to feel safe with him. I trusted him and had been able to look past the monster to the point where I had forgotten it was there beneath the surface.

I never wanted to be that naive again. I never wanted to give away my power. Antonio Vitale was a dangerous vampire and a criminal. His love for me clearly had its limits and I had bumped right into one. He didn't believe that I could know or understand something more about the supernatural than him. He didn't trust my visions. He didn't want to be helped by me.

A tear ran down my cheek. Everyone around me was too busy hatching plans and chatting to notice.

CHAPTER EIGHTEEN

FEBRUARY ARRIVED AND I TRUDGED THROUGH MY LIFE in a detached haze. I spent time at the restaurant and with the shifters but usually felt more like an observer than an active participant. Part of me almost wanted to experience the full change to become a shifter myself. At least then I'd really be one of them. I wouldn't be counting on them to protect me, or getting in the way of their important role in protecting the veil from demons and anything else that might threaten humanity. I knew I was semi-capable of protecting myself, but something still kept me feeling like a burden.

Antonio kept his distance, for which I was thankful. I wasn't sure how I would hold up if he tried to suck me back into his orbit. I missed him. There were times when I caught myself staring at old messages between us and almost reaching out to him, but it was best that we stayed apart. I knew I couldn't trust him, and in truth I didn't trust myself with him. Ever since he'd come into my life I'd been consumed by him and my judgement had been embarrassingly poor.

Peter's pack had a room set up at the back of Kirk's office. There was a back door that they came and went through so that they weren't seen by the other people who worked in the building. Peter took me there one day in the middle of February. He pulled open the door with a heavy clang and led me inside; the lights flickered on automatically as we stepped in. The walls were covered in photos and slips of paper with writing scrawled all over them. I gazed around at it all. There were pictures of Antonio and Marco De Luca blown up and taking up centre stage with a mess of threads leading away from them to show their influence and associates. I'd given the shifters some of the information on Antonio, and a little stab of guilt hit me as I looked at some of the names that had been crossed out. De Luca's side of the wall was less busy, and less impact seemed to have been made there.

Peter went to the large desk in the middle of the room and grabbed a pad of paper. He began scribbling on it while I looked over the complicated web of corruption displayed on the walls.

'It's like a game of whack-a-mole,' Peter said softly. He approached the wall and pinned up the paper he'd just written on. It was a list of names under the heading "Dirty Cops". It was a long list.

'Didn't you already deal with some of them?' I asked, pointing at the list.

'Nope. These are new ones. Each time we expose someone, a bunch of people pop up in their place.' He moved a few pins around and crossed off a couple of names. He put a big X through a photo of a young woman who looked naggingly familiar.

'Who's that, and what happened to her?'

'Michelle West. A journalist. She's dead.'

A painful lump formed in my throat. I remembered where I knew her from. She had been the one quizzing Antonio about his suit on the carpet on the way into the New Year's Eve ball at the castle. I hadn't seen her clearly at the time because of all the flashing lights, but seeing her smiling face with a thick, black line through it brought the memory to the surface.

'What happened?'

'We don't know. She had written a few puff pieces about Vitale and De Luca over the years, and we were going to approach her to see if she was one of the demon's puppets, but she was found dead in her flat this morning. Our guy at the morgue told us.'

'You have a guy at the morgue?' I raised my eyebrows.

'Yeah, he's a shifter. I don't think you know him. Anyway, it looks like a drug overdose.'

'Why would anyone take her out if she was helping them?'

'Want to help me find out?'

'Of course.'

'Good, because I have her address.' He flashed me a grin. We left the office, slamming the door behind us, and drove in Peter's car to a relatively new development on the edge of the city. Three buildings stood in a U shape, each containing a few dozen flats. It was late in the evening, but not a completely unsociable hour. Peter approached the building on the left of the trio and hit every button on the board by the door. A ripple of buzzes followed and the door clicked.

'I can't believe so many people would just let someone in without knowing who it is,' I whispered as Peter yanked open the door.

'People are stupid,' he said with a shrug. I eyed him cautiously as we entered the quiet, dimly lit entrance hallway. I didn't know he was so cynical. He'd always been an upbeat, optimistic guy before. He set off up the wide staircase, ignoring the two lifts down the hall. I followed him up; motion-censored lights flickered on to light our way. Luckily we stopped at the first floor and he led me down the hall, checking the numbers on the doors that we passed. 'Here we are,' he said, stopping at 4B.

'How do you plan to get in?' I asked. He glanced at me and tugged a cord out from under his shirt. A black key hung on the end of it. He hoisted it over his neck and slid the key into the lock. It hadn't looked like it would fit, but it morphed on contact with the metal lock and shifted shape. 'What is that?'

'A skeleton key,' he said with a grin. 'Like your coin, it's a talisman that has special properties. It can unlock any lock.'

'Handy,' I said, nodding.

'We figured something like this would be useful after we had to break into Vitale's basement.'

Peter opened the door and we stepped carefully inside. It was dark but a little light from outside and a couple of digital clocks cast an eerie glow over the empty apartment. A shudder ran up my spine. 'Do you think she was hiding something?'

'I'm certain she was. Iron Eyes, our guy in the morgue, said that she wasn't a habitual drug user, but the police report says they found drug paraphernalia here. It must have been planted.' He moved through the flat, opening doors and casting a sweeping look across surfaces. I passed him and went into the living room. It looked as though it had been ransacked. There were newspapers and magazines scattered everywhere except for one chair by the window that had a dark stain on it. There was a broken mirror on the wall next to the kitchen door and shards of glass all over the floor. My own reflection blinked back at me from one of the pieces still wedged into the frame.

My breath caught in my throat as a vision rushed into me. Michelle looked back at me in the mirror, her eyes wide with fear. She quickly looked away from the mirror and spun around. The room wasn't a mess, but neat piles of publications sat beside the coffee table and a few papers were scattered across it. There was a loud buzz: her doorbell. She rummaged through the papers and picked out a flash drive. She ran to the window and peered down into the car park below. She couldn't quite see the door but there was no sign of anyone further from the building who might be looking up to her window. She ducked down behind the chair and pulled up a floorboard. She stowed the drive underneath it and hurriedly slipped the loose board back into place. A loud thump on her door yanked her to her feet and she reached for her phone.

There was a click and the door opened. A deep voice called her name down the hall. Michelle's breathing was heavy as she shoved the chair slightly to cover the hiding place. She looked desperately down at the papers but it was too late to do anything about them. Heavy footfalls echoed down the hall and a tall figure appeared in the living room doorway. He was dressed in a smart suit, had light blond hair, pale skin and startlingly blue eyes.

'What are you doing here?' she demanded. It seemed she recognised the man. So did I. It was Celino. He rushed towards her in a blur and scooped her up. He threw her across the room and she smashed into the mirror. I gasped again as I rushed back into the present moment.

'What did you see?' Peter asked, his hand gripping my shoulder. I sank onto the paper-strewn couch.

'It was Celino. He killed her. Didn't your guy in the

morgue find blood loss?'

'Not that he told me, but he found some cuts.' His gaze raked over the broken mirror. 'What does Celino have to do with any of this?'

'I don't know, but he came in without an invitation, so he must have been here before. They knew each other.'

'If he was here on orders to make the death look like a drug overdose then maybe he restrained himself from feeding?' Peter suggested, still looking around.

'I guess.' I stirred from the numbness that soaked my muscles and pointed towards the chair. 'Under the floor, she hid something.'

Peter quickly moved the chair and fiddled with the floorboards until he found the loose one. He tugged it up and reached inside. He pulled out his hand, the thumb drive between his fingers.

'Let's find out what she was hiding.'

We left the flat and made our way back to the office. A heaviness hung over me. Questions about her involvement and whether Antonio was really still working with his old henchman bubbled inside my head. Peter fired up a laptop on the desk and took the only chair in the room. I perched on the desk beside him and watched as the laptop slowly booted up.

'Do you think she was going to write something they didn't want getting out?' I asked.

'I'm certain of it.'

The laptop finished loading and Peter plugged the USB drive into it. He navigated into the drive and found a handful of folders. The folder names just appeared to be dates, so Peter clicked on the most recent one. It contained photos of Isabel getting into the passenger seat of a silver Audi.

'I recognise that car. It's De Luca's. I saw it when he came to my house and tried to bribe me.'

'Uh-huh,' Peter said, scrolling through the images. There was another set with the same car in a different location. Isabel got out, then De Luca got out of the driver's seat and they walked away together into a large house. 'I think that's his house. We did some scouting a while back.'

'Why would she willingly go with him?' I asked, frowning. 'She looks at ease; cocky, even.'

'She didn't know what he was capable of.' Peter leaned in close as the next set of images scrolled onto the screen. He clicked on one to open it full size. The timestamp showed an hour's gap between the last one of Isabel going into De Luca's house and the next set. Antonio's car pulled up and he got out of it. It was all there like a stop-motion film. Michelle had documented it all.

There were no more. No suspiciously shaped object being brought out the front door and loaded into the boot of one of the cars. No smoking gun. But the date and time embedded in the image files would be useful to honest police if they were to investigate Isabel's disappearance.

'I wish we knew if the mayor has reported her missing. Is he in on this?' I asked, gesturing to the image on the screen that clearly showed Antonio entering De Luca's house.

'We might be able to find out. Her disappearance hasn't been reported in the press though. Now we know why. The one journalist willing to investigate was just killed for this.'

'I wonder if she had anything else?'

'I'll keep looking,' Peter said.

'I'm exhausted. I can't, Peter.'

'I know,' he said, turning to face me. 'Seeing such violent visions must really take it out of you.'

'It does.' I rolled my shoulders, making them both click.

'I'll take care of this. You go get some rest. I'll let you know if I find anything else incriminating.'

I gave him a quick hug then headed out. It was getting late and I was anxious to get home to my bed. When I arrived at my street, I scanned the parked cars without really thinking. Parked a few metres away from my front door was De Luca's Audi. I pretended not to notice it and made straight for my house. I thought I could see a figure in the driver's seat, but I didn't allow my gaze to linger and quickly went inside. I locked and chained my door and leaned heavily against it, my heart thumping at double speed. I waited but there was no knock. I hurried upstairs and went to my bedroom window without turning on any lights. I peered down into the street and he was still there. He must have seen me return home but wasn't coming to confront me. A shiver ran through me at the thought of him watching my house like that.

I stayed by the window, hidden in the shadows, and waited. It was almost midnight when his car finally lit up and pulled away from the kerb. He drove slowly down the street, turned around and drove back. I leaned back, afraid that his headlights would illuminate me. The lights swept past and I chanced a glance again to see him drive to the end of the street and turn out onto the main road.

I moved shakily away from the window and crawled into bed. I wanted to be done with dangerous men.

CHAPTER NINETEEN

'De Luca was at my house.'

'Excuse me?' Kirk asked, frowning. Peter, Kirk, and I were sitting around their kitchen table, a mug of freshly brewed tea in front of each of us.

'He was in his car and didn't approach me, but it was creepy enough.' I shifted my weight and lightly ran a finger over the handle of my mug, trying to look directly at Kirk. He was usually so kind but sometimes his protective, fatherly nature took on a more aggressive tone, especially when it came to the dangerous and powerful men in my life. I sometimes felt like he thought I'd invited this trouble into my life by associating with Antonio. I never dared to probe into his actual thoughts to confirm my suspicion; I was too afraid that I would be right and I couldn't bear to know that this fatherly figure in my life would think things like that about me.

'Anyway, I just thought the pack ought to know as it was on your territory.' I gave a nonchalant shrug and took a sip of tea.

'Yes, well, we'll keep an eye on the situation. He doesn't know anything about our kind, as far as we know, so it's best not to alert him to our existence.' Kirk fiddled with the top button on his grey cardigan before also lifting his mug to drink.

'What progress has there been on Michelle's murder?' I asked, focusing on Peter.

'Not much. I found a draft article on the flash drive. She was writing about Isabel's disappearance. She must have asked the wrong person the wrong question in her investigation. Possibly De Luca himself. There's no sign of a missing person's report, so if the mayor did report it, De Luca buried it, but it's possible the mayor is in on this and didn't report it.'

'What if I report it?' I asked, my eyes widening with the idea. 'I'm her friend, sort of. If multiple people report it they can't keep burying it, right? Isn't that how this works? People who are missed by lots of people are more likely to be looked for.' It was sad but true. No one cared about the invisible, forgettable people, but someone in a relatively public position, as the mayoress of the city and beloved friend of many people, couldn't just disappear.

'You could just be drawing more attention to yourself,' Kirk replied.

'I'm already in the spotlight. De Luca's already watching me,' I said, almost losing my temper. I took a breath.

'Yes, but by reporting Isabel as missing you'd be letting him know that you've noticed. As it is, he doesn't know that.' Kirk wasn't going to let this go.

'Dad,' Peter said softly. 'I think it's a good idea.'

Kirk pinched the bridge of his nose. His frustration seeped off his skin and was as real to me as my own frustration with the situation.

'You're an adult, Eve. You're not my child or my pack mate. I can't stop you, but I'm allowed to worry about you.'

'I appreciate that, Kirk,' I said, leaning across the table to rest my hand on top of his. Our eyes met and he nodded, his lips pressed together in a thin line.

'We should be looking for Celino ourselves,' Peter said, his voice low and dark.

'You're right,' I said, withdrawing my hand from Kirk's. 'We can't trust that Antonio's doing that.'

'You've changed your tune on that subject, then?' Kirk said, a wry smile on his lips.

'On trusting Antonio? Well, he's under the influence of a demon, so...' I didn't need to finish that sentence.

'Right,' Peter said, shifting his weight. 'Come on, while it's light, we can try to make some progress. We might get lucky and find his sleeping, vulnerable body.'

We got up from the table and marched down the hall towards the front door before Kirk could object.

'Stay safe,' came his one call from the kitchen.

'Will do, Dad. See you later.'

Peter led us out onto the street and to his car.

'What's the plan?' I asked as I climbed into the passenger side.

'So we know he killed that woman and dumped her in the river, and that drug dealer witnessed it. We know the drug dealer was in custody and talking about it, but then he was released and disappeared, right?'

'Right. And finding him is going to be like searching for a needle in a haystack.'

'Or it would be if we were normal people.' He set off driving and I let out a small laugh.

'True. So, what do you have in mind?'

'I have a pretty good sense of smell.'

'Do the vamps smell of anything?'

'Sure, I mean, they're harder to identify because they don't have body odour or hormones, but they smell of blood and any products that they use. Lucia reeked of hairspray.'

'Of course.' I nodded. I didn't want to ask about Antonio, or think about the blood issue.

'But we're going to look for the drug dealer first.'

He drove us back to the bridge we had met Antonio on, where I'd had the vision. He parked in the same spot that Celino had to dump the body, and we walked down the dirt track between the end house of the terrace and the high fence separating it from the field next to it. Halfway down the alley, once out of sight of the road, Peter shifted into his fox form. I never got sick of seeing that transformation. He shrank so quickly, his clothes vanishing to be replaced with ginger fur. He gave a gruff little bark and I sensed satisfaction coming from him, like he was pleased that he could shift like that in front of me. I let out a small laugh and let him trot ahead, sniffing the ground. He got to the bridge and whimpered as he sniffed where the body had been tipped into the river. He weaved back and forth along that little stretch of riverbank, sniffing carefully. I kept a watch up and down the river. A man was walking his dog in the distance and I tensed up, worrying about him seeing me near a fox.

'Peter,' I said softly, knowing he could hear me fine with his sensitive hearing. 'He saw it from the other side of the bridge. That's where I was in the vision, but there's someone nearby. I'm going to cross the bridge. I'll signal you when the man is looking the other way. Okay?'

He gave a gruff little "yip" of agreement and I set off across the bridge. I stepped down onto the muddy track on the other bank of the river and looked around for the dog walker. He was moving away from us and throwing a ball for the excited Labrador.

'Coast's clear,' I called gently. Peter came trotting across the bridge and started sniffing around at my feet. I stepped back from the bank and pointed to where I'd been standing in the vision. It had been a few weeks since the dealer had seen the body being dumped. I didn't know how good Peter's sense of smell was or how easily he'd be able to track it. He sniffed around the end of the bridge and dug his nose into the dirt a little. I kept watch, checking both ways for people. It was quiet and the dog walker was getting smaller in the distance.

Peter sniffed the ground near my feet again, nudging me aside, and I backed to the side of the path to let him past. He gave a low bark and set off at a trot down the path, the way we had approached the place when we met Antonio. I glanced over the bridge towards his parked car, but I had little choice but to follow him if he'd picked up a trail. I walked behind him, not getting too close. I knew how odd it would look if anyone saw us: a woman walking a fox would be an unusual sight in Oris. Even seeing a fox out in daylight was odd enough.

Peter continued along the path for almost as long as we'd been on it on our last trip here, but a little before reaching the city centre, he stopped and sniffed at a narrow, overgrown track away from the river. There were buildings right up against the edge of the path with narrow gaps between them. Peter slipped through the long grass and disappeared between the two, red-bricked buildings. I glanced over my shoulder at the opposite bank, which was lined with the backs of more buildings. Most of them had dark windows, but I didn't see any obvious signs of people who might be watching. I followed Peter between the buildings, picking my way carefully over the uneven ground.

It was largely overgrown, but the narrow track of bent grass suggested that this route was used by a small number of people. It was getting late in the afternoon and the sun had dipped lower than the rooftops. My teeth were on edge, clenched tight together as I inched carefully after Peter. I emerged on the other side of the passage into an almost empty car park. There was a small, black hatchback parked on the far side, and in one corner was an abandoned old estate with no tyres and several years' worth of dirt built up all over it. Peter was sniffing his way carefully along the front of the building to my right. Windows looked down on all sides, but the buildings looked disused; one of them had no glass in the windows at all.

Peter reached a door and looked up at it. I moved quickly and quietly over to meet him. He reached up a paw and scratched at the wooden door frame. The door was covered in faded, peeling, black paint and had a set of small, square glass panels in the top half of it, all filthy and impossible to see through. The building looked like it had once been some sort of factory; all stained brickwork and a tall chimney jutting out of the top. White paint had once signalled a company name across the top half of the front of the building, but it was too worn to read.

'You want to go in there?' I asked, looking down at the fox at my feet. He looked up, his bright eyes shining, and gave a little nod accompanied with a soft bark.

I tried the door handle and, to my surprise, it moved. I pushed the door open and the creak echoed inside. I took out my phone and lit up the torch, shining it around the shell of an entranceway. There had been a fire here once, long ago. The walls and floor were black and the smell of old smoke clung to the surfaces. Music was playing upstairs, some soft, progressive rock that I barely recognised. Peter moved inside, brushing past my legs. He ran to a metal staircase against the wall and dashed up it.

I held my tongue and followed, keeping as quiet as I could. The stairs felt firm enough, but there could have been fire damage that I couldn't see, so I wasn't taking anything for granted and proceeded with caution. The music grew louder as I approached the top of the stairs. Peter ran around the corner onto the landing and was shifting back into his human form as I rounded the top of the stairs. The air was thick with the heavy scent of incense and the unmistakable tang of weed.

Peter strode down the corridor and pushed open a door that stood ajar. A beaded curtain hung across it and the beads rattled against each other as the door pushed them aside. I followed close behind and covered my nose with a hand, not that it was an effective way to block out the smell. The room was lit with the undulating colours of a lava lamp and dull light coming in through the windows along the far wall. Cushions and mattresses lay around the edges of the room, and about half a dozen people sat and lay on them in various states of intoxication.

'Peter,' I said softly, reaching for his arm. He turned and looked at me with his sad, wide eyes. He moved away from me towards a pair of young men sitting leaning against the wall on a dirty mattress. They were the most conscious of the group and looked up as Peter approached them. Their dopey eyes and dirty clothes reminded me of Oliver Twist. Pity swelled in my chest and a tear tugged at the corner of my eye. Peter dropped into a squat in front of them and spoke to them softly.

'Hey, when was the last time Davey was here?'

'Davey? Is he here?' The boy on the left sat up straighter, looking around Peter hopefully.

'No. I'm asking when you last saw him.'

'Oh. I dunno. A couple of weeks I guess.'

I looked around at the others. There was a young woman in the corner passed-out next to a burned spoon and other clear signs of heroin use. She was deathly pale, a complexion I was all too familiar with. I drew a breath and knelt down next to Peter.

'Hi,' I said, trying to smile. The two boys looked at me; one of them managed a smile. 'What about a couple of Italian men? You seen them around here? One of them's tall and blond with light blue eyes, he's quite striking.'

'Yeah,' the boy on the left said, recognition dawning on his slack face. 'Yeah, we've seen him.' His smile dropped and he shuddered. I took a deep breath, braced myself and put a hand on his knee.

I rushed into his thoughts and saw exactly what I expected to see: Celino and Laguardia had both been here to feed. They'd have wiped their victims' conscious memories, but something residual was left in this poor kid's subconscious because he saw Celino lying with the girl in the corner, sucking on her neck while fucking her. I rushed back into the present and a wave of nausea rushed up inside me. I bolted for the door and made it onto the landing before emptying my stomach. I was hardly the first person to do so as the floor was stained with splash marks. Peter was beside me, a hand on my shoulder, in an instant.

'They were feeding here, right?'

I nodded and wiped my mouth.

'And raping. Or at the very least, taking serious advantage of. I'd bet my life that the body Celino dumped was someone from here.'

Peter nodded solemnly and we stood in uneasy silence. The weight of what I'd seen pressed down on my shoulders.

'Let's get out of here,' Peter said at last. 'We don't know who might be keeping an eye on this place. If the vamps come back we could be in trouble.'

It was almost dark when we emerged in the car park. We jogged quickly back to the river and along the path in the twilight. A light fog was moving up the river and the path wasn't lit. Peter took my hand to guide me in the gloom and we made our way swiftly back to the bridge and the safety of his car.

'What do we do?' I asked, staring out of the car as Peter drove us quickly away from the bridge.

'I don't know. I'm sorry. I'll talk to my dad. We'll figure it all out.'

I watched the lights of the city rush past the window as droplets of rain landed on the glass and raced in tiny rivulets towards the back of the car. Antonio had seemed to be genuinely searching for his progeny, so I had to believe he didn't know what they were up to, but it had been a while since I'd spoken to him and I didn't know how far his investigation had gone. Was it possible that he now knew what Celino and Laguardia had been up to? A shudder ran up my spine. I was going to have to communicate with him and I wasn't sure how well I would handle that.

CHAPTER TWENTY

Peter left me alone at my house and went to fill in his pack. I watched the road from my living room window, turning my phone over and over in my sweating palms. Finally I made myself hit "dial" on Antonio's number. He answered it surprisingly quickly.

'I'm glad you called. We should talk,' Antonio said without any preamble.

'Yeah, I agree.'

'Will you come to my place?' he asked, his voice heavy.

'Sure. I'll make my way there after I show my face at Piero's.'

'Very well. Are you sure you don't want me to send the car?'

'Yes, thank you. I'll make my own way there.'

I hung up the phone and tossed it aside, a scowl fixed to my brow. Everything felt heavy. I was carrying a burden that I couldn't put down anywhere. It had been weeks since we had attempted to stage an intervention and rescue Antonio from the clutches of the demon. I had hardly spoken to him since and hadn't seen him at all. I missed him, but I also knew that it was the right thing to do, to have space. Ms Rational was impressed with how little restraint she needed to enforce. I didn't even want to see him, for the most part. I missed what we'd had before, but there was no going back.

Going to see him might be a mistake, but it felt as though it was time. I had no desire to leap back into his bed, well, maybe a little desire, but not enough to overcome the caution I felt about being around him, or the frustration over him not believing my concerns.

I did as I'd said, and went to the restaurant to check on things there. Tina was really doing an admirable job and I had no cause for concern, but I liked to show my face and see everyone. I didn't stay long and soon set off on foot for Antonio's house. It wasn't a particularly long walk, but it took me right through the city centre and kept me grounded in the real world, as opposed to the sheltered bubble of Antonio's wealth and privilege. What I'd seen by the river was a stark reminder of the harshness of the real world.

It was a cool evening, but the biting cold of January and February had passed now that March had taken hold. The walk warmed me up and I even had to unbutton my coat. When I arrived at the mansion I was flushed and in need of a drink and a sit down. Lights were on in several windows, making the place feel more like it had used to when I first met Antonio. There were several cars parked by the garage, more than I'd seen in months. My gaze lingered on the familiar rear bumper from my vision of Celino dumping the body, and I approached the door with a cautious knot in my stomach. Frederick answered the door and greeted me with a stiff smile.

'Good evening. May I take your coat?' I quickly took it off and passed it to him. I tried to smile at him, but his slight frostiness halted the smile before it reached my lips. There were voices echoing in the cavernous ballroom; I craned my neck to see if I could make anything out through the crack between the double doors, but Frederick was quick to hang my coat up for me and held out a hand to indicate for me to follow him. He led me towards the back of the house, past the door to the basement, which I glanced at warily, and out to the parlour at the back. Antonio was sitting on one of the large, red, leather sofas, a glass of Scotch in his hand and the top two buttons of his dark grey shirt undone. His hair was loose and hung over one shoulder. He looked up as I entered the room, and his dark eyes met mine.

'Thank you, Frederick,' he said, nodding past me to his servant. The butler nodded back and closed the door on his way out.

'The house is a bit more lively tonight,' I said, making my way over to him. He stood up, placed his glass down on the table and opened his arms. I moved in for a hug, but quickly released myself and sat down on the sofa.

'Thank you for coming.' He looked at me with sad eyes and picked up his glass again. He took a sip and then quickly put it back down. 'Would you like a drink?'

'Yes, please, just a soda or something.'

Without a word of reply, he swept over to the bar and prepared me a lemonade with ice and a slice of lemon. He returned and passed it to me, still without saying anything. 'Thanks,' I said, taking the glass. The fizz made my nose tingle as I took a sip. It was cold and refreshing after my walk.

'Eve.' He sat down at the other end of the sofa and leaned forwards, propping his elbows on his knees. 'You shouldn't have broken in here.'

'No, I know. I'm sorry. We needed to get the barrier up before—' I stopped myself and took a drink. I couldn't talk about it in case we were being listened to. If there were vampires here, their hearing was good enough to pick up my voice from the other end of the house. Not to mention that the demon, or one of its minions, could be with Antonio at all times, listening to everything, watching everything. I gave an involuntary shudder at the thought of something watching us all the times we had had sex.

'I understand why you did it. I just think that your caution is misplaced.'

'I got that. I stand by it, though.' I looked around, wary of my surroundings. I shook my head. 'I shouldn't have agreed to talk here.' I took a long swig of my drink and stood up to leave. What was I thinking? I wanted to talk to him, but simply couldn't take the chance of saying the wrong thing without first protecting myself. Cogs clicked into place and I fixed my narrow eyes on him. 'Why did you agree to see me tonight? It's been weeks since that happened.'

'I'm worried about you and what you might be getting into.'

'Really? Are you keeping tabs on me?'

'No, Eve,' he said. He shook his head sadly, his long hair shifting on his shoulder. Fuck, he was sexy and distracting. I took a breath and firmed up my resolve. 'But I do know what you saw this afternoon.'

'Right. So you aren't keeping tabs on me except when you are.' I put my glass down with a little more force than was necessary and some of the remaining lemonade sloshed over the side.

'It was a coincidence. I swear.'

'Were you there? Or have you embraced Celino back into the fold? I saw your missing car out front.' I crossed my arms and glared at him.

'I did find them both, yes.' I didn't give him a chance to explain further. I turned and stormed towards the door. 'Please don't go. We need to talk about this.' He was after me in a blur of motion and caught hold of my arm. I pulled away and spun to face him.

'I agree, but I can't. I just can't. Something tried to kill me here. Something wants me dead. And the vile monster who tortured me is presumably in the other room! That isn't something I can just brush past and move on as if it's just another day at the office. You may have lived with threats like this around you constantly for two centuries, but it's all new to me. First your sister, now this, in just a matter of months. It's too much. Since you came into my life it's been in constant peril and I can't pretend otherwise. I was safer before I knew you.'

'But were you happier?'

'Yes!' I closed my eyes and tilted my face to the ceiling. I hadn't meant to say it. I wasn't even sure if it was objectively true. I had been unhappy with having to hide my gift, I always felt broken and detached because of it. I could never be close to anyone. I had never known love, but in hindsight, ignorance was bliss.

'I don't believe you. I've seen how much you've come into your own since we first met. How much more confident you are, how you've matured. I know that you've had intensely pleasurable times in my company.' He flashed me one of his wicked smiles. I shook my head.

'I don't deny any of that, but there is more to happiness. My life was simpler and I was never in a position to have to fight for it. There are good things about this thing between us, but I can't overlook the bad.' I turned and swept towards the door.

'What are you saying? Is it over between us?'

'I think so.' A lump formed in my throat and I regretted saying it out loud. His jaw tightened and one eye twitched. 'I don't know,' I said, backtracking in panic. 'I need more space to figure that out. I'm angry with you, Antonio. I'm frustrated that you are still up to your old tricks and that you keep putting off fulfilling your promise to me.'

'I told you when I made that promise that I had things I had to see through first. I was always candid about that.' His voice rose and sharpened, his Italian accent thickening as it always did when his temper rose.

'Yes and now I know what it was. It isn't something I can just sit by and allow to happen! It's just wrong, Antonio! Why don't you see that?'

'Because I have lived several lifetimes over, Eve, and my moral compass works a little differently than yours. That happens when you live so long that you see politicians come and go and things never change. When you see the world move on and yet always stay the same. You learn just how pointless most human actions are!' He jabbed his finger at me accusingly and his nostrils flared as he shouted.

'Don't try to act as though your lifetime has somehow elevated you! Living longer doesn't make you better than us. You aren't privy to some mystical truth that no one else has ever witnessed. Plenty of people get jaded about the system. It doesn't excuse rigging it. You can't just break the very core of our democracy because you feel like it!' I stomped to the door and grabbed the handle.

Antonio's hand was around my wrist before I could turn the handle. He slammed me against the door, his nose millimetres from mine, and his dark eyes flashed.

'Everything I've done, I've done for you.'

'No you haven't. You've done it for yourself. Let me go.' I spoke through clenched teeth. Anger swelled inside me like a tidal wave. He slammed the palm of his free hand against the door right beside my face and a snarl escaped his thin lips.

'I want you to stay.'

'No. Not while we're both this angry.' Even as I said the words I felt my anger ebbing away and a dream-like drowsiness began to seep into my body. I blinked hard and shook my head. The anger rose inside again like a wave of nausea. I pushed out with my mind, fury searing like fire. Antonio flew back across the room and tumbled over the sofa to land with a bump on the other side of it. I ripped open the door and stormed down the hall to the foyer. I didn't wait for Frederick to appear. I grabbed my own coat from the stand by the front door.

'Eve!' Antonio called from behind me and I wheeled about to see him hurrying into the foyer. 'I'm sorry.'

'You tried to use your power on me! How dare you!' I swung my coat on and dashed for the door. He stood in the middle of the chequered floor, his mouth hanging slightly open. The ballroom doors opened and Celino leaned there, a smirk on his cruel face. I turned my attention back to Antonio, too angry to care about the audience. 'Don't call me! Don't come near me. Don't come near my family or my business. You are not welcome at my house or anywhere near me. And if you continue with your plan to subvert the election, I will turn you in and I will ensure justice is done.' I yanked the door open and fled into the night.

My heart thumped wildly and my breathing felt tight as panic and rage coursed through my system. I put my head down and set off running for the gate at the end of the winding drive. It opened for me as I approached and I burst out onto the street and kept on running until my lungs couldn't take any more. I had just reached the city wall and I skidded to a halt under the arch through which the major road out into the suburb beyond passed. There was light traffic but no pedestrians about and I slid down the wall to sit on the cold pavement, with cars sweeping by on the road in front of me.

Tears poured down my face and I covered it with my hands. I was shaking all over and felt as though my chest was going to burst open. I let out a huge cry that turned into a roar. My heart was breaking, I realised dully: this is what that feels like.

After god knows how long, the tears stopped and I was left shaking slightly with a numb backside from the cold, hard ground. I tugged my phone from my pocket and called the only person I wanted to talk to: Weaver.

'Eve?' she answered almost immediately.

'Can I come stay with you for a while?'

'Of course you can!'

'I'll be on a train in the morning, if that's all right?'

'Yes, that's fine. Let me know what time you're due into Caerton and I'll meet you at the station.'

'Thank you.' My voice was shaking and fresh but silent tears leaked from my tired eyes.

'No problem. You can tell me what happened when you get here. Try and get some rest.'

'I will.' I got to my feet, the stone wall cold against my wet hand as I used it to help me up. My feet burned from the run from Antonio's house and I winced as I took a step. 'I'll call you again from the train. Thank you, Weaver.'

'Don't mention it. See you tomorrow.' I ended the call and put my phone away. I set off walking gingerly and it took me twice as long to get home as it would normally have done. I finally stepped into the hall in my house and locked the door behind me. It had been the longest evening of my life. I trudged up the stairs and got ready for bed in an exhausted blur.

I'd expected to toss and turn for hours, but sleep claimed me as soon as I lay down. I was too exhausted for my brain to get in the way of sleep.

CHAPTER TWENTY-ONE

BY 10 AM THE NEXT MORNING I was taking my seat on a quiet train. Before leaving my house, I'd boarded up the hidden trapdoor to the catacombs and put a heavy crate over it. I left a light on in the hall and made the house as secure as possible. I still hoped that my vocal rescinding of Antonio's invitation would have some power, but I couldn't be sure; I just had to trust that he would respect my decision and not try to enter my house. I let Tina know I was going away and that I was leaving Piero's in her capable hands, but as I sat there on the train waiting for it to set off, I had the most difficult conversation still to come. I found Peter's number and hit "call".

'Hey. You okay?' he asked, his voice heavy with sleep.

'Not really. I'm on my way to Caerton. I don't know when I'm coming back.'

'Oh. Right.' The hurt was clear in his voice.

'I'm sorry. I just have to get some space. I had a big fight with Antonio last night and I can't risk running into him. It's all got too much for me in Oris.'

'I get it,' he said, with a sigh. 'Take the time you need. I'm right here if you need me.'

'You guys don't really need me for what has to be done, right?'

'Right. I mean, you'll be missed, obviously, but we'll manage. I'll let my dad and the others know. I hope you get what you need from the break.'

'Thanks. I'll see you soon.' I hung up and felt a tightness in my throat that I didn't want to turn into tears. I gave a big sniff and shook my head.

An announcement came over the PA and a moment later the train doors closed. The steady hum of the engine intensified as the wheels started moving and soon we were speeding out of the station. Oris rushed past the window and I gazed at it, my brain as much of a blur as the streets and buildings passing by. The churning that my brain had been simply too exhausted to do the previous night began to happen as I gazed at the city giving way to countryside. The fight with Antonio played again and again in my mind. Part of me wondered if leaving was really the right thing to do. I was running away from a horrible problem, but maybe I should be facing up to it and dealing with it?

I couldn't deny that I genuinely needed breathing room. Being too close to a problem usually made it impossible to see a solution. The distance between Oris and Caerton wasn't just physical, it was also the mental space that I so desperately needed.

I returned my attention to my phone and let Weaver know my estimated time of arrival, which was in the middle of the afternoon. Then I let my mind drift away and begin to process everything I'd endured over the last few months. Silent tears tracked down my cheeks and I was grateful to not be sharing my seat with anyone. I listened to music through my headphones and let the feelings come through. It was long overdue.

The train ride was a little over four hours, and by the time the train slowed down and pulled into Caerton Central Station, I was all cried out. It was odd to be returning to somewhere both familiar and alien. I had been living in Caerton for over two years when I returned to Oris. I still had belongings in my shared house here but had had virtually no contact with my housemates except to periodically tell them I still didn't know when I was coming back. I would have to take this opportunity to box everything up and put it into storage. They would probably want to let my room to someone else. I couldn't blame them. To their credit, they hadn't nagged me. We weren't close. Until Antonio, I hadn't let myself get close to anyone really, because of my gift. My uni friends were no exception, but I would go and see them while I was in Caerton and get things squared up with them.

I got to my feet and moved along the train towards the door. The train slowed to a smooth halt and the doors hissed as they opened. I stepped out onto the cool and bustling platform and made my way quickly towards the exit. People brushed past me and I slipped back into the old habit of neatly swerving to avoid everyone who came too close. I made my way out to the large entrance to the station where there were newspaper vendors, a flower stall, a sandwich place, and the many stone arches out to the taxi rank. It was packed with people rushing in and out of the station and I craned my neck, searching for Weaver. There was no sign of her. I struggled through the crowd pressing in around me. I stepped out onto the wet pavement outside and into the light rain that was a permanent feature in Caerton. Standing at the rear end of a row of idle taxis was Weaver in a long skirt, long coat and her waist-length blonde hair lifting slightly in the breeze. She caught my eye and raised a hand and I ran towards her. She opened her arms and engulfed me in them. I allowed her to squeeze me and I held tight in return. When she released me I again had fresh tears on my face. I swiped them away quickly and let out an embarrassed laugh.

'How was your journey?'

'Oh you know, dull.'

She took one of my bags from me – I had a large shoulder bag with my wallet, keys, phone and all that junk, plus a holdall with my clothes and whatnot. She took the latter and lifted it as if it weighed nothing. She led me away from the line of taxis and over to the small car park that extended away from the front of the station and down the slight hill to the busy road beyond. We approached a dark blue pickup truck which took up two of the narrow spaces, and a guy jumped out of the driver's seat and lifted a hand in greeting.

'Eve, this is Claws.' I looked him over. He was medium height and lean, with short but unruly dark hair. He looked a little older than Weaver, early forties maybe, with slight grey streaks at his temples. His eyes were light grey and slightly lined. He exuded calm, like Kirk. I held out a hand, which was most unlike me, and he shook it.

Usually my visions would rush into me like a waterfall, causing me to stagger and sometimes even black out, but what I got from Claws was just a calm feeling of slowly sinking down into warm water. I released his hand and smiled.

'Nice to meet you.'

'Likewise.' He smiled back, then took my bag from Weaver and hoisted it easily into the back of the truck. We all climbed up into the cab, which had a wide front seat, big enough for Weaver and me to sit side by side while Claws drove. He pulled the truck out of the parking space to rude gestures from waiting drivers who seemed to object to how big the vehicle was. He wasn't fazed in the slightest and drove away without commenting or gesturing back.

'Where are we heading?' I asked, realising that I never really knew which part of Caerton Weaver and her pack claimed as their territory. I knew her from the university, where she was a physics lecturer.

'To our place. It's a closely guarded secret, so we have to blindfold you,' Claws said, completely deadpan. I glanced at him with wide eyes and looked to Weaver for confirmation. She was making a poor attempt to hide a smirk.

'He's kidding,' she said softly and gave him a gentle smack on the arm. He chuckled and gave a nod. I stared out of the window as we wound our way through the busy streets of the city centre. Caerton was such a contrast to Oris. My home town was old and still retained many of its Norman features, like the wall. The roads were narrow and many of them were filled with quaint, independent shops and restaurants. Caerton was at least four times bigger than Oris and more metropolitan. It was full of big chain stores and modern buildings. There were no tower blocks or skyscrapers in Oris, but Caerton had plenty. We sped past the tallest building in the city, a great glass tower that sat in the heart of the financial district. The roads were choked with double-decker buses and cars. People in suits marched along under black umbrellas and the rain sloshed up under the big wheels of the truck.

We drove out of the city centre on the dual carriageway that led north into St. Marks. It was an area I knew a little as there was some student accommodation there. The main university buildings were tucked in just north of the financial area that we had driven through. My own shared house had been near there, but I had friends who lived in St. Marks and had occasionally needed to go there. We skirted the edge of St. Marks and headed towards Crossway, a leafy suburb that bore little resemblance to central Caerton, but before we reached it we pulled off the main road and approached a vast circular complex of apartments. Claws drove us through an arch and into the car park in the centre. It was like a giant doughnut made from shiny glass and chrome. The car park could only accommodate a handful of cars, but around it was a lush green lawn and some well-manicured trees and hedges. We all hopped down out of the cab and Claws retrieved my bag from the back.

'Welcome to The Circle,' Weaver said, grinning and holding up her hands to indicate our surroundings. I looked around and nodded my approval.

'Which apartment's yours?' I asked, gazing up and turning on the spot to take in all of the windows. The cladding on the exterior walls looked new, the paint was clean and unspoiled.

'All of them,' Claws said as he swept past me.

'I'm sorry?' I scurried after him, Weaver skipping along at my side.

'We own the building,' he replied.

'Seriously?'

'Yep,' Weaver said, grinning. We followed a path

between two rounded hedges towards a pair of shiny, glass doors. Claws drew out a fob from his pocket and tapped it to the censor next to the door. There was a low pulse through the metal frame and Weaver pushed the door open and held it for me. I went inside, followed by the others, and a lift door on the right *dinged* open. Opposite was a huge bank of mailboxes with neatly engraved numbers on them. We filed into the mirror-lined lift. The doors closed and I rounded on Weaver.

'But you're a professor. How are you also some sort of property tycoon?'

She let out a throaty chuckle and shook her head. 'You know I'm a lot more than a university professor, Eve.'

'The pack owns it,' Claws said. 'Jointly.'

'Yes, quite.' Weaver nodded solemnly. I looked from Weaver to Claws and back again.

'Will I meet the others?'

'If you want to,' Weaver said.

'It might be a bit much.'

'Maybe, but I am taking you to a special party if you stay a few weeks.'

'Oh really?' I cocked an eyebrow.

The lift *dinged* and came to a halt on the sixth floor. We filed out and turned left. We passed through a set of doors and into a corridor that curved away to the right. I glanced over my shoulder to see a matching corridor going the other way beyond the lift. The corridor was lined in thick, blue carpet and the walls were covered in pale paper with a slight sheen to it. There were skylights at regular intervals and wall lights that flicked on as we approached them. It was surprisingly bright and cheerful for a block of flats.

Claws came to a halt and unlocked a door. He went inside and held the door for me. I stepped into a huge, open-plan living area with a kitchen to the right, a dining area to the left, and in the middle was a spacious sitting room with low, wide couches facing the floor-to-ceiling windows that looked out over the centre of the circular complex. The whole space was bathed in bright light, despite it not being the brightest day outside. Everything was white and navy and smelled new. The kitchen was made up of shiny white cupboard doors and chrome appliances that gleamed. There was a short corridor immediately to my left and another door at the window end of the left-hand wall.

'This is where I actually live,' Weaver said, grinning as she shut the door.

I let out a long whistle as I gazed around.

'How about you?' I asked, looking at Claws, who was busy making himself at home in the kitchen.

'I have another one down the corridor.' He looked up at me from buttering some bread. 'Want a sandwich?'

'You guys are going to feed me and everything? I could get used to this.' I grinned and Weaver let out a chuckle.

'You're here so I can look after you, so that's exactly what I intend to do.'

CHAPTER TWENTY-TWO

THE FOLLOWING FEW DAYS consisted mostly of Weaver bringing me food while I slept and journaled through my feelings. I didn't see much of Claws, nor did I meet the rest of their pack, although I picked up that they knew I was there. It felt as though they were trying to give me space, which I appreciated. I didn't feel much like socialising. Weaver gave me a fob to unlock the complex doors so I could come and go. After a week of hiding away to process everything that had happened, I went to my old house to see what the situation was.

It was a three-storey terraced house in a student neighbourhood. The street was narrow and packed with cars, and all of the houses were built from dark red stone that was common in this part of the city. A lot of the university buildings were made of the same stone. I stared up at the house, trepidation churning my insides. I approached the door and fished out my key. Before I could put it in the lock, the door flew open and Jenny, one of my housemates, stood there grinning at me.

'Eve! Oh my god!' She pulled me across the threshold and into a hug. I flinched but allowed her to have her moment of overfamiliarity. 'How are you doing?'

'Umm, yeah, good thanks. All things considered.'

'I was so sorry about your parents,' she said more soberly.

'Thanks.' I shut the door and followed her down the narrow hallway to the living room. The floors were all lined in thin and patched carpet and the whole house leaned slightly to one side, which was one of the things we'd liked about it when we looked around last year. The living room was stuffed full of two sofas that were too big for the room and had a large flat-screen TV mounted on the wall over an electric fire.

'Are you back for good?' Jenny asked.

'No, not this time. I thought I'd better come and sort my stuff out in case you want to let my room to someone else.'

'Oh no. I'm sorry to hear that. You paid up for the whole year, so the room's yours, hun. It's not the same without you here. What about your degree?'

'I want to come back, but I need to speak to the dean. I think they'll make me restart my final year in September.'

'That makes sense. You're so talented. You should finish the course.' My cheeks burned. Jenny had always been the sweet, bubbly sort. Even though I never felt close to her, I'd always liked her.

'Thanks,' I replied. Jenny flopped down onto one of the squashy sofas and I perched awkwardly on the other end. It didn't feel like my home any more.

'What have you been doing with yourself back home?'

'Running my parents' restaurant.' It was mostly true. That was what I was doing initially, but the truth was I had hardly done any work there in a couple of months. There was no way I could tell her what I'd really been doing – sleeping with my crime boss boyfriend, who it turned out was also a vampire, and hanging out with my new shapeshifter buddies. I didn't think any of that would go down well. I felt so disconnected from my old life now. It felt alien to be sitting in the living room with someone who knew nothing about the supernatural.

Jenny nodded and looked impressed, but neither of us had anything else to say. I got to my feet and she copied me.

'Do you want to go for a drink with us later?'

'Maybe. I'll see what's happening with the friend I'm staying with.'

'Why don't you stay here?' She looked stung. 'It's still your room.'

'No, it's okay. Thanks. I'll just go sort through some of my stuff and then get out of your hair. It's really weird to be back here, to be honest.'

'Yeah, I get that.' She followed me as far as the stairs then went her own way to the kitchen. I trudged up the stairs, glad to be on my own. My room was on the top floor and everything was as I'd left it. I'd loved this room when we moved in. It had a sloped ceiling and a skylight and was painted deep purple with a white ceiling and an exposed beam. The furniture was all pine and the floorboards were exposed and polished. My lamp had a light blue scarf draped over it and I'd hung star-shaped fairy lights up along the beam and around the wardrobe.

I closed the door, leaned on it and looked around the room, a small smile creeping onto my face. I'd made my parents' house as close to my taste as I could without making substantial changes, but this room was perfectly mine. This felt nice. I walked around it and ran my fingers over things. The wooden surfaces were thick with dust; the fabric was soft and familiar though. This had been my sanctuary when I was overwhelmed by all of the feelings and thoughts I was always picking up from other people. I tugged open the wardrobe, the door of which had always stuck a bit. I had grabbed a few essentials when I packed to go back to Oris, but left most of my clothes behind. I'd bought lots of new things to restock my wardrobe there. The remaining clothes hung limp and lonely in the wardrobe and I hurriedly picked out the things I wanted to take with me. I hastily boxed up my books and art supplies and made a pile of things I wanted to put in storage here in Caerton for when I came back properly. Some of my things were going back to Oris with me.

I stripped my bed to wash the sheets, which were a little musty after being left to gather dust for so long. I gathered them up and went down to the ground floor and through to the kitchen at the back of the house. There was no one around and the washing machine was empty, so I took the liberty to fill it with my bedding. I was just finishing up when Jenny returned with Clara and Helen, my other housemates.

They all squealed and took turns to hug me, which was getting tiresome. I went along with it and did my best to fake enthusiasm. I was pleasantly surprised at their reaction, as I had been pretty sure they would be frosty with me having been gone for so long. They were insistent that I go out to a cocktail bar with them that evening and I gave in to the peer pressure.

'It'll be just like old times!' Jenny said with a giggle. I nodded and smiled along with their excitement, while struggling to think when we had all gone out together before. My time in Caerton seemed like a whole different lifetime, but there had been a few nights out, back in our second year when we lived together for the first time. I leaned against the back door as the three of them rambled and giggled and reminisced. I felt just like I always had before: like the odd one out. Now it wasn't just my gift, it was my whole life. My whole sense of what was important. I hadn't considered them all that girly and superficial before, but right now they felt like a trio out of some cheesy teenage rom-com or coming-of-age-story. Was it being with a man two hundred years older than me? Had Antonio aged me prematurely? It was entirely possible. My chest tightened as I thought about him, and I could tell that my fake smile had become more strained when Jenny put a hand on my arm and looked into my eyes.

'Are you all right, Eve?'

'Yeah,' I said, forcing myself to brighten up and meet her gaze. 'I'm just tired.'

This excuse was accepted without question and the boisterous chatter resumed. I eventually pulled myself away and collected the things I wanted to take with me. It all more or less fitted in my holdall, plus one box. When I returned downstairs, the others had gone their separate ways. Music was coming from Helen's room, but I didn't know where the others were. I let myself out and ordered an Uber to collect me. That had been normal once too, but in Oris everything was within walking distance.

Later that afternoon I met with the dean of my department and made all of the arrangements to return full-time in September. I got through it without getting too emotional, despite having to talk about my parents, but it was a relief to get out of her office and get back to Weaver's.

I got myself dressed up for my big night out with the girls and set out to meet them. We met at a bar near the theatre in the centre of the city, and after a couple of cocktails it wasn't nearly as awkward any more. I ended up having a nice time. I let them do most of the talking and didn't get into any details about my life in Oris; it was just easier that way.

I spent the next few days shuttling back and forth between my old house and a storage unit I'd rented. I boxed up my things and took them to my unit. I collected most of my art from the university and packaged that up to store too. I was going to be away from the university for another six months and didn't want any of my work to get misplaced. There were some of my pieces on display around the building and I smiled when I passed them. They could stay where they were.

My old housemates insisted on taking me to karaoke, one of the social things we had used to do semi-regularly in our second year, and I grudgingly agreed. There was something nice and familiar about it all as I got settled back into Caerton. I was spending less time lost in my own thoughts, and a whole day passed without me worrying about what was happening in Oris.

I met the girls at the Japanese restaurant where we had a private room booked upstairs. It was complete with sliding doors and a low table surrounded by cushions. On the wall opposite the door was a projector screen on which music videos played, and a large folder of song choices waited for us in the middle of the table next to a pitcher of sake. The food was amazing at this place, but the private karaoke was the reason we went. It only took me three cups of sake and a large Midori to be willing to try my hand at singing something. We laughed at the cheesy videos that played on the screen, and Jenny duetted with me on a classic 80's rock number.

We left the restaurant and stumbled, giggling, into the bar next door for yet more drinks. Loud music shook the floor and thumped up my body, keeping me from tumbling into any visions from the bodies I inevitably ended up pressed against.

By midnight I was done and made my way back to St. Marks alone. It was a relief to be back in Weaver's clean, cool, neat apartment. I hadn't seen her all day, but she was sitting up at the table drawing when I got back. She looked up and smiled serenely.

'Good night?'

'Yes, thanks.' I dropped down into a chair opposite and peered at her drawings. 'Demon on the loose?' I asked, pointing at her pretty graphic and dark-looking sketches.

'Oh yes, but nothing to worry about. We've got it under control.'

'Glad to hear it.'

'I hope you're not too peopled out. I want to take you to the equinox celebration tomorrow night. You've been invited to take part in the coronation of the new Spring King and Queen.'

'I'm sorry?' I blinked at her in mild, drunken surprise.

'As our guest. Will you do it?'

'What's involved?'

'Nothing too complicated. You've helped in other shifter rituals. This'll be a walk in the park.' She grinned at me over her half-moon glasses.

'Okay.' I waved a hand in front of my face and exhaled heavily. I was too tired and a little too drunk to put up much resistance.

'How are you feeling about things?' I shrugged and looked down at her drawings. 'It's okay to not have any answers yet.'

'I guess. It's weird being back here, but it's starting to feel more like home again. I'll be back to finish my degree in September. The timeline feels good. Like there's a definitive end in sight.'

'End?' Weaver raised her gaze towards me.

'I said that? I guess I did. I guess that's how I see everything in Oris. Temporary.'

'Everything?' There was a small smile tugging at the corner of her mouth.

'Yeah, everything. I'm going to bed now.' I stood up and stuck my tongue out at her.

'Night,' she said, smiling fully.

I walked in a slightly wavy line to the guest room, my head feeling nicely foggy. As I got ready for bed, I wondered dully what I would have to do for this ritual and just what it would be like to meet all of Caerton's shifters at once.

CHAPTER TWENTY-THREE

Weaver led me towards a park surrounded by tall, wrought-iron fences. She placed a hand on the tall gate and pushed it open with a firm shove. The dark and empty park beyond the gate disappeared and a very different scene came into view as the veil between worlds opened for us.

A huge fire roared and the flames danced and licked the dark sky. Little sparks leapt up and then drifted in beautiful madness in the rising, hot air. Drumming filled the night and chanting, singing, laughter and banter accompanied the beat. We stepped into Hepethia, the shifter realm, which was made of crystal and could be shaped to meet the needs of the shifters who claimed a given territory. I'd had little glimpses into other realms before, but this was new to me and a little overwhelming. Shifters could cross the veil anywhere at will, but a special door had to be made for me, a relatively mundane human, to cross over.

I tried to smile and allow myself to be swept up in the

celebration, but I was too nervous. I had a role in the ceremony but I felt like an intruder. I wasn't even a shapeshifter. What place did I have to be crowning the Spring King?

'It's normally the previous year's king and queen who do it,' Weaver had said when I asked. 'But last year's Spring Queen isn't around any more.'

'Did something happen to her?'

'Yes. She died.'

'Oh.'

'You're our guest of honour, Eve. The council all agreed you should take her place.'

I understood and I felt honoured, but I was still nervous and uncomfortable about it.

'Don't introduce me to everyone,' I said, tugging at Weaver's arm as she led me towards the party. 'I won't remember everyone's names anyway.'

She chuckled and nodded in agreement.

I had never seen so many shifters. There were maybe only a quarter as many in all of Oris as there were here in Caerton. I was reminded of the memory of my parents that Weaver had shared with me: they had visited Caerton and attended a bonfire like this one once. I caught glimpses in that memory of the scale of the population, but seeing it in person was far more intimidating.

A dozen different groups cavorted together, dancing, clapping, cheering and shoving. Several of them were topless, many more were adorned with weapons. Tattoos gleamed in the flickering firelight on many an inch of skin, and bodies moved together to the pounding beat of the drums in the most erotic displays I had seen in my relatively sheltered and innocent life so far.

'Weaver!' A skinny guy in a long, black leather coat, with spiked up black hair and a pierced nose strode over and pulled her into a tight embrace.

'Scribe,' Weaver replied, grinning as they parted. 'This is Eve.'

'Hey,' Scribe said, smiling broadly and extending a hand. He had dozens of black bands around his wrists, each with a small charm on. I shook his offered hand.

'I didn't think you were going to be here,' Weaver said, her eyes wide with delighted surprise.

'I'm not really here,' he said, giving her a conspiratorial wink. 'I'm heading back across the veil in a minute, I just wanted to see you first.'

Weaver smiled and nodded; she tucked her long, blonde hair behind one ear and drew her bottom lip between her teeth. I watched the two of them, trying not to smile as they flirted awkwardly with one another. They were both a little old to be behaving like teenagers, I thought. Weaver was easily over thirty and he looked a similar age.

'Where are you supposed to be?' I asked, mainly to break the ridiculous silence between them.

'My pack, The Watch, we're on guard tonight. We'll be protecting the city while you lot celebrate.'

'Oh. Well, thank you for missing out.' I smiled and he grinned back at me.

'No problem. I have to go. I'll see you at the Scroll Archive tomorrow, right?' He was only addressing Weaver, and I turned away respectfully, feeling like an intruder in their moment. Out of the corner of my eye, I caught a chaste kiss on the cheek before Scribe walked away.

'Well aren't you two sweet?' I said, grinning at Weaver.

'Shush, you.' She gave me a playful shove. 'We're just friends.'

'No, you obviously aren't.' We both laughed and Weaver shook out her long hair.

'All right, maybe there's something there. A little on-again-off-again thing, but relationships are hard to sustain for our kind, Eve.'

I nodded. The giggles had evaporated. I caught sight of a young man dancing with fire poi a short distance away. He swayed and turned to the beat of the music, spinning the small balls of fire around himself. I was mesmerised as I watched him moving: he had rich, tawny-coloured skin; thick, dark, wavy hair, and a neat goatee. His chest and stomach were covered in curly, dark hair, and his body was fairly lean but with a little soft padding. His blue jeans were slung low on his hips and I could make out his hip bones in the undulating firelight. He had bare feet and moved over the bumpy crystal ground with no apparent discomfort.

'That's who you're crowning later,' Weaver said softly at my ear. I glanced at her, mildly surprised to hear her voice.

'Really? Him?' I asked, pointing at the fire poi dancer.

'Really.' She was smiling at me. 'He is to be our new Spring King.'

'Who's the queen?'

Weaver looked around, scanning the crowd. 'There,' she said, pointing in the direction that Scribe had appeared from. A tall, slender woman in a cream toga was surrounded by other women. They were painting her fair arms with delicate vines while she smiled and laughed at somebody's joke. She had long, wavy, brown hair and perfectly white teeth. A sick surge of envy pushed up inside me.

'Are they a couple?' I asked, surprising myself.

'Not as far as I'm aware. The roles are purely ceremonial. It's our way of honouring the coming of spring, of welcoming the fae of fertility and warmth. The Spring King and Queen don't have any authority and they aren't really getting married. We have a complex relationship with the concept of royalty around here. Traditionally, the Spring King would be the Green Man, but that's a big no-go for us too. It took a bit of doing to restart this tradition after a hundred-year hiatus.'

I glanced back towards the man, equally surprised and disconcerted by the relief I felt at learning that these two perfect creatures were not an item. A little stab of guilt over Antonio caught me somewhere near my navel.

Weaver took hold of my arm and gave it a gentle tug. 'Come on,' she said, 'drinks.' She led me away from the fire and towards a long table draped in a white cloth. There were platters of meat, pastries, olives, fruit, nuts, and sticks of carrot and celery to dip in the dozen or more pots of salsa, sour cream, and more. At each end of the table was a small mountain of paper cups and huge flasks of wine, mead, and punch. On the ground next to the table was a massive barrel with a tap in it that dripped strong-smelling beer.

'Just how drunk will everyone get tonight?' I asked, eyeing all of the alcohol.

'Not as much as you'd think. Our metabolisms actually burn through alcohol much more quickly than humans. I once saw one of my pack mates drink a whole barrel that size and walk away. He was a bit the worse for wear the next day, mind you.'

I chuckled as I poured myself some punch. Weaver was pouring herself some mead, and when we both had full cups we tapped them together before drinking.

The air was hot and smokey and the rhythm of the drumming changed, slowing a little. I watched as many of the shifters formed a procession and began circling the fire. The Spring King and Queen were each flanked by a small group of others, perhaps each of their packs.

'Come on,' Weaver said. She drained her cup and put it back on the table. I did likewise, the sour punch stinging my throat on the way down. I followed her back towards the fire and she led me to join the procession. Most of the assembly joined us, forming a great long tail.

Above the fire, a beautiful red and gold phoenix swirled, singing softly.

'What is that?' I asked, pointing up at it.

'Hope-for-a-New-Day,' Weaver replied, grinning. 'Our city spirit.'

'You'll have to explain that to me properly another time.'

The procession filed away from the fire and up a loose aisle between rows of tree trunks laid flat like benches. At the head of the aisle was a little raised platform with two wooden thrones. Between them stood a woman with long, bright red hair. She wore a scarlet dress with a plunging neckline, not unlike something Lucia might have worn. Unlike my old enemy, this woman looked wise and warm. She had bright green eyes, pale skin, and wore two long swords across her back.

The ceremonial King and Queen were led onto the platform and took up places on either side of the woman in red, their respective packs seeming to deposit them up there then retreat again like water rushing downhill. Weaver led me up the aisle, one hand gently resting on my back. We stepped up onto the platform and the woman in red passed me a thick, heavy wreath, smiling warmly at me.

'Welcome,' she whispered.

'Thank you,' I replied, taking the wreath.

Behind me was a young man with a shaved head and tattoos all over his sculpted shoulders. His skin was like black coffee and his eyes blazed. The woman in red passed him a smaller wreath and he took it with a courteous nod. I caught Weaver and the tattooed man bumping fists before going their separate ways.

Weaver led me to where the Spring King stood and positioned me next to him. I smiled nervously at him. He was a little taller than me; his eyes were brown and glinted in the flickering firelight.

'Hi,' he said, a nervous smile on his full lips.

I nodded and turned to look at the assembled crowd. At least sixty shifters stood before us. I had always shied away from the limelight and felt extremely uncomfortable with all of those people staring up at me. Weaver stepped down off the stage and went to stand in the front row. I glanced again at the topless man beside me and smiled awkwardly.

The woman in red raised her hands and the crowd fell silent.

'We are gathered here tonight to celebrate the turning of the wheel of the year. When we last met, it was to pay the Danegeld at Imbolc. Now we gather at the equinox to welcome the coming spring and the strengthening sun. We honour the fae of fertility and feasting. We welcome Persephone back from her time in the underworld and ask her to watch over and protect our ritual tonight. We also acknowledge those who we have lost. Sadly, this year, our previous Spring Queen is no longer with us. We welcome, in her place, our honoured guest, Eve Rawling.'

My cheeks burned and the wreath grew heavier in my sweating hands. Every eye was on me, and whispers rippled through the crowd.

'We thank Glaive-of-Night for his service as our Spring King.' The woman in red gestured towards the man who had followed me onto the stage, and he nodded in acknowledgement, a severe expression on his dark face. 'But as the wheel turns, we welcome the new court. I give you all Rising Mist, our new Spring Queen!' A huge cheer burst from the assembled shifters, clapping and whoops of celebration. Glaive-of-Night stepped in front of the woman in the toga and placed the delicate wreath he was holding on the top of her head like a crown. She grinned and her cheeks flushed. The two shifters embraced, and after he released the new Queen, Glaive stepped down from the stage and joined Weaver in the front. They gave each other friendly nudges and I saw his face relax for the first time.

Perhaps he was as nervous as me.

The cheers began to subside and I looked at the woman in red: she was smiling affectionately, the corners of her eyes creasing with kindness. I thought she looked about my mother's age, but there was something about her eyes that told me she was older than she looked.

'Beside our Spring Queen stands our Spring King,' she said, her voice ringing with clear authority, and the last of the noise petered out. 'Blade Heart.'

The roar that erupted from the crowd dwarfed the jubilation that had followed Rising Mist's announcement. I was a little shocked. People leapt in the air, pumping their fists; they hugged each other and shouted joyfully. The woman in red gave me a friendly nod and I stepped in front of the man whose name I finally knew. He ducked down a touch so that I could reach to place the wreath on his head. He smelled so good, musky and sweet, like smoke and mead.

'Thanks,' he said, standing up straight. 'Eve, right?'

'No problem,' I replied, nodding and again feeling the heat in my cheeks and on my neck. 'You're popular,' I managed to say with a small smile. He grinned back at me. I was about to turn to go when he caught my hand and gave it a squeeze. I looked up into his brown eyes.

'Don't worry, you are very welcome here tonight. I know we can be an intimidating bunch, but your parents were heroes and we all know that.'

'Oh, thanks.' I tried to smile, but my cheeks wouldn't cooperate. He released my hand and I rushed down to Weaver's side. She threw an arm around me and pulled me close. I flinched, waiting for a vision, but nothing came.

'Well done,' she said loudly at my ear over the din around us.

'Our Spring Queen and King have been crowned,' the woman in red called over the noise. The two of them moved together in front of her and clasped hands, smiling warmly at each other. They then parted and each took a seat in one of the ornately carved wooden thrones. Blade Heart and Rising Mist looked like the perfect couple. She sat straight and regal, giggling slightly as she watched the cheering crowd. He sat with his weight on one elbow resting on the arm of his throne, his legs sticking out with his bare feet crossed at the ankles. His wreath was slightly lopsided and I suppressed a chuckle.

'How were they chosen?' I asked Weaver as the crowd began to break up into smaller groups.

'They have to have changed between one and two years ago, and honoured their pack in some way. Glaive-of-Night here,' she said, giving him a gentle shove, 'joined my pack two and a half years ago. He saved my life and our Alpha's, just weeks after joining us. Made quite the impression, didn't you?' He shrugged and smiled a lopsided smile.

'Do you talk?' I asked, thinking of Dante.

'Sometimes,' he said, grinning more broadly. When he smiled he didn't look severe at all. He ran his hands over his bald head, then turned and bounded away.

'Is she a priestess?' I asked, pointing at the woman in red, who was talking animatedly to Rising Mist.

'Crimson? I suppose you could call her that. She's a ritualist. She's the Alpha of her pack and one of the city's Elders. She often leads our ceremonies because she's one of the most powerful shifters in Caerton.'

'Oh,' I said, staring in awe at the stunning woman. 'Did she know my parents?'

'Yes, she did.' Weaver squeezed my hand.

'Blade Heart said something to me up there. He was trying to put me at ease, saying I was welcome. He said everyone thought of my parents as heroes. Is that true?'

'What your parents did, or laid the foundation for, is known here, yes. There were people here who wanted to do more to help the cause in Oris, but it was decided that it was too far away and not our fight. There was near unanimous support for what you had to do, though. They all think you're a hero too.' She smiled.

'He didn't say that.'

'No? I'm sure he didn't want to overwhelm you.'

I looked up at him again. He was holding a cup and leaning over the arm of his throne to talk to Crimson and Rising Mist. His muscles were taut beneath his golden skin, and I drew my bottom lip between my teeth as I stared at him. Weaver chuckled.

'What?' I asked, suddenly aware that I was almost drooling.

'Well, I certainly think he's better for you than a vampire.' She shook her head and began to move away. I wasn't sure whether to follow or not. I looked back up at the stage, longing to go and talk to him, but with no clue what I would say.

However bad things were between myself and Antonio, it wasn't entirely clear if we were still together. I'd yelled some pretty final-sounding things, but I couldn't be sure how he'd taken them. Besides, it had only been a couple of weeks. Even if we were absolutely over, it was far too soon to be looking at other men. That nasty twist of guilt turned me away and I followed Weaver into the crowd.

CHAPTER TWENTY-FOUR

I'D HAD SIX CUPS OF THE PUNCH and midnight had been and gone. The fire danced higher and higher and became fuzzier around the edges as I gazed at it.

Shifters kept coming up and shaking my hand. The alcohol dulled the visions but didn't stop them entirely. One after another they invaded my thoughts. I saw brutal fights, eviscerations, death, and when one particularly large man grasped my hand, I got a vivid image of him in his wolf form mounting his mate. With a grimace I moved away from him and wandered around on my own.

I swayed to the music that filled the air, veering away from anyone who came too close. The heat of the fire warmed my skin and I tugged off my long-sleeved shirt and tied it around my waist, over my jeans. I was wearing a vest and the heat on my bare arms tingled.

I saw Weaver dancing with her pack mates, lost in the music, and a smile crept over my lips. She looked happy, at home.

My cup was empty and I stumbled towards the table to

refill it. I poured punch from the flask and overfilled my cup, spilling the bright pink liquid over the white tablecloth. It was far from the first spill of the night. Amber and pink stains marked the fabric.

'Oops,' I said dully. I picked up my cup and spun around to leave the table. I bumped headlong into a bare-chested shifter, spilling my drink again all over his hairy chest. 'Shit!' I looked up as his hands caught hold of my bare arms to steady me. Blade grinned at me and let out a throaty chuckle. His crown had been discarded.

I would have either laughed or died of embarrassment, but I was sinking into his mind. My head lolled and my eyes rolled back in their sockets as I fell into the vision. He and Rising Mist were facing each other, their hands clasped, and Crimson was tying a purple cord around their joined hands. They were all grinning and waves of love rushed over me.

'Eve?' His voice sounded like it was coming from the other end of a long tunnel, far away and echoing. 'Eve? What's wrong with her?'

'Let go, Blade. Put her down.' Weaver's voice cut through my dull hearing. I was lying on the bumpy crystal ground, and my eyes began to flicker open. 'Are you all right?' Weaver asked. I pushed myself up to sitting. My head throbbed.

'Fine.' I clambered to my feet and avoided looking at Blade.

'I'll take you home.' Weaver placed a careful hand on my back.

'I have a car on the other side of the veil. Let me drive you.'

'No, we're fine, thank you,' Weaver said, her voice still sounding far away.

'Are you sure?'

'Yes, honestly,' she replied.

I looked over my shoulder at Blade as Weaver led me away. He stood watching us, frowning and chewing his bottom lip. Weaver took hold of my shoulders and I winced, but no vision struck. She led me through the gate and across the veil with her. There was a strong tug at my navel, and my head spun painfully as I took a horrible step that felt like stepping off a cliff. When my feet landed on tarmac I stumbled sideways away from the iron fence and trees that lined the park and towards one of the many parked cars at the kerb. An unpleasant lurch from my churning stomach sent me reeling away from Weaver. My clammy hands made contact with the cool metal of a parked car. I vomited spectacularly into the gutter next to the car. The aftertaste was sour and the watery vomit was bright pink – the colour of the punch.

Weaver rubbed my back. I groaned and dry-heaved. Away from the heat of the fire, the night air was cool on my bare skin, which had broken out in goosebumps. It was late and the street we had emerged on was dark and quiet. I stood up straight and wiped my mouth with the back of my hand.

'What did you see?' Weaver asked, her voice gentle.

'A possible future. Nothing bad, and not really any of our business.'

'I see. Let's get you back to the flat so you can sleep it off, yeah?'

I just nodded, too exhausted and intoxicated to do anything else. The walk from the park to The Circle seemed to take forever. Weaver gently guided me, catching my arm when I drifted sideways towards the road. Gradually, the buzz of the alcohol wore off and I pulled my shirt back on over my goosebumped arms.

We arrived at the large estate under a star-dotted sky sometime in the small hours. Weaver, to her credit, didn't ask a single question about my vision. I tried not to think about it. When I did glimpse the future, it seemed malleable, not fixed. Maybe Blade would marry Rising Mist, maybe not. We had just met and I was technically attached to someone else, so what did it matter anyway?

Weaver led me in through the main entrance of the tower block and called the lift. The light in the lobby was too bright and I closed my eyes as I leaned against the wall to wait.

'I can probably get you his number,' Weaver said. I wearily opened my eyes to scowl at her.

'Not interested,' I said. My voice croaked and my

throat stung, sore from puking. I wrapped my fingers around my neck and gently massaged it.

'Really? You seemed interested.' She flashed a smile at me.

There was a *ding* and the lift doors opened. I rolled my eyes at her and staggered inside. The motion as we moved up to the sixth floor turned my stomach some more but I didn't think I was going to be sick again. When the doors opened I stepped forward ahead of her and looked both ways along the corridor, unsure which way to go. Weaver chuckled and set off to the left.

'How do you not get lost in this place?'

'I've lived here for nearly ten years.'

I followed her along the gently curving corridor. Every flat we passed was silent. I had no real sense of what time it was, but evidently everyone was asleep. Weaver came to a halt next to the door to her apartment and unlocked it. It was dark inside and she flicked on a lamp by the door.

Exhaustion overtook everything else. I stumbled, unseeing, through the lounge and into the bedroom that Weaver had provided for me. I collapsed on the double bed, still fully dressed.

When I woke, daylight poured in through the open curtains, stinging my eyes. My throat ached and my head pounded. Voices filtered through from the other side of the door, and I made my way cautiously out of the bedroom. Weaver laughed, far too brightly for the state I was in. A deep chuckle accompanied her light laughter; I paused at the corner, peering around it.

Blade sat at the dining table, smiling his handsome smile. He and Weaver both turned as I entered the room, both grinning as if it were the best day ever.

'What time is it?' I managed to croak.

'Noon,' Weaver replied. Blade stood and scooped up a flask from the table.

'I brought you some soup. It's a special recipe to help with days like these.' He was dressed in black jeans and a Pink Floyd t-shirt, heavy boots on his feet. Part of me was a little disappointed his feet weren't bare. He passed me the flask and I took it, smiling awkwardly. I unscrewed the top and smelled the rich, creamy soup.

'Thank you.' I took a sip. It was hot and soothing. 'Oh, wow, that's so nice.' I smiled more warmly and Blade grinned back at me.

'Let's go for a walk,' he said. He didn't wait for a response, he just strode for the door and held it open for me. I glanced at Weaver, who was resolutely not looking at me as she tidied away their teacups. I was still in the previous night's muddy jeans and wrinkled shirt. My hair was a tangled mess and I felt dirt on my back from where I had fallen to the ground during the vision. I'd managed to kick off my boots, and looked down at my socks. I was mortified, but I grudgingly went, shoeless, with Blade into the corridor.

We walked slowly along the brightly lit hall. The soft light through the frosted skylights overhead was slightly easier on my eyes than the blazing sunlight that had been spilling into the apartment, but still not pleasant. I sipped the soup some more and it warmed my aching throat.

'I'm sorry about last night,' I said after a minute of uncomfortable silence.

'Oh, no, I'm sorry,' he said, turning his head to look at me with wide eyes. 'I didn't know about your ability or what triggered it. I wouldn't have caught hold of you like that if I'd known. I'm sorry if my brain caused you any distress.'

'Weaver explained?'

'She did.'

'I see.' We walked on. Televisions buzzed behind some of the doors we passed, some movement, signs of life in this vast, circular tower block. 'It didn't,' I said, not looking at him.

'Sorry?'

'Your brain didn't cause me any distress.'

'Okay, I'm glad to hear that.'

'I'm not going to tell you what I saw.'

'I wouldn't dream of asking.'

I looked at him quizzically, trying to read in his face if

he was serious. He seemed earnest enough.

'Most people would want to know.'

'Not me. I'm happy working it all out as I go. Knowing the future would be a burden I don't think I could bear. You must be incredibly strong.'

'Thanks.' I drank some more soup as I let his compliment sink in. I hadn't always been good at accepting such encouraging words, but if the last few months had taught me anything, it was to value my strengths. 'I don't often see the future. It's usually the past or particularly strong emotions in the moment.'

'That's interesting. I wonder what Artemis intends it to be useful for.' He was watching me again.

'Artemis?'

'Well, yeah. She grants us all these gifts.'

'I'm not a shifter,' I said, whispering and glancing over my shoulder. We were quite alone, but I couldn't risk being overheard.

'I know, but you're shifter-blooded. It's no coincidence that you have this gift. It's all Artemis's doing, I'm certain.' He grinned at me and I found myself smiling back. Weaver had suggested the same thing.

'Well, it doesn't feel like a very useful gift. The fainting, disorientation, and often horrifying visions haven't helped me out much.'

'I bet. I'm sorry that it's so hard for you.'

'Thanks.' Thinking about it, while an awful lot of what

I had seen over the years was useless and frustrating, my gift had led me to the truth about my parents, and it helped me to be a fairly good judge of character. I considered sharing this with Blade, but as I looked at him I decided to keep it to myself.

'It must make it hard to be around people,' he said after a while.

'Yeah, it does, but it's got easier. It was a secret for seven years. Now it seems like everyone in my life knows about it, so I don't have to work so hard at keeping contact to a minimum. People know not to hug me and stuff.'

'Sure...' he said, nodding. There was a 'but' coming and I looked at him, waiting. 'But what about, you know, intimacy?'

My cheeks flared with heat and I returned my gaze to the dark blue carpet ahead of my feet.

'Yeah, that's a bit of an issue.' The sparks between us were undeniable. I was going to have to broach the subject of Antonio before this went any further. My stomach turned painfully and my mind raced over the words, but I couldn't voice them. I didn't want to tell him I was involved with someone else. I was scared to close this door that stood open before me.

As we walked, Blade drifted slightly closer to me and my pulse quickened. He didn't reply; he didn't need to. I felt his desire to touch me oozing out of his pores. He wanted to give me something he felt I was lacking. He didn't know the truth and I didn't want to set him straight. The backs of his fingers brushed lightly against mine. My breath caught in my throat and I held it. No vision struck, and I allowed my fingers to entwine with his. Unmistakable butterflies were making figures of eight in my stomach.

We were approaching a set of double doors and Blade released my hand to open one of them for me. I passed through into the vestibule where there were lifts and access to the stairs. There was a *ding* and the lift doors opened. A man in a suit stepped out, glanced at us warily and hurried away the way we had come. Blade smiled at me and we went on our way, through a matching set of doors past the lifts and into the next curved corridor.

'Does that happen a lot?' I asked. 'People scurrying away from you?'

'All the time. Humans don't deal so well with our naturally intimidating demeanour.' I let out a hearty laugh. I had rarely met anyone less intimidating than Blade. He was so obviously kind and warm to me. He gave my shoulder a playful shove and glared at me in mock offence.

'Sorry,' I said, still chuckling. I passed him the empty flask and he tucked it into the back pocket of his baggy jeans.

'Besides, who says he wasn't fleeing from you?' He raised an eyebrow and waved his hand in the general direction of my bedraggled appearance.

'Hey!' I shoved him back and it was his turn to chuckle. His laughter subsided and we walked on in silence for a while. 'So, when did you change?' I asked at last.

'About eighteen months ago. I'm glad you didn't see that.' He wasn't smiling now. His gaze was fixed on the corridor ahead.

'Was it awful?'

'Sort of. Not compared to some people, I guess. It was during a school play. There was a fire when something went wrong with one of the stage lights and the rig fell onto the stage. I was in the audience. There was a lot of panic, people running and lots of smoke.' His voice had taken on a faraway tone. 'The cast were trapped on the burning stage and my girlfriend was up there. I changed in the chaos but I didn't entirely lose myself. I charged up onto the stage and lifted the burning rig up so that the cast could get out. They escaped, but they were never the same afterwards.'

'I bet. That's awful. I'm so sorry that happened.' At the mention of a girlfriend an ugly shot of disappointment fired in my chest.

'Thanks,' he said, glancing sideways at me. My eyes had been fixed on him as he spoke, but I looked away, suddenly aware that I had been staring.

'You got out okay?'

'Yeah. Once the other kids were off the stage I dropped the rig and ran for it. I ran through the empty school rather than following everyone out to the car park. I made it right to the other end of the building before I shifted back. I hid in a bathroom; my clothes were wrecked. I had to steal some spare clothes from the changing rooms next to the gym.' His cheeks had gone red.

'What happened with your girlfriend?'

'She couldn't look at me any more.' There was sadness in his eyes. 'She didn't exactly remember the beast, but she remembered the fear and she associated me with it. Plus, I got pulled into this life and had to leave everything behind.'

'How old were you?'

'Eighteen.'

'So was Peter.' I didn't mean to say anything and was a little surprised. We looked at each other.

'Is he your boyfriend?'

'No,' I replied, a little too quickly. 'He's my best friend. We grew up together. He changed just before we were supposed to go to uni together. I left, he stayed behind.'

'You came here?'

'I did. I had to go back to Oris last year, but I'm coming back in September to finish my degree.'

'I am extremely pleased to hear that.' He grinned broadly at me.

We passed through another vestibule and I realised we were halfway around the huge complex. Neither of us had mentioned where we were walking to; we just kept going, as if silently agreeing. It was now obvious that we were making a complete circuit of the sixth floor.

That knot was back as Antonio popped back into my thoughts. I had to mention him. I took a deep breath.

'Look, Blade, I do have someone back in Oris. Not Peter, someone else.'

'Oh, right.' The disappointment was evident in his voice.

'It's complicated, though. I mean, I don't know if we're...' I stalled and stopped walking. I blew out a heavy breath, causing my lips to shake. My cheeks felt suddenly heavy. Antonio had betrayed me. I had left in anger nearly two weeks ago and hadn't spoken to him since. He hadn't even tried to call me.

'Hey,' Blade said softly. My gaze moved up to his. He stepped closer and looked searchingly into my eyes. 'Do you want to talk about it?'

'I really don't, but thanks for offering.' I tried for a smile, but my lips wouldn't make the right shape.

'Okay. Can I hold you?'

I nodded, my eyes tingling with the threat of tears. Blade closed the gap and folded his arms gently around me, holding me against his chest. He was so warm. I wrapped my arms around his back and sank into his embrace. It was firm but tender and his palm held my head under his chin. His steady heartbeat thumped against my ear. I waited for a vision, but mercifully, none came. His embrace was like coming home, tucked inside the best hug I had ever experienced. The real world felt like it was a hundred miles away. Yes, I could stay right there forever.

CHAPTER TWENTY-FIVE

'LET ME KNOW WHEN YOU GET BACK, OKAY?' Weaver patted my shoulder and passed me my bag.

'Sure. Thank you for everything.'

'Any time. I really hope everything works out smoothly.' We exchanged a brief, one-armed hug before I turned and headed for the ticket barrier. It was strange to be returning to Oris so soon. Caerton was just beginning to feel familiar again. I really wasn't sure where home was any more.

I found my train and boarded. It was packed with people and I was glad that I'd booked a seat. I found the right one and stowed my bag. An older man was my travelling companion and I grudgingly took my seat in the window next to him, wishing I were seated alone. I briefly entertained the idea of doing something obnoxious to get him to move, but wisdom prevailed and I put my headphones on and tuned out the world instead. A message lit up my phone as I stared at it.

"Hey. Safe journey back. I was sorry not to see you

again before you left. Keep in touch, Blade xx"

I couldn't help but smile, but the moment faded and a tangle of guilty roots tightened around my insides. Nothing untoward had happened with Blade; not really. There was an undeniable spark there, though, and I wanted more of it. We'd exchanged numbers, and although I pretended that it was just in the name of new friendship, part of me yearned for more. Had Antonio hurt me that badly? Yes, he probably had. A few months ago I was infatuated with him and would never have dreamed of meeting anyone else, but the problems had been there since the beginning and had only festered over the months. Now it felt as though the whole relationship was rotten to the core.

I read Blade's message again and quickly tapped a reply.

"Thanks. I was really glad to meet you and spend time with you. I think we'll be great friends. I'll be back in Caerton before you know it."

"Good," came his reply.

I liked the feeling of simplicity with him. Everything was straightforward in a way it never had been with Antonio, but I would have to get everything straightened out with him before giving in to temptation and acting on these feelings. I locked my phone and turned it face down. I wasn't going to churn over this mess the whole train ride back to Oris.

At the next stop, the man next to me left and I had the

double seat to myself. I stared out of the window at the passing countryside as the day grew steadily darker. My eyes grew heavy and the weight of everything I had been through settled on me at last and forced me into a sleep.

'Next stop is Oris, change here for all other destinations. Oris next stop.' The voice seeped into my consciousness and my eyes flickered open. I was still sitting alone and the rocking of the train increased as it slowed to enter the station. I rubbed the sleep from my eyes and picked up my phone. I had a string of messages, but scrolling through them I didn't see anything urgent. I gathered my things as the train came to a halt and made my way to the nearest door. The train was much quieter than it had been when it left Caerton. I was the only person to leave by that door and the platform I stepped onto was cold and relatively empty. Trains rumbled around the station and the tannoy blared out announcements every few seconds. I walked across the bridge, trying not to think about when I had returned to my home city after my parents' deaths. People rushed past me, hurrying for their trains or wherever they were going to, but my feet dragged. The sleep on the train had left me with a crick in my neck and a groggy feeling.

I carefully navigated the steps at the other side of the bridge and made my way to the taxi rank at the front of the station. Peter wasn't there to collect me this time. If things hadn't been left so sour with Antonio he would have insisted on collecting me, but I was happy to make my own way home. I got a taxi and looked properly at my messages as we drove the short distance to my house. Peter was asking what time I got back. Crystal wanted to know if it was okay if she collected something from the cave under my house. Tina had a question about the menu. I replied as briefly as possible to each of them. The taxi pulled up outside my house and I paid the driver. As I turned to get out, someone opened the door for me and I looked up into Antonio's face. He tried to smile, but it faltered on his handsome face.

'Welcome home,' he said, his voice low and husky, charged with emotion. I climbed out of the back seat and dragged my bag with me. I thanked the driver and slammed the door shut before turning to address Antonio.

'How did you know when I'd be home?'

'A contact let me know.'

'So you have people watching my movements? Really?' I rolled my eyes.

'I was worried about you, and I felt we should talk.'

'I'm exhausted. Can it wait?'

'If you prefer. I wanted to make sure you were all right also. Are you?'

'I'm okay. I'm hurt, Antonio. Really hurt.' I passed him and approached my door, fishing my keys out of my bag.

'I'm so sorry.' He followed me and stood close behind me as I unlocked the door. I looked at him and saw the honesty in his eyes, but I'd been fooled by that look before, all too recently.

'I don't know if I can believe you.'

'Which is why we should talk.'

'Yes, but I'm tired,' I snapped at him, and he blanched, taking half a step back. He had the decency to look away for a moment. When he looked back, his dark eyes were blazing and his nostrils flared.

'Whose scent is that?'

'I don't know,' I replied, recoiling from him. 'The taxi driver's?' My heart lurched down into my stomach. I had a horrible feeling I knew who he could smell on me.

'No,' he said, his voice low and dangerous. He leaned in and took a big sniff near my hair. 'That's a shifter I don't know.'

'It's Weaver,' I snapped. 'She hugged me at the station. Are you seriously doing this?' I turned and opened my door. I didn't know if he still had an open invitation into my home. I wanted nothing more than to slam the door in his face and for him to be stuck on the other side of it with no choice but to leave before sunrise.

'It's not Weaver,' he snarled. I stepped inside and wheeled about to face him, my own eyes blazing angrily at him. 'You met someone, didn't you?'

'I met a lot of people. I got very drunk. I vomited. I passed out. It wasn't pretty. Your wise and mature twenty-one-year-old girlfriend made a tit of herself in front of a hundred shifters. Some of whom, by the way, were virtually naked. I think I danced with someone. I don't really remember. I had to perform a role in their ceremony. It was a great honour and I'm glad I did it, even though I was terrified. I was on my own down there. I only knew Weaver. If someone else I met was kind and treated me well, and brought me recovery soup the next day, that's no crime. Nothing happened that shouldn't have happened.' I slammed the door hard in his face and the knocker rattled against the wood.

'Eve,' he murmured through the door. 'I'm sorry. Please can we talk about this?'

'No! And don't forget, I took back my invitation. You can't come in!' I screamed my last words and stalked away from the door. I didn't know if it would work. I didn't even really care that much. I wanted to vent. I wanted to sting him. I stormed into the kitchen and dropped to my knees.

'Well this is awkward,' a cool voice said from the shadows. I toppled backwards into the hall doorway and looked around for the source of the voice. Crystal appeared in the pool of light from the hall. I took a steadying breath and it burst out in the form of mildly hysterical laughter. She extended a hand and helped me to my feet. 'Are you all right?'

'Eve?!' Antonio called from the other side of the front door. 'Who's there? Are you okay?'

'Oh for fuck's sake! Would everyone stop asking me

that?! Sorry, Crystal,' I added quickly. She didn't look remotely bothered by my outburst and nodded as if to let me know it was no problem. I stormed back to the door and slammed my palm against it. 'Go away! I'm fine. It's a friend. Go and mind your own business.'

I swept back up the hall to the kitchen and flicked the light on.

'Sorry to intrude.'

'No, it's fine. I said you could come in my message. Although I wasn't expecting you to come right into the house.'

'Yes, sorry about that. Peter asked me to make sure you were all right when you got back. I didn't mean to alarm you. I'm afraid I forced my way in down there. I didn't realise you'd covered the trapdoor.' She gave me a regretful smile. I waved a hand to dismiss it. I didn't have the energy to object. 'I hate to ask, but, seriously, are you all right? Is there anything I can do? Like maybe rip one of his arms off?' She flicked her head towards the door. I had the horrible feeling that he was still there. I hadn't seen his car outside, so I wasn't sure how he had got here or how he was going home. That wasn't my problem.

'Right, yes. No. It's fine. I mean obviously it's not. We're a mess!' I burst into tears and in an instant her arms were around me. I braced myself and the vision rushed through my head and out the other side in a split second.

Crystal was sprinting through the catacombs. Dark

shadows surrounded her and clawed at her.

Then I was back in her arms, tears streaking down my face.

'I'm sorry,' she said softly, releasing me. 'You had a vision, didn't you?' All I could do was nod. I sank into a chair at the table and cradled my head in my arms. I was sick of it all. The tears fell freely and I clenched my eyes tightly closed. I was aware of Crystal moving around me. The kettle clicked on and slowly began to boil. A few agonising minutes later, a steaming mug of tea was placed in front of me and I lifted my head and opened my bleary eyes.

'It's enough,' I whimpered.

'Sorry?' she asked, seating herself next to me.

'I'm done. I can't help everyone all the time. I can't be with him any more. I can't stay here.'

'You just got back.'

'Yeah, and I already want to go back to Caerton. It's hard to explain.'

'No, I get it. Oris is full of ghosts.' I looked at her and she sipped her own tea, watching me shrewdly. I nodded and reached for my tea. It was hot and a little sweet. Just how I liked it.

'There's all this pressure on me. It's good that I don't have to work so hard to keep my gift a secret, but I'd honestly trade that discomfort for being in constant danger and feeling as though I'm somehow responsible for everyone's safety.'

'I wasn't going to ask you what you saw in your vision just now, but I feel like you want to tell me and don't know how.' I shrugged and focused on the tea. She was right. I had to tell her, in case it was important, and that's exactly what I was talking about as I rambled through my disjointed thoughts.

'I saw you running through the catacombs. It felt like you were in danger. I don't know if it was past or future, though. Anything like that happened to you recently?'

'Not since we fought Lucia, no. Could it have been then?'

'You were with the rest of us that night. In the vision you were alone and it was dark, no flickering light.' I shuddered.

'Well, thanks for the heads-up. I'll be careful, but Eve, you are not responsible for my safety, or anyone else's besides your own. We shifters are very capable of taking care of ourselves, and now that we're free we have to do just that.'

'I suppose. Thanks.' I wrapped my hands around the mug and breathed in the lingering steam. 'I just want to be free too.'

'You feel trapped?'

'Yes.' We made eye contact and there was something almost solid in the air between us, something tangible about that acknowledgement, the weight of it suddenly enormous.

'Then you have to break free. How can I help?'

CHAPTER TWENTY-SIX

'Have you ever done this before?' I asked, eyeing the tattoo needle warily.

'Of course!' Crystal said, grinning from ear to ear. I let my gaze roam over her heavily inked skin. Almost every inch of her was decorated in some way, and she always wore clothing that kept as much skin as possible on show.

'Doesn't someone else do yours?' I asked, waving a hand towards the arm nearest me.

'Well, sure, for the most part, but no one gets this many tattoos without learning how to do it themselves. It's a tradition among shifters to get tattoos to celebrate the epic deeds that we do, and because we heal a lot quicker than humans we can't always go to human tattooists. So I learned how to do it so I could ink up my friends.'

'Which of yours are for shifter stuff, then?' I asked, genuine curiosity making me lean closer to look at the details.

'This one here is for last year.' She tapped a black, tentacled demon across her left shoulder. When I looked closer, it did resemble the demon we'd sent back to hell together, even down to the huge mouth filled with fire. Skilfully woven between the tentacles were drops of blood, which I assumed represented Lucia, who we'd tossed through the hole in the veil after the demon.

My kitchen table was covered in sketches, plastic gloves, and the ink Crystal would need. I'd also set up a bright lamp on the table, and Crystal nudged it to get it at the right angle. With a nod of resolve, I tugged my shirt off over my head and turned in my chair to present the back of my right shoulder to Crystal. The lamplight was warm against my bare skin. Crystal wiped my shoulder with an antibacterial wipe and the cold contrast brought me out in goosebumps. 'Ready?' she asked.

'Let's do it.'

'Okay, just relax.' I could hear the smile in her voice and I held back a laugh. Relaxing was much easier said than done. The buzz of the machine echoed suddenly in the kitchen and I took a deep breath and held it, waiting for the needle to make contact with my skin. 'What will you have to do to finish your art degree?'

'I have to complete 120 cred—ah!' I winced as the needle made contact, but Crystal had done a good job of sneakily distracting me with a question to answer and I had to give her credit for that. I took a breath as she set to work. 'Credits,' I said, picking up where I left off. 'When I go back in September I'll have one core class to take and the rest will come from my final project.' I kept taking slow breaths as I adjusted to the scratching sensation of the tattooing process. Other people made it look so easy, but it was a challenge for me.

'What will you do for your final project?'

'I'm not sure. I did have some ideas before I left, but things have changed. I'll have to figure it out.'

Crystal kept me chatting while she worked and for the most part it effectively kept me distracted. We steered clear of my love life or anything difficult to talk about. I'd enjoyed the superficiality of the time I'd spent with my old housemates in Caerton, but talking with Crystal was easier, despite the pain I was in. I could be myself and I needed that so badly.

'All done,' Crystal said, turning off the buzzing needle and wiping the back of my shoulder again. 'Want to see?'

'Will it be all bloody?'

'Nope.' She passed me a mirror and held another up behind me. I adjusted the one in my hand so I could see her handiwork. A black and purple triquetra of intricate Celtic knotting now adorned my alabaster skin. She wiped it again, picking up a little loose ink and blood before it could gross me out.

'And the extra surprise?' I asked, raising an eyebrow as I looked at her face in the reflection in my mirror.

'Try it.'

'On you?'

'Sure.'

I turned around in my chair and made eye contact. I took a breath and let it out slowly, reaching out with my thoughts. I imagined the new tattoo glowing faintly purple as I called on its power. Mixed with the ink was crushed black onyx powder straight from Hepethia. I had a little of the shifter realm in me now. Wherever I went my shifter friends and parents would be with me, lending me their power.

Inside Crystal's head was a lovely place. Despite an appearance that some might find intimidating, she was all light and bubbles really. Butterflies fluttered through her thoughts with their brightly coloured wings and swift changes of direction.

'Butterflies,' I said. 'You're thinking about butterflies.'

'I am. You're not even touching me and you're controlling it.' She grinned. 'It's not going to completely stop all the unwanted visions. I want you to have realistic expectations. Nothing can stop Artemis sending you a message when she needs to, but you'll have more control over the lighter stuff now, the surface thoughts and feelings. You'll be able to pick and choose which ones you tune in to more easily and won't need physical contact.'

'Thank you,' I said, grinning almost as broadly as she was. This was going to change everything.

The giddy euphoria of getting the magical tattoo wore off more quickly than I'd have liked. The next few days dragged painfully as I limped from grief to rage and back again. In my absence, the shifters had all been checked for corruption and all come back clean. Whatever the demon was up to, it hadn't tried to go anywhere near the shifters. Perhaps it had realised it would be discovered and dealt with if it tried anything so brazen.

Antonio tried to call me several times, but I ignored his calls and messages. My chest physically ached with grief at what had happened between us. I wished I was completely ready to part ways with him, but I wasn't there yet. I knew it was for the best, however, and I tried to stay strong. It didn't matter what he had to say. There was no apology he could offer, or compensation he could make to put things right after everything. Of course, I hoped he wanted to tell me that he had called things off with De Luca and was going to let democracy take its course, but I had difficulty believing that after everything that had been said he would suddenly come around on that score.

The election was fast approaching and we still didn't know exactly what they were going to do to rig it. If I had one regret, it was not using my position to discover that before cutting ties with him, but there was no way to change that now.

Something that did brighten my days and nights was the messages and calls from Blade. I found myself smiling whenever he got in touch. He was delightfully persistent without being creepy. He asked me questions about myself; he seemed genuinely interested in me as a person. It wasn't all about my gift, or the shifters, either.

'Show me your art,' he asked one evening during a video call.

'I don't have much here. Most of it's back in Caerton.'

'Is it on display anywhere?' he asked, like an eager puppy. 'I'll go view it!'

'There are some pieces up in the Art faculty building. There's a big display there, but it's lots of students' work, not just mine. You'd have to look at all the labels to find mine.'

'I can do that.'

'Aren't you terribly busy defending the veil?'

'My pack does keep me pretty busy, it's true, but I have my free time.'

I giggled. For some reason that I couldn't quite put my finger on, I was yet to tell him that things were definitely over with Antonio. Maybe because of that lingering feeling that things weren't quite done yet. I wasn't sure how things were going to go with the election and banishing the demon. On some level, perhaps I still felt as though Antonio could be redeemed and wanted to be around for that.

Blade was patient and kind with me. He never asked for more than friendship, respecting the boundary I had put in place that last day in Caerton, but his eagerness was undeniable. We joked together; we stayed on the phone to each other for hours some evenings. He was affectionate and flirtatious, without ever pushing things into sleazy. I wondered where he had been before I'd returned to Oris. How different might things have turned out if we'd been together then?

One day when I was washing up, there was a sudden tap on the window. I startled and looked up to see a large, black bird on the windowsill. It tapped its beak hard on the glass and gave a squawk. I frowned and reached for a towel to dry my hands. I kept my eyes fixed on the bird as it bobbed its head up and down and pecked again at the window. I leaned across the sink and undid the catch on the window. The bird hopped along the sill to get out of the way as I opened the window, almost as if it understood what to do. Once there was a gap big enough for it, the bird hopped inside and dropped a rolled-up and sealed scroll of paper from one of its clawed feet. I blinked at it and carefully reached for the paper, wary of it trying to peck my hand, but it hopped back and left my hand alone. I grabbed the scroll and pulled my hand back quickly. The bird, which I was sure must be a raven or something due to its size, gave an extra loud squawk and then hopped to the window and took flight.

I watched it fly out of sight, then looked down at the strange message in my hand. I slid my finger under the seal to break it and uncurled the paper. Neat but unmistakably masculine writing covered the paper, and there were three sides all rolled-up together. I read the first few lines and a smile gradually crept onto my face. I moved away from the sink and dropped down onto a chair at the table.

Dear Eve,

I hope this little note finds you well. I've been enjoying our phone calls so much, but there's really no substitute for the good old-fashioned written word. Text messages aren't the same. What can I say? I'm an old soul. Or so people keep telling me. Don't you just think there's something being lost from the world today? So I'm doing my part to try and keep some old traditions alive.

I hope you didn't mind the method of delivery. It's much quicker than the regular post! But if you want to reply by snail mail, my address is on the back page.

I flipped through the pages to check, and it was indeed. I grinned as I read on. Blade wrote about his day, about taking part in a ritual. He mentioned socialising with some people, and a game of football in the park. He regaled me with a blow-by-blow account of a stupendous goal he had scored to win the match. I laughed so much that it brought tears to my eyes.

I had to take advantage of my captive audience. No one here is interested in my athletic prowess. Sorry, not sorry. I hope you found it a little entertaining. I'd better sign off here, lots to do. I'm very busy and important.

Lots of love,

Blade.

I was grinning as I rolled it back up and looked up, surprised to find myself in my kitchen. I'd been so transported back to Caerton by his words. I wiped a tear from my eye.

'This is what it's meant to be like,' I said out loud to myself. 'Easy and light. This is better.' I went up to my room and took out a shoebox from the bedside cupboard. I had a few keepsakes inside and added the letter to it. I promised myself I would reply. First, I had the corruption demon to deal with.

CHAPTER TWENTY-SEVEN

DAYS PASSED. The shifters were still feverishly working on their investigation into the complicated web the corruption demon had woven. I drifted in and out of their activities, numbness causing me to drag myself around, a burden to those around me. I wanted to be useful, but couldn't figure out how I could help. I felt as though I was in the way, although no one said or did anything to make me feel that way, it was all in my own head. I knew that really and didn't direct my frustration towards any of my friends.

'Have you seen this?' Peter asked one evening, bursting into the office at the restaurant, where I was hiding out and trying not to get in anyone's way. He closed the door and strode to my desk.

'What?' I asked, looking up with a frown. Peter brandished a newspaper at me. It was the local evening paper, the one Michelle used to write for before she died. Splashed all over the front page was a photo of a crime scene and the headline read "DRUG DEALER'S BODY FOUND IN RIVER!"

'No way!' I cried, taking the paper and scouring the short article next to the photo. 'They're reporting three missing teens, the kids from the drug den!'

'I know.'

'This is good news. Isn't it?' I looked up, my eyes wide and a surge of hope rushing through my veins. Peter wasn't anywhere near as excited as I was. He wore a deep frown, killing my buzz before it really took hold.

'It's potentially good, yeah, but it could really get in the way of what we're doing. As a general rule, we prefer it when humans don't get mixed up in shifter business.'

'I get that, it's a matter of saving lives and sanity and all that, but this is different, isn't it? Humans are already being killed. This dealer, the addicts at the den, Michelle, Isabel.' My voice caught in my throat with an uncomfortable lurch.

'Yes, I know, you're right. There was no hiding this. De Luca didn't get to it fast enough, I guess. People saw the body floating down the river this morning, there were loads of witnesses.'

'That's pretty awful.' A swell of empathy rose in my chest for the people who had had their morning interrupted by such a grizzly discovery.

'Go to the main article on page five.' Peter gestured to the newspaper now lying on my desk. I flicked to the right page and began skimming it. 'They're reporting blood loss as the cause of death. Obviously they don't know what they're really seeing and wouldn't ever admit it, but this is getting dangerously close to truths being exposed that certain people really wouldn't want to get out.'

'Do you think De Luca knows now, about the vampires?' I asked.

'I don't know. Maybe.'

'Antonio said he didn't at New Year. He knew about the crime stuff, obviously, but not the supernatural. I don't know, though, maybe that's changed in the last few weeks.' We stared at each other for a moment. My distance from Antonio suddenly presented us with a problem we hadn't had before. I'd been on the inside, almost. I'd been able to pick up things about what he was doing that I simply wasn't privy to any more. It was a blind spot that was deeply uncomfortable to be in.

'We'll have to play it by ear,' Peter said with a dismissive wave of his hand, as if sweeping away the troublesome idea.

'They might move, you know?' I said softly, the dark thought intruding.

'Sorry?'

'The vampires. This might prompt them to do something. I think Antonio has the sense to lie low, but I can't say the same for Celino or Laguardia. This might make them do something reckless. Something we can catch them doing.'

'What are you thinking, Eve?' Peter leaned forward

against the desk and fixed me with his bright eyes.

'I want to deal with them. Get rid of them once and for all. Especially Celino.'

'Are you talking about killing them?' His voice was deeper than usual and barely above a whisper.

'Well, they're technically already dead. Right?' His eyes widened and he sat back in his chair, studying me carefully. I was a little surprised at myself. It hadn't been that long ago that I was defending Antonio fiercely against such ideas, but I was sleeping with him and had to stop myself from going anywhere near the idea that he was a living corpse, for the sake of my own sanity and stomach lining. Things had changed somewhat. Besides, it was easier to think that way about the creature that had broken my fingers in the cave below the city. I flexed my hand like I often did when I recalled those events. The ghost of the pain haunted the digits from time to time. I had to remind myself that they were no longer injured and could move freely.

'Eve, while I kind of welcome this attitude, it's not like you.'

'I know.' I drew a deep breath and glanced at the ceiling. 'It's time to take action and deal with the situation.'

'If they're back at the mansion, then they're back in Antonio's employment. Right?'

'It seemed that way, yeah.'

'Won't he be protecting them?'

'Maybe, but he's never been able to control them. If they step out of line he might even end them himself.' I didn't really believe that. He'd chosen to bring them back into the fold, rather than sending them to their final death already. I wondered what they would have to do to merit a death sentence from him, if abducting and torturing his girlfriend wouldn't do it.

'I wonder if we can draw them out?' Peter asked, gazing into the corner of the room.

'I think I probably could. Celino seemed curious when I was at Antonio's last time. He showed his face to get a good look at me on my way out. I think he might be tempted out of his hiding place if there was a chance to get his hands on me again.' A shudder ran up my spine. I couldn't quite believe I was offering myself up as bait to catch that monster. What would we even do if he did emerge?

'I don't want to put you in danger, Eve.' Peter's voice was low, his gaze downcast. He picked at the skin on the side of his fingernail.

'I know, but I've been in near constant danger for months now, and I have a chance to regain a sense of control here. Maybe it's a terrible idea, but maybe there is a way to make some progress.'

'I guess.' He raised his thumb to his mouth and chewed at it, his hallmark nervous habit.

'I don't want you to worry about me, but I know you

will anyway.' I gave him a sad smile. He nodded, still not looking directly at me. I looked back down at the newspaper, the words a jumble before my eyes. The fact that this had made it to the press and that a full police investigation was under way was a huge blow to De Luca's plans. My eyes widened as I made the connections.

'What?' Peter asked, staring intently at me. I tapped the newspaper hard with one finger and sat up straight in my chair.

'Peter! We can leak Michelle's research.'

'Can we?'

'Of course! There was no point trying before because we knew De Luca would block any investigation, but this has run away from him. Now's the time to leak the rest. It'll spur the police on if they have the mayor's wife to look for as well. How much do they really care about a drug dealer and his user friends who are missing? They think Michelle's death was connected to drug use, so that's the link. Once they go looking into her death they can find what she was working on and follow it up. We just have to get her research to the journalist who wrote this piece and get them to connect them. The police will have to investigate.'

'That's a good plan. What does it have to do with Celino, though?'

'He killed Michelle. He'll know he's at risk of being caught. He wasn't that careful, he didn't have to be with De

Luca covering his tracks. Without the commissioner's protection, Celino's at risk of being discovered. It'll draw him out.'

'Okay. Let's do it. Keep that talisman close and use it if you need me at any time. Deal?'

'Deal.' I flashed a grin. I finally felt as though there was something I could do about everything that was threatening to overwhelm me: Michelle and Isabel's deaths, De Luca, Celino, the demon, even Antonio. Maybe there was still a way to get him out of this mess. 'Just, could we leave Antonio out of it?' I asked. Peter rolled his eyes.

'I knew you'd ask that. Yes, we can, but Eve, what if you can't save him?'

I didn't want to answer that question.

We left Piero's and went to the secret office to collect Michelle's research. Peter put the printed files and a copy of the thumb drive with all of the photos, except the ones that implicated Antonio, into a large envelope and sealed it with tape. The news article was credited to a member of the editorial staff, Steve Wright. It was getting late and the city was draped in a velvet sky pricked with stars. Peter and I didn't talk much as we made our way towards the newspaper's offices.

My phone vibrated in my pocket and I pulled it free to see Blade's name on the display. I pressed my lips together to hide the girly grin that threatened to break out.

'Do you need to answer that?' Peter asked, giving me a sideways glance.

'No, but I want to.'

'Go on then.' He picked up the pace and went ahead of me. I answered the call and pressed the phone to my cheek.

'Hey. Everything okay?' I asked.

'Peachy. How are you? I haven't heard from you since the letter.'

'I'm going to pen a proper reply and send it in the post,' I said, smiling to myself. 'You'll have to be patient.'

'Yeah, I'm not great at that. I've been spoiled by having other ways to communicate.'

'So have the normies, you know? Since these hand-held devices we're using right now came along, patience has been growing increasingly thin for most people.'

'True. What are you doing? Sounds like you're on your way somewhere.'

'I am. It's actually not the best time. We've got a thing to deal with.'

'Fair enough. I'll leave you to it. Will you be safe?'

'Yeah, I will. I've got Peter with me. We're just going to talk to someone; a regular person.'

'Well now you've taken all the fun out of it. That doesn't sound like a *thing* thing.' I let out a hearty laugh and Peter looked over his shoulder at me. He slowed down and fell into step beside me with his head cocked to one side in curiosity. I glanced up at him and a blush rose on my cheeks. There wasn't much traffic on the streets and I got the feeling he might be able to hear Blade on the other end of the phone with his heightened senses.

'Sorry to disappoint you,' I finally replied.

'Should I be jealous about you spending time with Peter?'

I glanced up at my companion again. He was looking down at me with a slight frown.

'No,' I said firmly, knowing for certain that Peter was party to the whole conversation now. He had understandably fallen back at the sound of his own name. We shared that look again, the one that good friends develop over time that lets the other know that all is well with the friendship. 'I told you about him, he's my best friend.' I was still looking right at Peter. He gently wrapped an arm around my shoulders and steered me around a corner.

'I know. And I'm not really the jealous type, I swear. I'm just playing.'

'Okay,' I said with a nod and a knowing smirk. I didn't entirely believe him. I liked that he felt a little threatened by Peter. It reassured me that he really liked me. It's not as if I hadn't felt that green-eyed monster myself over the vision I'd had of Blade's possible future.

'I'd better let you go, then.' There was reluctance in his voice. I knew the feeling all too well.

'Yeah. I do have to go. Thanks for calling, though. I'll get that letter written and posted soon. I won't leave you waiting too long, I promise.'

'I'm looking forward to it.' There was a smile in his voice. I hung up the phone and looked up at Peter again.

'So?' He asked, grinning. 'Who was that?'

'Someone I met in Caerton,' I replied, unable to stop myself from smiling.

'Well, anyone who makes you smile like that is a welcome addition to your life.' He squeezed my shoulders and released me. We came to a halt at the foot of a four-storey, red-brick building with a huge, digital clock lit up near the top of it. The newspaper logo was emblazoned above the wide, glass doors at the top of the shallow flight of steps leading up from the pavement. 'We're here.'

CHAPTER TWENTY-EIGHT

Peter and I approached the glass doors to the newspaper building. The inside was dark, but there was a single lamp on behind the reception desk and a sleepy guard sat there, his gaze fixed on the soft glow of what must have been a screen just out of sight. Peter tried the door; it rattled but was locked. The guard looked up with a frown. He was a portly, middle-aged man with a moustache. He tapped his watch, indicating to us that it was late. It was barely 9 and I had a feeling there would still be people busily preparing the following morning's paper. Peter and I looked at each other. I gave a shrug.

'What do we do?' I asked.

Peter knocked on the door and beckoned the guard over. He got up from behind the desk, hitched up his trousers over his belly and made his way slowly across the dark foyer to the doors. He made no signs of opening the door for us but came to a halt on the other side and crossed his arms.

'Well?' His voice just about carried through the thick

glass.

'Is Steve Wright still in the building, please? It's urgent that we speak to him.' Peter put on his extra polite voice, the one he'd used with my parents. I pressed my lips together to hide a smirk.

'Can't it wait until the morning?'

'I'm afraid not. Please could you check? If he is here, could you call him down? We don't have to come inside.'

The guard heaved a sigh and made his way back to the desk.

'What if he's not here, or won't see us?' Peter asked me.

'Then we leave the package for him and hope for the best.' We met each other's gaze. Movement on the other side of the glass caught my eye and I turned to see the guard approaching us again, this time with his keys in his hand. He unlocked the door and opened it.

'Come in and sit down over there.' He pointed a stubby finger at a seating area to the left behind a row of potted plants. He flicked on a light over the square of squat, grey, padded chairs so we wouldn't be sitting in the dark. We sat awkwardly, the envelope clutched tightly in my clammy palms. The guard returned to his desk and we waited. The world slowly ticking by outside with the swish of lights from passing cars and the second hand of the clock on the wall behind the reception desk echoing in the nearly-empty lobby.

A loud *ding* broke the silence and Peter and I turned in unison towards the row of lifts at the other end of the lobby. The doors of the middle lift slid silently open and out stepped a tall, thin, balding man in a short-sleeved shirt undone at the top, beige trousers and, jarringly, battered old trainers on his feet. I got to my feet and Peter followed suit. The man approached us, running a hand over his bald patch.

'Steve Wright?' Peter asked as he approached. I glanced at him as he slipped a large piece of smokey quartz from his pocket. He clenched it in his fist.

'That's right. Do I know you?' He looked us both up and down, his gaze lingering on my face and a frown of partial recognition crossing his brow. As he got within the range of Peter's shifter aura he slowed to a halt just a little further away than would normally be considered optimal for a conversation. He shifted his weight warily.

'Could we speak somewhere privately?' I said, glancing at the security guard, who was watching the exchange from behind his desk.

'What's it about? It's late. I'm on a deadline.'

'It's about the headline in tonight's edition. We have more information,' Peter said, still using his polite voice, but an edge of impatience creeping into it. I gently put a hand on his arm to try to calm his nervous energy.

'It's also connected to Michelle,' I added on a hunch. Steve's eyes widened and he cleared his throat.

'Okay. Come on up. It's all right,' he added, waving to the guard, who had sat up a little straighter. Steve led us back to the lifts and hit the call button. The one he had arrived in opened immediately and we filed inside. Peter leaned against the back wall and Steve stood just in front of the pair of us, his back to us. Peter lifted the quartz talisman slightly and little black motes drifted out of it. They floated towards Steve and bounced off his back before falling to the floor and disappearing. Peter gave me a nod to let me know that Steve was clear of the demon's influence. I knew he must be to have written the piece he had, but it was reassuring all the same.

The rest of the short ride up to the fourth floor was tense. Both men were bristling with nerves which my gift could read as clearly as if the pair of them were saying as much out loud. The lift glided to a smooth stop and the doors opened. Steve stepped out and led us along a short corridor and into a large newsroom packed with desks, computers, filing cabinets, and printers. Along one wall was a bank of TV monitors, all black, but I could imagine them during the day looping the news. There were a handful of people at their desks, furiously typing away. A teenager who had to be an intern scurried past us with two coffees in her hands, which she deposited on people's desks before rushing off to collect a stack of papers from a whirring printer.

'It's busy,' I said softly.

'You should see it at noon,' Steve said with a grunt before steering us to the right towards a row of offices partitioned from the main room with glass panels. His office was at the end and he led us inside and closed the glass door behind us. His desk was covered in stacks of folders and copies of the newspaper. His bin was overflowing and the shelves behind his desk were covered in books and more folders. There were a handful of awards hidden amongst the clutter, and the little wooden sign on his desk declared him "Senior Editor". Steve sat down behind his desk and waved a hand at two chairs opposite him. There were three more against the glass partition, all covered in stacks of research. Peter and I sat down and I handed the envelope across the desk. Steve took it and frowned at me.

'It's the research Michelle was gathering for a story before she died,' I said. His eyes widened and he opened the envelope eagerly. 'You knew her?'

'Of course I did. She was a friend.' He didn't look up. He flicked through the papers and held up the thumb drive. His surface thoughts betrayed him. She was more than a friend.

'She wanted to write other things,' I said, speculating and hoping to win his favour. 'She hated being stuck on the gossip column and was chasing something meatier.'

'How do you...did you... know her?' He corrected himself, closing his eyes briefly.

'I only met her once, but I understood her.'

'She told me she was putting something together but wouldn't tell me anything about it. What's on this?' He waved the thumb drive.

'Photos,' I said and shifted my weight in preparation for the truth bomb. 'Of the mayor's wife meeting the police commissioner the night she disappeared.'

Steve's eyes narrowed and he glanced past me to the newsroom beyond the glass.

'How do you know the mayor's wife is missing? No one knows that.'

'Apparently you do,' Peter replied with a cluck of his tongue.

'Fair enough,' Steve said. He looked back at me, expecting an answer.

'We were friends. I'm very confident that she's dead, and that Michelle's investigation is what got her killed. You know as well as I do she wasn't taking drugs.'

'No she wasn't,' he said stiffly.

'The person who killed Michelle was looking for that information and wanted to stop it from getting out. We need you to print it.'

'Let's say for a second that I believe you and that there's enough here for a solid story, what does it have to do with tonight's front page?'

'The person who killed Michelle also killed that drug dealer, and the missing kids. The dealer saw him dumping a body in the river. The police need to drag it to find the others. I'm hoping they'll find Isabel Shaw too.'

'You can't just say stuff like that,' he said, leaning back in his chair and running his hands over his head. 'You need evidence. Or I do if I'm going to put it in the paper.'

'Michelle had most of the story written,' Peter said, pointing at the file on the top of the mess on Steve's desk. 'Can't you print it as a tribute to her?'

'Not like this. I need verified sources.' He leafed through the pages we'd given him. 'Who killed her? Can you give me a name?'

'I can, but you won't find evidence of his existence,' I said. 'He's protected by powerful people. I'm afraid there isn't much more we can give you.'

'How do you know all of this?'

'I'm just good at connecting pieces of a puzzle,' I said with a wry smile.

'Who are you both?' Steve was leaning on his desk and eyeing us both eagerly.

'This is Peter Wilkes. My name is Eve Rawling,' I said, squirming slightly.

'Fuck!' Steve pushed away from his desk and his chair rolled back towards the shelves behind him. He knew my name. Damn.

'Excuse me?' Peter said, raising his eyebrows.

'You're Antonio Vitale's girlfriend!' *Shit.*

'How do you know that?'

'Your parents died in that awful flood, I'm so sorry.' To his credit, he had the decency to blush and lower his tone as he dragged his chair back into position at his desk. 'And Wilkes?' He turned his attention to Peter. 'Didn't you lose your mother recently?'

'That's right,' Peter said, shifting his weight.

'You two know each other?' I could see his shrewd mind making connections too, like a good journalist.

'Yes, childhood friends. Our families have known each other for years. Terrible coincidence.' I rushed through my words, hoping to get off the subject quickly. I didn't dare look at Peter, but I felt his grief rushing to the surface. 'How do you know about my connection to Antonio Vitale?' I pressed.

'I connect pieces too.' He rummaged through a stack of newspapers and found the one he was looking for. He flicked through its pages and folded it open near the back. He tossed it across the desk to me; among the many pictures on the page, I saw myself, standing next to Antonio outside the castle in my glamorous dress. Isabel and the mayor were in the picture beside ours, and a lump rose in my throat. Antonio hadn't given my name to the press, but they had printed my picture with his name below it. 'I saw this, and my editor-in-chief was at that event. Apparently people were talking afterwards about Vitale's girlfriend dancing and seeming to argue with the police commissioner. Michelle was trying to figure out who you were for a follow-up piece, and I figured it out from the articles about your parents.'

'Oh,' I said, that lump pressing painfully at the back of my throat.

'Is that how you know what happened? Was it to do with Vitale?'

I closed my eyes for a second to compose my thoughts. Peter's knee bobbed anxiously up and down beside me.

'Yes and no,' I said. 'Yes I see and hear things, in part, because of the circles I sometimes move in, but no, Antonio had nothing to do with the deaths. Have you ever met him yourself?'

'No, I can't say that our paths have crossed.' He crossed his arms and fixed me with his shrewd eyes. He was telling the truth, despite his defensive posture. His surface thoughts were easy to read. He knew Antonio by reputation only.

'Look, I'll be your anonymous source on this, but you'll have to do some more investigating if you want more evidence than we can give you. Michelle had a ton of stuff on Isabel Shaw. It's all there. The photos have timestamps on and show her meeting De Luca the night she disappeared. How did you know about that, anyway?' I narrowed my eyes at him. Peter tensed beside me; in my peripheral vision, I caught sight of him inching the quartz out of his pocket again.

'The mayor filed a missing persons report, but my

source at the police station says it's not going anywhere. My boss wouldn't let us report it.'

'Well, if you were wondering why, now you know,' Peter said, impatience snapping through in his tone. 'De Luca is hushing it up.' Little black sparks drifted up from his clenched hand below the line of the desk, but they fell away without glowing. I watched Steve carefully; he was too busy glaring at the glass behind us to notice anything.

'Isabel was my friend. She came to me for help,' I said. 'But what I told her didn't help her and now she's gone.' A tear prickled at the corner of my eye. The guilt over what I had done was a pain I would carry for a long time. 'There may not be anything I can do to see justice done for Isabel, but maybe I can for Michelle.' I lifted my chin defiantly and Steve nodded appraisingly.

'All right.' He raised his hands in surrender. 'All right. I'll see what I can piece together and will try to get something in the paper soon, but it'll have to get past the editor-in-chief.' At his words, the little sparks drifting out of the talisman turned gold and hit the ground with a faint hiss. I tapped the nearest one with my foot, hoping they wouldn't burn the carpet.

'I understand,' I said, nodding. 'Thank you for your time.' I got to my feet and Peter did likewise, subtly pocketing the talisman.

Steve showed us back to the foyer and the guard let us out. Once we were clear of the building, Peter took me by the elbow and pulled me around to face him.

'I think we can assume that the chief is under the influence of the demon.'

'I thought that too. Maybe Steve will get something past him.' I looked back up at the building. My thoughts raced over what we knew and what we still needed to uncover. 'I should meet with De Luca before Steve prints anything about Isabel.'

'What?!' Peter tugged on my arm and my head whipped back to face him. 'You can't go anywhere near him.'

'Excuse me?' I pulled my arm free and glared up at him. 'I can and I will, but it has to be tomorrow. Once the story breaks I'll have lost my chance. He's bound to know that I had a hand in getting this information out there.'

'Why do you need to meet him?'

'I need to see the demon in him for myself and confirm his role in Isabel's death.'

'Why, Eve?' His voice was pained.

'I just do. I'm responsible.' A tremor in my voice betrayed my appearance of grit and determination. 'I told her about the election. She needed something to bargain with to get out of an agreement with De Luca and Antonio. I gave her something that got her killed. It's my fault she's dead.'

'That's not true. You didn't know De Luca was capable of that.' He squeezed my shoulder.

'No, but I knew Antonio. I knew the risk and I told her anyway. I have to live with that.' A tear escaped and I swiped it off my cheek.

'Eve, you aren't responsible for everyone. Other people make their choices. You didn't make Isabel confront De Luca and you didn't cause Antonio to be what he is. Stop trying to shoulder the blame for everything that happens.'

'I know,' I said with a sigh. 'I know that, but I can't help feeling like this about certain things. I need to speak to him myself. I have to do this. None of your people have got close to him, right?' He reluctantly nodded. 'So let me be the one to wave that crystal at him and confirm that the demon is controlling him. I might even be able to get something out of the situation. He offered me a favour and I didn't take it. Maybe I should?'

'He was trying to bribe you,' he said with a smirk.

'Yes, and it's too late to buy my silence, isn't it? But he doesn't know that yet. Let's let him think he can win me over for a second before his world explodes.'

CHAPTER TWENTY-NINE

My stomach churned and kept lurching dangerously. I was pretty sure I wasn't really going to be sick. It was that horrible feeling of nerves.

'I'll be right out here if you need me,' Peter said. I glanced sideways at him from the passenger seat of his blue Honda and gave a mute nod. His grip was tight on the wheel, his own nerves showing.

'I have my talisman,' I said, holding up the big, gold coin he had given me. He grudgingly smiled and his hands loosened on the wheel a fraction. 'And this one.' I held up the smokey quartz and he gave a nod of acknowledgement. I pocketed the coin and the quartz, and opened the car door. With a final quick look at Peter, I stepped out into the sunlit car park in front of the police headquarters. It had seemed like the best plan, to approach De Luca in his place of work with other people around, during the day when Antonio couldn't intervene. I really didn't know what he would do if he knew what was going on, whose side he would ultimately be on. After our recent arguments and the way things had been left between us, I wasn't convinced that his love for me, if it had even been genuine, would overcome his corruption and his loyalty to his friend.

I took a deep breath and marched up the steps to the main door of the building. I pulled it open and stepped into the cool, bright entrance. There was a reception desk with two busy staff behind it, both in uniform. My spine stiffened, immediately cautious of their authority. It was an old reflex. A lesson learned from my parents at a young age: conceal your weirdness, they'll never understand. Now I understood exactly where their attitude came from.

I approached the desk and waited for one of them to break off from their work to address me. The woman was on a call, the man was going through a stack of papers. I gazed around the reception while I waited, taking in the waiting area where around a dozen people sat, tapping their feet, chewing gum, and leafing through old magazines.

'Yes?' The male officer finally addressed me and I looked sharply around at him. 'Can I help you?'

'I have a meeting with Mr De Luca. It's Eve Rawling.'

'Just a moment.' He looked at his computer screen, nodded, then picked up the phone and hit a few buttons. Every action grated on me. I wanted to just be transported to where I needed to be and get on with this foul task. 'I have Eve Rawling here to see you.'

I looked away and waited, my stomach turning in knots. 'He's on his way down to meet you,' the officer said.

I nodded and moved away to take a seat in the waiting area but changed my mind at the last moment. I was too anxious to sit down. I didn't want to be near other people when I was trying to get my mind ready to tune in to someone specific. I stood near the glass doors and looked out into the car park. Peter's car was in the nearest space and I caught sight of him staring up at the building. He didn't seem to have seen me. I didn't want to wave or draw attention to myself, but I wanted him to notice me. That feeling of desperation surprised me and I wondered where it was coming from. I turned away and clutched my bag strap tightly in both hands.

A bell *dinged* and I looked for the source. There were a pair of lifts to the right of the reception desk, and one set of doors slid open. Out stepped Marco De Luca in a grey suit and dark tie. He smiled broadly at me, showing too many teeth.

'Eve,' he said, striding towards me with his hand outstretched. I took it and braced myself. No vision struck me; I was getting better at controlling it. 'So good to see you.' We shook hands and he was a little slow in releasing mine.

'Likewise,' I replied, trying to smile. He finally let go of my hand and I quickly withdrew it, sliding it into my coat pocket. Considering the nature of our last encounter, I was repulsed by the fake cheeriness of his greeting.

'Well, shall we head on up to my office?' I glanced at the two officers behind the desk. The man was eyeing me with surprise, the woman was still on the phone and seemed to be getting more and more agitated with the caller. I followed De Luca back to the lift and the doors re-opened for us immediately. We stepped inside and the doors closed slowly. I backed myself against the wall and crossed my arms over my chest. I didn't know what would happen to his demeanour once we were alone; I braced myself for it to turn sour, but he continued smiling my way and rocked on the balls of his feet.

'How have you been?' I asked, breaking the uneasy silence.

'Not too bad, thank you. How about you? I gather you went out of town?'

'How did you know?' I asked, a little too much snap in my voice.

'Oh, Antonio mentioned it last time I saw him. He seemed a bit down about it. I guess he missed you.' He was entirely too casual. The lift came to a smooth halt and the doors *dinged* open again. He stepped out and I followed him down the corridor and into an office at the very end. It was a huge room with great, glass walls on two sides looking out over the centre of the city. It wasn't a very tall building, but it commanded a good view of the river and part of the wall. The minster was visible in the distance over the roofs of some shops. He snapped the door shut behind me and strode around his large, black desk. The walls that weren't glass were lined with immaculate bookshelves. He sat down behind his desk and indicated the chair opposite. I inched towards it and cautiously took a seat. I slipped my hand into my coat pocket and turned the quartz over in my fingers, wondering how to take it out without him noticing. 'What can I do for you, Eve?'

'I was thinking again about what we talked about before.'

'Oh? Outside your house?'

'Yes.' I looked over my shoulder. We were quite alone and no one could see into the office. My mind was racing and I needed it to be calm. 'I didn't properly accept your apology.'

'No, I suppose you didn't.'

I waited. I wasn't going to apologise when it was him who was so much in the wrong. I slowly started to reach out with my mind, just touching his surface thoughts carefully. He was looking at me with his brows knitted together; his fake smile was gone. I caught glimpses of caution and curiosity, nothing unexpected given the situation.

'Perhaps there was something I should have asked for, to solidify your apology.'

'Really? That surprises me, Eve.' He raised his eyebrows and leaned back in his chair. His thoughts turned to appraisal. He wasn't suspicious.

'I seem to have a habit of surprising people.' I smiled nervously. I pushed a little deeper into his thoughts, looking for some sign of the demon. The waters of his mind were crystal clear, but even as I looked, they became slightly cloudy. I wasn't sure what I was seeing.

'Do you, indeed?' De Luca steepled his fingers in front of his face and fixed me with an intense look of curiosity. I defiantly glared back at him but tried to soften my expression into something a little flirtatious. I had to be careful, but I was determined to get to something useful. I crossed one leg over the other and leaned forward. I reached deeper into his thoughts, sifting through them. My hand was still on the quartz in my pocket and it was growing warmer.

'I think most women are surprising to men. I don't quite know why. Take Isabel, I had the measure of her pretty quickly after we met, but I get the feeling she keeps surprising Antonio. I haven't seen her in a while though. Have you?'

'No, I haven't seen her since New Year's Eve.' His whole body stiffened slightly and he leaned forward on his desk, moved a pen from one side to the other and avoided eye contact. 'I didn't realise you two had become friends.'

That was it. Swimming beneath his surface thoughts of wondering what colour my underwear was and whether I was coming on to him or not, was something darker. I saw those inky black tendrils winding through his mind, tugging here and there like strings. I saw Isabel confronting him, and his rage and fear pulsed through his veins. She was going to undo everything he had worked for. She was a threat. I stopped looking, almost turning away physically before catching myself. The quartz in my pocket flared white hot and I quickly withdrew my hand, hoping he hadn't noticed anything.

'A little. We relate to each other on a couple of things,' I replied, shaking my hand by my side and trying not to show any signs of pain. His anxiety rolled off him in waves. I'd set him on the back foot and he wanted to know if I knew something. My own insides squirmed. This had got too close to the danger zone way too fast.

'So, about that favour. What did you have in mind?'

'It depends if you're going to renew your apology or not.'

'Of course. I'm so sorry for alarming you, both at the ball and at your house. It was certainly not my intention. Antonio is a good friend and ally and I would hate for there to be a rift between the two of us that would place him in the middle or cause any offence.' He almost sounded sincere. He certainly didn't seem aware that Antonio and I were as good as dead. I might have believed him if I couldn't see the panic behind his eyes and that black fluid seeping forward into his surface thoughts.

'Thank you, I appreciate that. If you would really like

to make amends, you could introduce me to the editor-in-chief at *The Oris Post*. I gather you know each other.'

'Is that all? I'm sure we can arrange that.' There was a flicker of relief at the simplicity of my request, but then something else. That darkness under his skin swirled and consumed every thought, every feeling. The demon was right in there, controlling his every word now. I had dragged it to the surface from whatever depths it was previously hidden. It was looking right at me through his eyes.

My heart thumped wildly and my pulse raced. I could feel my cheeks heating up under that penetrating gaze. The demon was trying to read me right back. Was it aware that I had seen it in there? I got to my feet so abruptly that De Luca jumped. He stood up, pushing his chair back with a little too much force. It almost rolled right into the window behind him.

'Good, well, I'll be going.' I moved quickly towards the door, but De Luca caught up to me and placed his hand on the handle before I could open it.

'Eve...' He stalled, looking into my face, searching it. He was too close. Cold darkness radiated from him. I was close to breaking down. I had seen those eyes before. The same dark hunger that De Luca was examining me with. Yes, the demon knew. It knew about my gift, how it worked and how I was when I used it. I had seen it before but never knew it. I had seen it looking at me through

Antonio's eyes. I had to leave.

'I really should go,' I said, breathlessly.

De Luca released the door handle and grabbed my face in both of his hands. He planted his mouth on mine and pushed me against the door. I whimpered and resisted his kiss; he promptly released me but stayed much too close.

'I'm sorry. I thought you wanted me to. I misread the signals. I'm sorry.'

I patted my trembling lips and shook my head. He was lying. It was the demon. It was all a show. I had to play along, for whatever shred of subterfuge still remained to me. 'There's no need to tell Antonio. Is there?' De Luca looked worried now. His own eyes, not the demon's, were looking at me, but not quite meeting mine. They raked over my lips.

'He would literally kill you,' I whispered.

'Or he'd try to,' he said, his voice shaking. His own rage pulsed alongside the demon's, the two twisting together like a double helix. De Luca was only loyal to his friend to a point. If Antonio ever got in the way of what De Luca wanted he wouldn't hesitate to end that relationship, just as he had with Isabel. I saw the demon's fear then, burning white hot inside De Luca's thoughts. It was intricately linked with Antonio. His puppet vampire would do whatever he was instructed to do. Antonio was the demon's tether to this world. I knew its name now. Coming face to face with it through De Luca was like an introduction, a bit like the way Kirk knew the names of demons and fae on sight. The thing's name sent a shudder up my spine: Spectre-of-Maleficence. It was more powerful than I'd imagined and it knew me as well as I knew it. But it had its limits. It could control only so much, and in that moment it was afraid of what it couldn't control. The thing it feared most was De Luca's thoughts of killing Antonio.

If Antonio dies, so do I.

CHAPTER THIRTY

I BOLTED OUT OF THERE AS QUICKLY AS POSSIBLE. The ride down in the lift seemed to take forever. My knees were trembling and I cast my gaze up to the ceiling, willing the lift to descend faster. He didn't accompany me out, which I felt was probably against regulations, but I was deeply thankful. When the doors opened I dashed out before they had fully parted and scurried straight for the main doors without bothering to sign out or speak to anyone.

Fresh air and sunlight hit me and I ran to Peter's car. He looked up as I approached, full of concern as I leapt into the car.

'What happened?'

'Drive. Get us out of here now. Please.' The tears began to fall and I squeezed my eyes tight to try to stem the flow. It was pointless.

'Eve, talk to me.' Peter's voice was desperate.

'I can't. Give me a minute.'

To his credit, he didn't ask me any more questions, but he didn't drive us home either. I realised after a few minutes that we were heading out of Oris. I glanced sideways at him and tested his mind. There was no sign of the demon, so I didn't think I was being abducted. He put his foot down once we reached the quieter roads and drove hard until we were surrounded by hedgerows and fields. He pulled into a lay-by and turned off the engine. My tears had stopped and my breathing settled. I opened my door and stepped out into the warm sunshine. He was at my side in a flash.

'Ready?'

'The demon was possessing him. He definitely killed Isabel, and I realised that I've seen the demon inside Antonio before, I just didn't know it because of what he is. I always thought it was the vampire. Maybe it was in part, but there was too much familiarity. I felt like I'd seen the demon before, talked with it, made eye contact with it.'

'Oh, Eve. I'm sorry.'

'There's more.' I drew a deep breath. 'Do you know about tethers? Anchors for demons?'

'Yeah. Some really powerful demons need to be linked to something from this world in order to stay here. Oh...'

'Yeah.'

'What's it tethered to?'

'Do you really need to ask?' I looked up into his blue eyes. My lip trembled. He grabbed me and pulled me against his chest. I started sobbing again and pressed my face against his shirt. I shook and he held me tight.

'I'm sorry. I'm so, so sorry. You know what this means?' All I could do was nod. I was sure he would understand. I knew exactly what it meant. The only way to get rid of the demon was to sever its connection to this world, to separate it from its tether by destroying it. Antonio had to die the final death. My knees gave way and I crumpled. Peter held me up, taking my full weight. He stroked my hair and let me get it all out. There was no judgement, no vindictive smugness or relief. Only compassion for me. Dimly, I was aware of this change in him, but in that moment all I could do was grieve over what had to happen.

When I was all cried out it was drawing dark. The shadows lengthened across the ground and there was a nip in the air. Peter helped me back into the car and quickly got back into the driver's seat. We drove home in silence. My face was numb from crying so hard. My eyes ached and I had to close them. When the car came to a halt in front of my house I peered blearily at my front door. I put my hand on the handle to open the car door but stalled there.

'Peter, I can't. I don't want to be alone. It's nearly dark too.' I wasn't going to say it, but he would know what I was thinking. He didn't need my gift to know that I was scared now of what the demon would do in Antonio's body. I still had no idea if my verbal rescinding of his invitation into my house would keep him out, but I couldn't risk being there alone. Antonio had never been invited into Peter's house. Without another word he started the car again and drove around the corner to his house. He skilfully parked in a tiny space, two wheels up on the kerb like every other car on the narrow street.

We went inside together and he made me a cup of tea. I took the quartz out of my pocket, which now had a burn hole in it, and passed it back to Peter. I didn't need it any more. It was an age before either of us spoke again. Finally he heaved a sigh. I braced myself for whatever he was about to say.

'We can try to find another way.' I wasn't expecting that. A strained laugh escaped my dry lips.

'I love you, Peter. Thank you for suggesting it, but we both know the truth.' He hung his head and I exhaled slowly, letting out all the tension I'd been holding onto. This was how it had to end. It had been inevitable since Antonio had walked into my life. It was crazy to ever think we would get some sort of happily ever after. That was never our fate. I got to my feet, despite how heavy my body felt. 'I'll be right back.' I moved slowly to the stairs and made my way up them to the bathroom. I turned on the light and locked the door, leaning heavily back on it and closing my eyes. The weight of the day was crushing. I was shrivelling up inside. I went to the sink, ran the hot tap and gazed at my exhausted reflection. There were dark circles under my eyes, and my cheeks were pale and drawn.

The mirror began to steam up and I gazed at my face

as it disappeared under the condensation. The light gave a slight flicker and I glanced up at it. When my gaze returned to the mirror, the light went out completely, plunging the room into darkness. The street light outside cast a dim, orange glow through the heavily frosted glass.

'Eve?' Peter called from downstairs. 'You okay?'

'Fine. Has the power gone out?' I called back.

'Yeah. Stay where you are. I'll be right back.'

I wiped the mirror and stared at myself again. My face was illuminated by the street light and I looked truly ill. I stopped the tap running and scooped up a handful of water from the pool of it in the sink. I splashed my face and winced against the sting of the hot water. I blinked droplets from my eyelashes and gazed at myself again. My eyes looked back at me with a dark glaze over them. I squinted, blinked, and looked again. The darkness deepened. I jumped back from the mirror, my pulse pounding.

'I'm not going to hurt you,' my reflection said in a voice that didn't belong to me.

'What do you want?' I grasped my throat, which rasped painfully.

'It's not what I want. It's what you want, and what I can do to give it to you.'

'I don't want anything from you.'

'I think you will when you hear my offer.'

'Peter!' I screamed at the top of my lungs. I couldn't

tear my eyes away from my evil reflection. Every time the demon spoke my throat burned; I wasn't in control of what came out of my mouth.

'He won't hear you just yet. Scream again in a minute, when you've heard my offer.'

I opened my mouth to object, but no sound came out. A tear leaked out of the corner of my eye and I swiped it away. I was done with crying. The fear was like a tight hand around my throat. 'I know what you want, Eve. I can see inside your heart. You've wanted one thing for months.'

'Have I? And what is that?' I spat angrily, challenging the demon.

'A normal life.'

I tried to object, but I knew deep down that it was right.

'It doesn't matter what I want. That isn't something I can ever have.'

'Oh but you can. I can give it to you.'

'How?' The anger had slipped down a notch and there was more curiosity in my voice than I would have liked.

'I can take away your curse, Eve, stop you from hearing other people's thoughts and seeing their ugly pasts and desperate futures.'

'It's a gift, not a curse.'

'Is it? Are you sure? If you were rid of it you could be with anyone... enjoy normal intimacy with regular people.

You could get as close as you wanted to whoever you wanted. You could live a normal life with healthy relationships. You could have children, a partner, a career. Just like you've always wanted. I can give you that gift.'

I hesitated, my breath held tight. I inched closer to the mirror, squinting in the dark.

'What would it cost me?' I was surprised at my response and stared wide-eyed at myself.

'Not a thing. It's a gift. Go live your life. Go back to art school, do what you like.'

'Just leave Antonio alone, with you controlling him?'

'You don't want to become a murderer, Eve. I know you don't. I'm saving you from that fate. You know you can't have a life with him in either case. This way you get to have a fresh start in another city and move on with your life without ever having to hurt anybody.'

I swallowed against the pain in my throat and stroked my neck. I longed for that life. I could see it playing out in my mind's eye. The demon was right. It was what I had always wanted, but Peter's face entered my thoughts, and Weaver's, and Blade. Without my gift, would I still have a place with my friends? I thought of what the demon was planning to do with Antonio, about the spread of even more corruption, of the theft of democracy, of the hidden bodies.

My darkened eyes stared back at me expectantly, a hungry expression on my drawn face. The demon grinned back at me, knowing how tempted I was.

'No!' I roared with all my might. I thrust out a hand and pushed with all of my mental strength and the mirror shattered into a thousand pieces. The glass scattered all over the sink and the tiled floor, tinkling like tiny bells.

'Eve?!' Peter called from the other side of the door. He hammered on it with his fist and I ran to it and unlocked it. The lights flickered back on and he surveyed the broken mirror. 'What happened?'

'The demon is desperate. It just tried to corrupt me, but I resisted. It can't control me. We've got it scared.'

'I see,' he said, looking past me at the pieces of mirror all over the floor. He disappeared and returned with a broom and dustpan and brush. Peter and I cleaned up the broken glass. We kept catching each other's eye and smiling. Despite the job that had to be done in order to beat the demon, it felt entirely possible that we could win this fight.

'How did the demon communicate with you?' Peter asked me as we finished cleaning up.

'It spoke through my reflection,' I replied, not thinking much of it.

'That's why you broke the mirror?'

'Yeah.'

'But the demon was in the mirror, right?' Our eyes met and I couldn't answer him. We both realised in that moment that breaking the mirror may have been pointless.

I looked down at my pale fingers and turned my hands over. How would I know if the demon was inside me? Would Peter be able to see it in my eyes as I had seen it in De Luca's? Peter raised a finger to his lips and I nodded mutely. He reached into his pocket and tugged out the quartz. He held it in his palm between us and sparks began to float out of it. They moved towards me, glowing gold. Peter closed his eyes. I watched the sparks bounce off me and sizzle faintly.

'Peter? We should go our separate ways for a bit,' I said softly. He nodded and opened his eyes.

'Will you be all right on your own?'

'Yeah. I'll be fine.' I didn't know how much the demon could sense from inside me. Was it just my thoughts? Or could it see and hear everything that I experienced? I couldn't risk cluing it in any more than it already had been. I also wondered how it had got into me. It might have been free to possess anyone at any time, but I suspected it needed a way into someone's life in order to do what it did. Had it been when De Luca kissed me? Or could it have come from Antonio before that? There was also the chance that my own actions had invited it into me. I didn't want to believe that, but I had to consider the possibility. It was somehow more palatable to think that it passed from person to person, like some sort of contagion. If you stayed away from anyone who was infected, you could escape its evil clutches. If it could come for anyone, any time, what hope was there then?

I wondered if taking away its tether would be enough. Would it just jump hosts and find a new one? I had to trust that the shifters would think of that and could handle it. This is what they were made for.

Peter and I went back downstairs and I gathered my things to go home. 'Tell your dad I'm sorry about the mirror.'

'I will, thanks. Are you really sure—'

'I need to not be around you right now, just in case. You had the same thought I did back there, and it isn't worth the risk.' Peter nodded and his Adam's apple bobbed noticeably. He was worried about me. 'Make sure you're ready, all of you. You know what I mean.'

'I will, I do.' He grabbed me and pulled me into his arms. I was getting used to that now. I let him hug me and only eased out of his arms when my back began to creak from how tight he was holding me. He grudgingly let me go.

I gave him what I hoped was a reassuring smile and left the house. I still didn't really want to be alone. I didn't trust myself. I felt unclean, like my veins were filled with toxicity. The ugly reflection I had encountered kept reappearing in my thoughts, and the temptation I had felt was too uncomfortable to deal with. The demon had made a compelling offer and I had genuinely been tempted to take it, if only for a few seconds.

I pulled out my phone as I walked and opened up my chat with Blade. I stared at his last message, which was just something light and disconnected from all of the drama unfolding in my real life.

"Lovely to speak to you last night. Had to tell Peter about you. You're not my secret any more. I will write soon, but things are hotting up here." My thumb hovered over the send button as I reread it a few times. It was fine. I hit the button and put my phone away. I wanted him to ask what was happening. I wanted to tell him everything about Antonio and what lay ahead, about the demon invading my body and how terrified I was. I hardly knew him really, but we had talked so much since we met that there was that connection and I craved more of it.

If I took the demon's offer I would never have to be scared of holding Blade's hand, of letting him stroke my face and press his lips to mine. I arrived at my house with a little start of surprise. I'd been so lost in my thoughts that I had lost track of where I was on my route. I went inside and sank down onto the floor, leaning back against the door. Why did it have to be so complicated?

My phone buzzed and I tugged it from my pocket. Blade had replied already.

"Wanna talk about it?"

Yes, desperately. Instead I wrote, "That was quick. Don't you ever have pack stuff to do?" I added a cheeky emoji just to make sure he got the right tone.

"I do but I always have time for you x"

Could I really be doing this? My feelings for Antonio hadn't exactly evaporated, but it was easy with Blade. I didn't have a future with Antonio. Even if he survived what was coming we couldn't be together. The demon was right.

'My offer still stands,' the demon's voice croaked out of my own throat.

'Piss off,' I hissed. I got to my feet and made my way to the kitchen to make a cup of tea. What did this mean for our plans? Did the demon know everything now? As the steam billowed out of the kettle, I lost myself in my thoughts, wondering what it would take to break free.

CHAPTER THIRTY-ONE

I HIT REFRESH ON MY BROWSER FOR THE HUNDREDTH TIME. It was growing dark outside my kitchen window and my laptop sat open on the table with *The Post's* website loaded and displaying sports results that I couldn't care less about. The evening edition of the paper would be hitting news-stands about now, and their website should be updated at the same time. Steve's article from the previous day was still displayed in the recent stories section and had attracted a fair amount of comments, not all of which were sympathetic to the fate of these unfortunate souls.

At 6:01 pm, after another impatient click on the refresh button, the page changed and my breath caught in my throat as I came face to face with a stunning photograph of Isabel and the bold headline: "Mayor's Wife Missing!"

'Thank you Steve!' My voice echoed around the empty kitchen. I scrolled past the picture to read the article. It mentioned Michelle's death, and there were quotes from the mayor himself and frustrations about the police department not taking Isabel's disappearance seriously. Steve had even managed to sneak in one of Michelle's photos of Isabel and De Luca getting out of his car. Tears streaked down my face and I laughed my way through the story, my senses overwhelmed with relief. It was everything we needed.

My phone rang, making me jump. Peter's name lit up the display.

'Did you see it?!' I asked.

'Yeah. It's exactly what we wanted.'

'I hope he's okay,' I said, sobering slightly. 'He could get into trouble for this.'

'He knows what he's doing.'

'I hope so.'

'How are you doing?' Peter asked gently, pulling me back to my current situation.

'Fine,' I lied. 'Nothing to report here.'

'Okay. Let me know if that changes. Deal?'

'Deal. Is everything in place for luring out Celino?'

'Yeah. I've been talking to my pack about it. We're ready when you are.'

'You probably shouldn't tell me any more details than I need.' I gazed at my reflection in the window over the sink. The garden was bathed in darkness beyond the glass, and the light in the kitchen reflected back into the room. Dark circles below my eyes betrayed my lack of rest, and poor nutrition, but the demon didn't make an appearance.

I couldn't take the risk, though.

'Okay. You know where we like to do this shit.'

'I do.' I battled with my own thoughts, trying not to consciously recall the catacombs. I pushed a thought of the city wall into my mind instead, just in case. I really didn't know how this thing worked, or if the demon could be hoodwinked. That frustrated me and I slammed my palm down on the kitchen table.

'You all right?' Peter asked.

'Fine. I'm heading out now that it's dark.'

'Okay, be safe.'

'I'll do my best.' I ended the call and ran my fingers over the coin talisman in my pocket, knowing that Peter was a breath away if I needed him. Metal clinked against metal and my fingers brushed against a key. With a frown I took it out and found Peter's skeleton key in my hand. I clucked my tongue. He must have slipped it to me. I tucked it back in my pocket beside the coin.

I turned to head for the front door, but my phone rang again, stopping me in my tracks. I went to answer it, expecting it to be Peter with something he forgot to say, but Antonio's name lit up the display instead. With a painful swallow, I answered the call.

'My phone is busy this evening,' I said with a wry smile.

'I wonder why?' he replied in an acid tone. 'Eve, what did you do?'

'I don't know what you're talking about.' I set off for the door and went about putting on my coat and shoes, with my phone tucked between my cheek and shoulder.

'Yes you do. That news report could do a lot of damage.'

'You had your chance to put things right. I was very clear on what I expected. You let me down, Antonio. You failed.'

'Dammit, Eve. You have no idea what forces you're messing around with here.'

'I do, actually. I know full well what I'm doing and, believe it or not, I'm still trying to help you, despite everything you've done, despite how badly you've hurt me. Despite what you are and the life you've lived. I still want to save you. God! What is wrong with me?' I flung open the door and stepped out into the night. I slammed the door behind me and stood there for a moment, rage rushing through my veins.

'How I've hurt you? How *I've* hurt *you*?! Eve! You left me. You didn't give me a fair chance to fix things. You ran away and met someone else in Caerton. You shut me out. I have been trying to meet your expectations for months and nothing I do is ever good enough for you. You say I've hurt you, but you've hurt me too. You've pushed and pushed and nothing was ever enough for you. *Porca miseria!*'

I was shocked into silence, tears streaking down my cheeks. Antonio had rarely been angry with me like this.

I'd seen flashes of a temper, I'd even had his hand around my neck once, but his anger had always been the quiet kind, which felt dangerous enough. This was different. I swallowed hard and tried to reach out with my thoughts towards him, despite the physical distance between us, I hoped it would work, either through the phone connection, or the ether itself, maybe the icy tendrils of Spectre-of-Maleficence could even be used as conduits between the people that the demon was controlling. I closed my eyes and tried to reach into his thoughts.

'Eve?' His voice had softened. My focus was broken without reaching his mind. 'Say something.'

'I don't think there's anything left to say.' I hung up and switched my phone off. I had another way to reach the only person I would need and didn't want to be bothered again. I set off at a brisk walk, not really knowing where to go, just that I had to move my body. I wiped my face and no more tears threatened to fall. It all seemed pretty final with Antonio now. There was no going back. Sadness was heavy in my bones, but the lack of doubt and confusion was simultaneously a relief.

I was barely aware of where I was going, just that the traffic on the streets was heavy. There was a hint of rain in the air and the wind whipped my long hair around my face. I tucked it back behind my ear and looked up to find myself within sight of the police headquarters. People rushed past me, a crowd gathering at the foot of the steps leading up to the door. A lectern had been set up, surrounded by microphones. The press formed a semicircle at the base of the steps. I made my way cautiously to join the back of the crowd. Speculation buzzed excitedly between people as I caught snatches of conversations.

'Any minute now... Expecting a statement... He's going to deny it...' On and on it went, like static hissing from an old radio.

I hung back at the edge, wary of being swallowed up by too many people for my senses to cope with. I craned my neck, looking for Steve in the press pack, but I couldn't make him out in the sea of people.

The station doors opened and De Luca stepped out, surrounded by a cluster of officers in uniforms and a few stiffs in suits. A woman at his side in a suit and holding a folder had the distinct look of his legal representation about her. The group made their way to the lectern, to the flashes and clicks of a couple of dozen cameras. A spotlight shone bright white on the pallid face of a man very much not in control of the situation as De Luca stepped behind the stand. A hush fell over the crowd.

'Thank you for coming at such short notice,' De Luca said, his voice amplified by the microphones clustered around him. 'I am saddened to be standing before you this evening under such grave circumstances. The breaking news of the disappearance of Isabel Shaw has shocked

Oris. Rest assured, our diligent officers are throwing the full weight of the police department behind this investigation. I, as much as anyone, am eager to find Ms Shaw alive and well. She is a good friend and I will cooperate in any way that I can with the investigation. I have made extra funds available for the Herculean effort the department wishes to make in order to bring her safely home to her husband.'

I rolled my eyes and let out a rush of breath into the cool night air.

The press erupted with questions, their cameras flashing madly.

'I won't be taking any questions at this time, thank you,' De Luca called over the din. He turned and was escorted by his people back inside.

'I did my best,' a voice said dully beside me. I turned to face Steve Wright. 'It's almost as if an invisible hand is wrapped around him, protecting him. Isn't it?'

A frown creased my brow. It seemed an odd thing for him to say, but disturbingly accurate.

'It is a bit, yeah. Are you okay?'

'Oh, I was fired. I put that piece out without running it past the chief. It was too important. He was given a dummy article for the front page of the print edition and then my story ran in its place. He tried to order the online article taken down, but an assistant pointed out that it had already had six thousand views and was bound to have been screen captured so it would look bad if it got taken down. It'll be edited instead, I expect, but not by me.'

'I'm so sorry,' I said, the regret evident in my voice.

'I knew the risks,' he said with a shrug. 'It had to be done. Maybe the court of public opinion will do its thing. He might not win the election now.'

I looked away and shook my head. 'That invisible hand is already working on that.'

'Sorry?' he asked, looking at me quizzically.

'Nothing. Just that I hope you're right.' A creeping sensation moved up my spine and I spun to look behind me. People had gathered there but were drifting away now.

'You all right?' Steve asked, following my gaze.

'Yeah, just a bad feeling. It's nothing.'

'Is she definitely dead?'

'Isabel?' He gave a nod. 'Yes. They won't find her alive.'

'Can you tell me how you know?'

'Off the record?'

'Funny.' He scoffed and scowled at me.

'Sorry. I just know.'

'The same way you just know that Michelle was murdered?'

'Pretty much, yeah. I wish I could tell you more.'

'Me too.' He looked down at his feet and kicked at the pavement.

'What will you do for work now?'

'I'll figure something out, don't worry. Take care of yourself, Eve.' Steve gave me a nod, turned, and walked away. I watched him go and turned back to the doors of the police station. De Luca was out of sight. I didn't know if he'd seen me, or had any clue that it was me who leaked the information. I couldn't worry about that now. The tingling up my spine was still there and I had a pretty good idea what was causing it: Celino. I hadn't seen him, but there was a blank spot in my extrasensory perception, a body nearby that I couldn't read. Like a cold spot on a heat map.

I set off walking in the opposite direction to Steve, not wishing to get him further embroiled in this mess. I grabbed fistfuls of my long hair as I walked and casually tied it back with the band that I kept around my wrist. I kept to the busiest streets, not wanting to give him an opportunity to strike too soon. I made my way to the part of the city wall that formed a bridge over the river, the spot where Peter and I had first learned about Spectre months ago. People brushed past me and cars chugged by on the clogged, narrow streets. The cold spot was following me, always just beyond my reach. I was sure it was Celino. He radiated energy in a particular way. Or maybe it was the demon inside me connecting me to him.

I came to a halt on the bridge and leaned against the stone wall to stare down into the black water rushing by beneath my feet. I glanced back the way I'd come, into the light flow of pedestrians walking towards me. There was no sign of Celino, but I could feel him there somewhere. People brushed past me and I set off again just ahead of a couple holding hands, half concealed by them. At the riverbank was an ancient guard tower with steep steps down to the riverside path. I slipped through the gap in the wall and jogged carefully down the steps into the shadows. An orange street lamp glowed beside the river, gently lighting my way into the shadow of the bridge. At the foot of the guard tower was a wooden door behind a metal grate. I only had seconds, alone in the dark beside the river. I took out the skeleton key and fumbled with it in the dark. I found the padlock on the metal grate and slid the key into it. There was a loud *click* and the key turned. I flung it open and tried the door, but that too was locked. I used the key again and pushed the door open with a groan of ancient wood against the stone floor. I turned and yanked the grate shut, clanging it hard against the wall just as Celino emerged at the foot of the steps. Our eyes met, a hungry sneer on his cruel face. I gasped. My heart pounded. I slammed the wooden door shut and ran.

CHAPTER THIRTY-TWO

IT WAS PITCH-BLACK and I ran straight into the cold, stone wall. I stumbled backwards, my head pounding. I fumbled for my phone, but I'd turned it off and nothing happened when I swiped the screen.

'Fuck,' I muttered. I reached out and touched the rough stone in front of me. I set off walking, using my hand to guide me, and I tried desperately to get my phone to come on. My clammy hand wouldn't cooperate. The door behind me scraped open and dim, orange light spilled down the passage. I looked over my shoulder at Celino silhouetted in the doorway. My breath caught in my throat.

'Eve,' he called, almost singing my name. 'Don't run from me.'

My phone came to life at last, gently illuminating my face. I tapped through to the torch and shone it into the passage ahead of me. I sprinted away from him; the instinct to flee was strong, despite knowing there was no way I could outrun him. The passage narrowed through an archway and my foot almost gave way as I plunged down a steep step. With a cry, I hurried down the narrow, spiral staircase, my torchlight bobbing on the sandstone walls. Celino was silent behind me. He wasn't even bothering to use his super-speed. My breath hitched in my throat. I kept my free hand on the wall, guiding me through the darkness. I hit level ground and the light shone up the narrow passage. Water ran in narrow rivulets down the wall; I threw my gaze upwards to where droplets of water clung to the ceiling. I was under the river. I sped onwards, Celino following silently behind me, his coldness oozing along the passage towards me.

I hurriedly tugged my coin talisman from my pocket as I sprinted on. I brought it to my lips and whispered, 'Peter' against the warm metal. The passage widened as I reached the other side of the river, the walls drying out again in my bobbing torchlight. A rush of icy wind brushed past me and before I could react, I slammed straight into Celino leaning against the wall in front of me. He lazily grabbed hold of me by my shoulders and spun me to slam me hard against the wall. The coin tumbled from my fingers and rolled away across the slightly uneven ground. He didn't seem to notice. His face was an inch from mine, a snarl on his lips.

'I've been looking forward to this.'

I squirmed in his grip and turned my head away. He let out a throaty chuckle and took a slow, deliberate sniff of my neck.

'Get off me,' I said through gritted teeth.

'Oh no, I think I'm going to take my time and enjoy this. Why should dear Antonio be the only one to get to taste you?'

I thrust my knee up, aiming for his groin, but he was too quick and dodged my attack. He shoved me hard against the wall and pressed his body flush against mine, pinning me so that I could hardly move. His ice-cold tongue ran slowly up from my collarbone to just below my ear. I grimaced, trying to pull free, but he was painfully strong, gripping me so hard that every part of me ached. I could hardly breathe. The points of his fangs grazed against my skin.

Rage and desperation surged up inside me and it took all of my strength and bravery to resist using my power on him. Something stirred inside my mind. A consciousness that wasn't my own. It was curious and inched towards the surface. Spectre.

Celino let out a low groan that made my stomach turn. He took hold of my chin and turned my face towards him. I could hardly make out the details of his face in the dark. The light from my phone in my hand cast eerie shadows from waist-height. His eyes locked onto mine and my head began to spin.

'I'm going to fuck you, Eve, while I bleed you dry. You need to learn not to tell tales to nosy journalists.' His voice echoed dully in the stone passage as my head drifted into the woozy space of being under a vampire's thrall.

Stay awake a voice inside my head urged. I wasn't sure who it belonged to. It sounded like my own. Could it be Ms Rational looking out for me? Or was it the demon? I remembered the plan and gently pushed back against Celino's psychic attack, careful not to push too hard and alert him. I gazed into his eyes and allowed my muscles to relax. His teeth pierced my skin and I gasped. My whole body tensed and energy swelled up inside me; the urge to force him off me was almost impossible to resist.

My blood rushed through my veins and his hungry gulps were all I could hear. His hands roamed down over my body and I had to let him. I remembered my vision of him in the drug den and revulsion coursed through me. It wasn't like being with Antonio. This wasn't erotic. I wanted to escape with almost my whole being, but I had to be strong and let this go just a little further. I saw the cave where we had banished Lucia swim through his thoughts as he fed from me. Fury drove him, nothing else.

'Hey!' a voice in the dark yelled. Peter. I sighed with relief and Celino recoiled from me with an animalistic hiss. My hand darted to my neck. Slick blood coated my fingers and I drew my shaking hand away, staring at it in the strange light.

I was dimly aware of the fight, but the remnants of Celino's thrall lingered in my head, making it swim dully. The blood loss had weakened me enough to leave me clinging to the wall to keep me upright. My head lifted slowly and my eyes focused on the pack of shifters trying to land a hit on Celino as he blurred between and around them, leaving them stumbling in the dark. He vanished up the passage in another blur and the shifters staggered after him. Peter hung back and approached me cautiously.

'Eve? Can you hear me?'

'Hmm.' I nodded slowly. He turned my head to one side to examine the wound on my neck.

'It's not too bad. You'll be all right. Come on, we have to follow him. We need you.'

I stayed there, leaning against the wall, his voice slow and muddy in my head. 'Eve?' he snapped. I gave my head a shake and drew a breath.

'I'm okay. I'm good.' I pushed forward, taking my weight on my feet. I swayed slightly.

'You sure?'

I nodded, took his hand in my bloody one and set off at a slow jog after the rest of his pack.

'I know where he's going. Come on.' My senses returned to me as we made our way through the catacombs, and by the time we reached the cave that the shifters favoured as their meeting place, I was back to normal. The bleeding had stopped and I gingerly felt for puncture marks, but they had already healed. Dry blood was crusted to my skin though. I ran ahead towards the cave Celino had been thinking of.

'Eve,' Peter called, tugging on my arm to slow me down. 'My pack. They're not here.'

'I know, but we have to get to him.' I ploughed on and he did his best to keep pace with me and not leave me in the dust.

We reached the vast cavern. Remnants of old underground development clung to the ceiling, black tiles smoothing out the rough stone. Flickering torches blazed in brackets on the walls, casting their warm glow on the black tiles. A great crack remained across the floor of the cave where the veil had been ripped open. It wasn't a gaping chasm into a fiery hell realm any more, but a jagged, dark line spanned the width of the cave.

Celino stood on a craggy platform at the far end of the cave, in the spot where Lucia had been tossed through the hole in the veil into hell right in front of him. His normally immaculate hair was ruffled, his shirt and tie were loose and one of his jacket sleeves had been torn in the brief scuffle with the shifters. He glared down at us with blazing eyes. His fingernails had lengthened into sharp talons and his fangs were bared. He looked like a beast about to lash out. He was cornered, but there were only two of us. I didn't know how far wrong the rest of Peter's pack had gone in their pursuit of the vampire.

'Where's your pal?' Peter called out, his voice echoing around the vast cavern. 'Laguardia isn't here now to back you up, is he?'

'This is between me and her!' Celino shouted.

'You've been killing people,' I said, not bothering to raise my voice. I knew he could hear me just fine. 'Michelle, the addicts, the dealer. You have to answer for that.'

'You stupid bitch!' Spittle sprayed from his mouth. 'It's what we do, all of us, even your precious Antonio.'

'He doesn't kill any more,' I said, shaking my head.

'Really? You sure about that?' A nasty sneer spread across his face. I couldn't answer that. I had been sure, but now there was doubt.

'Well, if that's the case then he'll pay too. We won't let any of you carry on terrorising the people of Oris.' Peter took a step forward to speak, squaring up to the vampire.

'Who told you to kill Michelle?' I asked, stepping alongside Peter. We both took another careful step forwards.

'Who do you think?'

'De Luca?' I asked, taking a small step. Peter followed. We were gradually getting closer to Celino.

'Oh.' His sneer disappeared for a second, replaced by surprise. 'Well, yes, as a matter of fact.'

'Did Antonio know about it?'

'Not beforehand. He knows now.' There was a flicker of something there. Pain? Anger? It was gone in a fraction of a second, but there was definitely a reaction. Antonio hadn't been happy about Celino killing Michelle. He had expressed his displeasure somehow. 'I've been cleaning up messes, that's all.'

'Is that what I am? A mess?' I took another cautious step forwards.

'You're a problem!' Celino leapt into the air, pouncing like an animal across the remaining space between us. Peter pushed me aside and planted himself in Celino's path. The two of them collided and tumbled across the dusty ground. Snarls and rips filled the air.

I was rooted to the spot, tense but not panicked. The gut-wrenching sounds issuing from the two of them bounced off the cavern walls and out through the passage behind me. I hoped Peter's pack would hear and come to his aid. This had been the plan, after all, to lure Celino here and take him on, but we'd intended for the whole pack to fight him, not Peter alone.

I pressed down into my feet, grounding myself as I drew upon my power. My hands tingled as energy pulsed into the muscles and tendons. I raised my hands out in front of me, clasped together, then with a great force of will, threw them apart. Peter and Celino flew apart too, both rolling away in opposite directions. Celino thumped into the wall of the raised platform we'd found him standing on. Peter scrambled to his feet first. He'd shifted into his Agrius form and stood seven feet tall with a huge jaw salivating as he panted to get his breath back. Celino rose gracefully to his feet and brushed down his suit. His long nails were dirty and had tufts of Peter's long hair caught under them.

'Are you all right?' I asked Peter. He let out a grunt in reply. That was about the best he could do in that form.

'Interesting trick,' Celino said, his voice thick with bitterness. In the blink of an eye, he vanished from view, once again moving in a speeding blur. He was too fast for Peter and my breath hitched in my throat as he crashed into me, dragging me away from my friend.

His clawed hand wrapped tight around my throat and the cave blurred past us both. Dizziness consumed me and nausea flooded my stomach. I clung to Celino's hand, wrestling with it to loosen his grip on my throat, but his fingers were as strong as iron. He slammed me down onto the ground and the wind was knocked right out of me. I lay there gasping for breath with Celino's claws digging into the soft skin of my neck.

A growl broke through the fog in my head as Peter charged towards us. Celino's head snapped to one side and his other hand jutted out towards the oncoming shifter. Blood sprayed hot and sticky across my face and a scream died in my throat. I strained to look to the side in time to see Peter collapse on the ground beside me, his throat ripped open. He writhed, gurgling, his huge hands wrapped tightly around the wound.

Celino ran a blood-soaked finger over my pale cheek before raising it to his lips and slowly, carefully, licking the blood from each finger. His eyes rolled back in his head as he took in Peter's potent blood. Shifter blood made vampires even stronger, faster, and more invulnerable. I thrashed beneath the weight of him but he had me pinned tight. Now was the moment to draw on my abilities again and push him off me with my telekinesis, but I was still winded and in shock. Fear for Peter flooded my veins. I looked again at his prone form beside me. His eyes were still open and he was fighting for life.

Hang on, Peter, I thought, pushing the words into his mind. *I'll get us out of this.*

Celino broke off from licking Peter's blood from his hand, and began unbuttoning his clothes.

'No,' I rasped, still held by the throat. I kicked and thrashed to no avail. Black spots appeared at the edges of my vision and I struggled to keep my eyes open. I wasn't getting enough oxygen and I knew I was going to pass out. Once that happened I wouldn't be able to stop him doing what he wanted to do. Panic rushed through me then, clearing the fog. I pushed back with my mind, but he didn't budge. My hands pushed against his shoulders as I fought for breath. I tried again to force him off me with my mind but the lack of oxygen was sending me spiralling down towards unconsciousness. He went for the belt on my jeans and tears spilled from my eyes.

His grip on my throat loosened as he fumbled with my clothes and I drew a great gulp of air. I screamed with all of my might and he went flying back across the cave, crashing into the wall with a crunch that would have broken human bones. He landed on his knees and his eyes locked back onto me. His shirt hung open, exposing his creamy skin. He lunged back towards me but a blur of motion intercepted him, slamming him back into the wall. I scrambled backwards, my hands skidding on the loose dirt under me. Peter was still moving but his eyes were closed. His Agrius form could heal remarkable wounds at incredible speed. I'd seen him get up from a broken neck before. His fur was matted with drying blood, but the skin of his neck was closing up and healing already. He would be all right.

Celino was locked in a speeding battle with another vampire. Dust rained down from the wall of the cave where they kept bumping into it. The blond went skidding across the ground in a cloud of dust and Antonio stalked over to him, his long, dark hair partially covering his face. The rage in the eye that I could see burned almost red in the torchlight. Celino lay prone and unmoving. I made it across to Peter and checked him over. As I'd thought, he was healing.

'Are you okay?' I asked, my throat rasping painfully. He nodded mutely, his eyes still closed. I patted his shoulder and tried to push myself to my feet.

'How dare you,' Antonio hissed dangerously at Celino. His young progeny raised his head and spat blood onto the ground beside him.

'You're so weak,' Celino said. 'When it comes to her.' He jerked his head in my direction. 'You've been fucking it all up for months since you met her. All of our plans laid to waste.'

'Shut your mouth, *stronzo!*' Antonio stooped down and grabbed Celino by the throat. He hoisted the younger vampire up in one hand as easily as lifting a rag doll. Celino resisted, writhing in Antonio's grasp, his feet thrashing against thin air. Strong as Celino was, he was no match for Antonio. He spun Celino around and smashed him face first against the wall. He thrust his other hand into the back of Celino's neck, his sharp claws ripping straight through the flesh. He withdrew his clawed hand with a squelch and spurt of blood, Celino's spine clenched in his fist. With a sickening ripple, Antonio parted Celino's spine from his body, tearing it right out. What was left of Celino collapsed to the ground in a mushy mess.

I retched and turned away, focusing instead on Peter, whose eyes were now open. He tried to sit up to look at what was going on.

'No, don't,' I whispered. 'You're still healing.' He shifted before my eyes, rippling back into his human form. His neck was still healing and a surge of panic rushed up my body at the sight of torn flesh.

'I'm all right,' he said, rasping as air leaked out through his wound.

'Don't speak, for fuck's sake,' I said as I checked the rest of him for other injuries. 'Let your vocal cords heal.' I spoke from some experience there. I glanced over to Antonio, who stood over a heap of clothes and blood-spattered dirt. His whole body shook and blood dripped from his hands. I got slowly to my feet and moved cautiously towards him. 'Antonio?'

His gaze flickered towards me and back to the mess at his feet. As I drew nearer all I could see of Celino, besides his ruined suit, were some bones with rotten flesh clinging to them. I gagged against the stink of blood and rot.

'Are you intact?' Antonio asked stiffly, not looking at me.

'I'm fine. Thank you, Antonio. You saved me.' He looked at me between the curtains of his hair.

'He had to be stopped.'

'Yes he did. We planned to do that. It wasn't my intention to involve you.'

'Laguardia told me what he was doing. I had to stop him from hurting you.'

'How did you know where we were?'

'I heard you.' He tapped the side of his head.

'Oh.' We were connected after all.

'Not everything we create turns out as we intend,' he said, his voice barely above a whisper. He had made Celino a vampire. The pain of having to destroy him flowed out of every pore of Antonio's body. His dangerous eyes landed back on me and there was hunger in them, intense desire for me. It was hard to resist that look. The anger I had felt towards him ebbed away. He had saved my life, again. He had destroyed Celino for me.

'We should get out of here,' I said, gathering my wits. I looked around at Peter, who was climbing to his feet, clutching his throat. I rushed over to him and scooped his arm over my shoulders to take some of his weight. Together we shuffled towards the passage out of the cavern, leaving Antonio behind. I glanced over my shoulder and our eyes met. He watched me leave with that need in his eyes.

CHAPTER THIRTY-THREE

I MANAGED TO GET PETER UP THROUGH THE CATACOMBS and into my kitchen. I sat him down at the table. He was drenched in sweat; I got him some chilled water from the fridge.

'I need to call your dad,' I said as I sat down next to him with a drink of my own. Peter nodded and took a long drink from the tall glass. I knew Kirk wouldn't get my call if he was still under the city somewhere, but I had to hope that it had been long enough without the pack finding their quarry that they'd return above ground to check in with us. My phone was coated in dried blood and dirt, and I gave it a hasty wipe before finding Kirk's number. Mercifully, it rang and he answered quickly.

'Kirk, we're both okay. We're at my house,' I rattled before he could panic.

'Thank Artemis. What happened?'

'Celino attacked. We were both hurt. Then Antonio appeared. He killed Celino.'

'I see. Where is he now?'

'We left him down there. I think he was in shock afterwards.'

'But you and Peter are both okay?'

'We are. Peter was hurt pretty badly but he's healing. He can't talk right now, but I'll bring him home. Are you there now?'

'No, we're on our way though. Be careful, Eve. It's still dark out and there are other forces still at work here.'

'I know. I will.' I hung up the phone and downed my water. Peter had finished his already while I was on the phone. 'Ready?'

He nodded and got to his feet. He was steadier now and led the way to my front door. We walked quickly to his house, not speaking. The hairs on the back of my neck prickled and I glanced over my shoulder every few yards. We made it to Peter's house at the same time as Kirk, Strikes Twice and Crystal. I was bear-hugged by Kirk and Crystal in turn and we all filed inside before speaking.

A hurried breakdown of what had happened followed, and Peter was soon talking as animatedly as the rest of the shifters. Dawn broke outside the living room window and my eyelids grew heavy. I got wearily to my feet and headed for the door. Peter followed me and caught my arm.

'You all right?'

'I need to sleep, Peter. I don't have super-healing like you.'

'Of course. Want me to walk you home?'

'No, sun's up. I'll be fine. Here, this is yours.' I passed him his skeleton key.

'Thanks. Just reach out to me if you need me.' I nodded and left the house. The walk home was painful. My muscles burned with the effort. I got inside and had one foot on the bottom step when a scrape of wood stopped me. I cocked my head and listened. Another sound from the basement reached me.

I changed course and made my way slowly into the kitchen. Everything looked as it should. I opened the door to the basement and flicked the light on. Antonio stood at the foot of the stairs. His shirtsleeves were rolled up and his hair tied back. He was filthy, with dirt and blood all over his hands and clothes.

'Can we talk?' he asked, his accent thicker than normal. He was in my basement, inside my house. The revocation of his invitation hadn't worked. I stepped back and held out a hand, indicating for him to come up the stairs. Morning sunlight lit a patch of the kitchen through the window; I closed the blind to make it safe for him. His footsteps were light on the wooden steps up. When he'd almost reached the top, a ripple, like heat haze, filled the kitchen doorway and he stopped, frowning at the door frame. He tried to take the last step but again met resistance. I smiled and crossed my arms.

'Huh. Looks like that's as far as you get now.'

'Fair enough.' He leaned heavily against the wall and

crossed his own arms, mirroring me. 'Are you all right?'

'I will be. I'm exhausted. I was about to go to bed.'

He nodded slowly.

'I am so sorry about Celino coming after you. I did not want that to happen.'

'I know.'

'He overheard our argument and took matters into his own hands.'

'You don't have to explain.'

'I do, because I bear some responsibility. He was mine to control and I failed.'

'You can't control everything.'

'No, I suppose not.' Our eyes met.

'Thank you again, for coming to my rescue. It can't have been easy for you to do that.'

'Eve,' he said, uncrossing his arms and looking right into my soul with earnest eyes. 'I would move heaven and earth for you. I always will.'

A tear prickled at the corner of my eye and my cheek trembled. It seemed a lifetime ago that we had been in love and not haunted by Spectre-of-Maleficence. I wished more than anything that I could feel the bliss of being the centre of Antonio's attention again. A silent war raged inside me between Ms Rational and the swell of emotion flooding my veins.

I dove forward through the doorway and into Antonio's arms. Our mouths collided in a deep and feverish kiss. His arms encircled me, keeping me safe.

I need you. Antonio's voice echoed inside my head. *I want to be with you forever.*

I broke the kiss, panting hard, my body pressed against his. I searched his eyes. He nodded. It had been his voice inside my head for real. He kissed me softly and tears spilled down my cheeks. Our lips parted again and we stared into each other's eyes in the dim light of the dusty stairwell.

'I made you an offer once when I wasn't in my right mind.' His voice was soft against my lips, my thoughts fuzzy from the euphoria of our reunion so soon after the exertions of the night. I blinked and it took me a moment to cotton on to what he was saying. 'Eve, be with me forever.'

I pulled back, a frown creasing my brow.

'Are you offering to change me?'

'I am.' I untangled myself from his embrace and stepped back up into my kitchen, out of his reach. He frowned up at me, pain in his eyes.

'No, Antonio. That might have tempted me a few months ago, but not now. Not after everything.'

'But—'

'I'm sorry if that hurts you. That isn't what I want, but I don't want to become like you either.'

His face sagged for a moment before hardening again. His blazing eyes looked up at me and he nodded firmly.

'I understand. I apologise. You're quite right. You need to move on and live your life. Get some rest and feel better soon.' He turned without waiting for a response and disappeared in a blur into the shadows beneath my house. I tentatively followed him down and covered up the hatch into the catacombs. I retreated back upstairs with a heaviness in my bones that went beyond physical exhaustion.

CHAPTER THIRTY-FOUR

SLEEP TOOK HOLD OF ME and held me captive right through the morning. When I finally peeled my eyes open again, bright sunshine filled my room. Groggily, I crawled from my bed, showered, dressed and made my way downstairs. I cleaned my phone properly and plugged the dead device in to charge. Once it had a little power, my phone lit up with a barrage of notifications. Before I could open any of them, furious banging on my front door split the deathly quiet of the house.

I went cautiously to the door and pressed my hands against the wood.

'Who is it?'

'Peter. Are you all right?'

I unlocked and opened the door. His hair was ruffled and his clothes hung off him as if he'd dressed in a hurry.

'I'm fine. What's wrong?'

'They dragged the river and found her.' He brushed past me and went into my living room. I closed the door and followed him, my tired brain not quite keeping up with his frantic energy. He turned on my TV and switched it to the lunchtime news.

'Police are waiting for confirmation from the coroner's office, but it does look as though foul play was involved.' The correspondent was standing outside the police station where De Luca had given his statement the previous night. The buzz of other newscasters around him filled out the soundscape of the broadcast. People rushed in and out of the building behind him.

'Wait,' I said, frowning at the channel logo in the top corner of the screen. 'Is this the national news?'

'Yeah,' Peter was crouched in front of the TV but looked up at me like an eager puppy. 'This is big news, Eve!'

Photographs of Isabel came up on the screen and the anchor in the studio was saying something about her disappearance.

'Shit.' I let out a heavy breath and dropped onto the sofa, my elbows on my knees, riveted to the coverage.

'Obviously, we're all waiting anxiously for that official report,' said the correspondent at the police headquarters. 'But Steve Wright, who broke the story, suggested when we spoke to him that this was connected to a series of other deaths and disappearances recently in the city, and that the Police and Crime Commissioner has been implicated in the death of Ms Shaw. Local journalist, Michelle West, was working on the story when she suddenly died under mysterious circumstances. Mr Wright is calling for her death to be re-examined. Given that the role of the PCC is to hold the police accountable to the public, this does look very bleak indeed for Marco De Luca, the commissioner here in Oris, who is standing for re-election this May.'

My hand had drifted up to cover my gaping lips.

'This has to have hurt the demon,' Peter said, grinning broadly.

'Yeah,' I said absently, still transfixed by the news.

'I had to make sure you knew what was happening, but I have to get back to the pack.' Peter stood up straight and put a hand on my shoulder.

Pain shot through me at his touch and I flinched away from him. Ice filled my veins and a rage that didn't belong to me pounded inside my skull. 'What's wrong?' Peter asked, concern knitting his brows together.

'Nothing, sorry.' I ran my hands through my hair and got to my feet. 'I'm still tired and was a million miles away then. You shocked me, that's all. I'm all right.'

'You sure?' He was still frowning, not entirely believing me.

'Yeah. I'm good. I need to eat and I'll be right as rain.'

'Okay. Call me if you need anything.' He set off for the door and I followed him.

'I will. Thanks for letting me know.' I saw him out of the door but he hung there on the step looking at me with concern. 'Go do what you need to do. Call me if you need me to help. Okay?'

'Sure. I hope eating sorts you out.' He gave me one of those meaningful looks that told me he knew there were things that couldn't be said, or possibly even thought, in my case. I gave him a reassuring nod and watched him head up the street. I shut the door and sank down to the floor, leaning back against the warm wood.

'What did you do?' the demon hissed inside my head on my shaking out breath.

'What I had to. You have to be stopped!'

'I've been patient, Eve. I've tried to help you. I still could. Let me take your curse away and you can go to Caerton to be with that nice shifter boy.'

'Get out!' I screamed. I slammed my head back against the door and pain shot through my skull. I cried out and clutched the back of my head.

'That won't do anything.'

'Get out of my head! Get out!' I leapt up and ran to the kitchen. I scrambled around for a big knife and found one in the utensil drawer. I grasped it in both hands and looked feverishly around the room. What was I going to do? I wasn't going to hurt myself. The demon wanted me out of the way, so it would only play into its hands. But more than that, I wanted my life.

'Put it down,' my own rasping, wretched voice said. 'We both know you won't use it.'

'Is that right? How do you know I won't slit my own

throat to shut you up?'

'Because you don't want to die. Put the knife down, Eve.'

My fingers opened and the knife clattered to the floor and skidded away from me. I hadn't done that. I gazed down at the gleaming blade. I began to shake. I bolted for the basement door, flicked the light on and thundered down the stairs. I found the ring-shaped handle of the trapdoor. I pulled it open and let the door drop to the floor on the other side of the hole in the ground. I stepped carefully down onto the uneven steps into the catacombs.

The demon had gone quiet and I was pretty sure it wasn't controlling me. I looked around the cave at my parents' old stockpile, lit from the bare bulb hanging above the hole. There were still a few weapons leaning against crates and my eyes settled on a wooden stick chiseled to a point. I picked it up. It was about two feet long and the tip was perfectly sharp. Without another thought, I set off down the passage that led down to the big cave deep under the city, and broke into a run.

The darkness swallowed me and I realised that I didn't have my phone, but I was sure of my footing after months of using the passage. The air grew warmer and a faint breeze reached me as I neared the opening. I burst out into the huge cavern and bolted straight across it. It was dark and empty but the torches burst to life for me. The flickering light filled the cave with a warm glow and I headed straight for the narrow opening. I ran as fast as I could for as long as I could. I didn't know how long I had until the demon figured out what I was doing. It probably already knew.

My legs began to tire and my chest ached with the effort of breathing in the confined space. For once I wasn't thinking about Lucia or what happened that night. I was completely focused on the task at hand. I couldn't let this go on another minute longer. I had to free myself before the demon used me to do something terrible. I had to slow to a walk eventually but I kept on going. The walls of the tunnel felt too close and my breathing quickened. I pushed the panic deep down and pressed on through the darkness.

The passage began to slope up towards the tight spiral steps into the basement of Antonio's mansion. I reached the door and took a few steadying breaths. This was it. This was where the last few months had been inevitably leading. I awkwardly held the pike in one hand and grasped the handle with my other. I turned it, but the door was locked. Antonio had repaired it from when we broke in.

'Fuck,' I muttered. Of course he wouldn't have left it open to intruders. What had I really expected? I no longer had Peter's skeleton key. I placed my palm against the door and focused my mental energy on the lock. I hadn't tried to do anything this refined before and I didn't know if I could, but it was all I could do other than turning around and going home, or blasting the door open with a force that would alert anyone in the mansion. Neither of those were viable options. I closed my eyes and imagined the lock turning. I reached out with my mind and pictured it happening.

There was a soft click and my eyes popped open. I felt for the handle again and turned it. The door gave an inch; it was unlocked. I held back a celebratory cry and pushed, but the door was stuck just slightly ajar. A small groan escaped my lips and I slipped my fingers into the crack and ran them down the edge of the door. They connected with the top of something wooden. It had been partially blocked. I frowned. It seemed a half measure, considering that Antonio knew that the only people or things that might come through this door had supernatural strength.

I pushed out with my mind and whatever was blocking the door scraped away across the floor. I shoved open the door and cocked my head to listen for signs of movement above. There were none. I walked silently over to the stairs and adjusted my grip on the stake. I placed my other hand on the wooden banister and made my way softly up the wooden staircase, careful not to make it creak. Light shone under the door into the hall and I stopped right against it, listening intently.

Footsteps approached the door and I held my breath. They passed by it, along with a shadow in the shaft of light coming under the door. From the heaviness and slow speed of the footfalls, I guessed that it was Frederick. I didn't want him to get hurt. I waited, still holding my breath until I was sure he was gone. I gingerly turned the door handle and slowly opened the door. I peered out through the gap and craned my neck to look around the partially open door. Frederick's back was disappearing into the parlour at the back of the building. I didn't know where Antonio would be but hoped he was alone.

I stepped softly out into the hall and closed the door, careful not to let it click. I looked both ways and listened carefully. I reached out with my mind and tried to sense who was in the house and where. My mind touched Antonio's. It was still and empty—he was sleeping. The grand entrance hall was bathed in sunlight and I moved swiftly towards it. I ran quickly up the carpeted stairs, my feet barely making a sound. I reached the landing and moved slowly, cautiously towards Antonio's bedroom door. I stopped and reached out with my mind again. Frederick was humming to himself downstairs, his thoughts calm and mundane. Nicholas was nearby too, but not in the house. He was leaning over a car engine, tinkering. There was someone else. Dark thoughts racing in a jumble, like a nightmare. Voiceless but horrifying, needing to scream and being unable to do so. Dante. I quickly slipped out of his thoughts. I couldn't tell where in the mansion he was. I had never been into the other wing of the upstairs, the rooms above the ballroom. That had been Lucia's domain when she'd lived here. Perhaps Dante had a room down there. I couldn't be sure. I glanced over my shoulder at the empty corridor behind me. This was my best chance, but was it utter stupidity to have come here alone?

The demon, if it was still inside me, was quiet. I wished I could tell whether it was in there or not, watching my every move, monitoring my every thought. If it knew what I was doing, surely it would try to stop me? Either by manipulating my behaviour directly, or by leaping into someone more controllable to get in my way. I shook off my hesitation and crossed the corridor to Antonio's bedroom door. I put my hand on the handle; the metal was cool against my palm. I turned it as slowly and silently as I could. It gave the tiniest creak. It might have been enough to wake him, so I stopped, my breath held tight, and I waited. Nothing but silence. I turned the handle further and the door gave. I pushed it open and carefully peered into the darkened room. The blackout blinds were closed and the drapes drawn across the windows as well. It was almost pitch-black. I hadn't considered that. I stepped inside and softly closed the door behind me, wary of the light waking Antonio. I could just make out a sleeping form under the silk sheets. He slept silently, no trace of a snore due to his lack of breath. There was no gentle rise and fall of his chest to clue me in to how deep of a sleep he was in.

My feet were silent on the thick carpet as I walked slowly towards the bed. The pike in my hand was smooth and warm. The sweat on my palm made my hand slip slightly as I adjusted my grip on the wood. I couldn't get this wrong, it was my one chance. I was standing at the foot of the bed looking down at him. His black hair was loose and spread out over his bare back and the pillow beneath his face. He was lying on his front, his head turned towards the closed dressing room door.

Slowly, I moved around to the side of the bed and took a long, deep breath. I turned the stake over in my hands, grasping it in both and raising it, point down, over his torso. A painful lump rose in my throat. My breath caught and a tiny sob escaped my trembling lips. A tear filled my left eye. I didn't want this. I wished there was another solution, but I was fresh out of ideas and so was everyone else. The demon had to be stopped and this was how we could do it. I took a sharp breath in and held it. I blinked away the tear and raised the stake again, gripping it so tightly my hands ached.

I glanced from his back to his face for one last look at the man I loved so deeply. His dark eyes were open and fixed on me.

CHAPTER THIRTY-FIVE

I LEAPT BACKWARDS and dropped the stake with a soft thud.

'Eve?' He sat up and tossed his hair over his shoulder, exposing his smooth, caramel-coloured chest. He flicked on the lamp on his bedside table and its warm light filled the room. 'What's going on?'

I'd lost my chance. The tear that I blinked away had fallen and my cheek was wet. My whole face shook and I crumpled to the floor and covered it with my hands. Antonio leapt from the bed and wrapped his arms around me. 'Hey, *cerbiatta*, talk to me. What's happened?'

I couldn't speak. All I could do was shake and cry. Finally I gasped for air and pulled free of his embrace. Our eyes met and there was such softness and concern in his that I knew the demon couldn't be behind them.

'I'm sorry, I came here to kill you.'

'I guessed.' He glanced over to the discarded wooden stake on the floor. 'I know we've been fighting, but has it really come to that?'

'The demon is inside you, Antonio. It's controlling you

and has been for a long time, maybe even years. It feeds off the corruption you create; it feeds off you. That's why it tried to kill me, because you were going soft since you met me.'

'Eve, no, I promise you—'

'I'm right!' I shouted. 'Please stop trying to convince me I'm mistaken. Trust me. I know what's going on. I've had visions, I've read minds, I've had the demon inside my head confirming it! I am right. You are infected with it and can't see it. It's tethered to you, though. You're the reason it can stay in this realm. For the shifters to banish it, you have to die.' My tears had dried up. My voice had levelled off leaving only a rasp.

He blinked at me, his mouth hanging slightly open. I wished he would breathe or show some sign of life that I understood. I hated that our relationship had come to this. Part of me regretted ever meeting him. It was impossible not to love him, but it was the most painful thing I had ever endured.

'I believe you. I didn't want it to be true for so long, but I've known in my heart for a while that you were right.' Relief washed over me and my shoulders sagged. I didn't have to fight with him any more. 'What do the shifters want?'

'They want to banish it from this world,' I whispered, checking his eyes for clarity.

'Do they want me dead?'

'I expect some of them do, yes, because of your history, but no one has said that to me.'

He took hold of my hands and laid several small kisses on them. He cupped my chin in his hand and looked deep into my eyes.

'Eve, what do you want?'

'I just want a way out of this mess. I want the demon out of you and out of Oris.'

'Anything else?' I gazed into his eyes and saw them growing darker. For a split second I thought I was going to break down in renewed tears, but a steel resolve settled into my chest instead. I placed my hands on his bare chest and leaned in for a kiss. Antonio welcomed it and tried to deepen the kiss, but I pulled back, shaking my head. I looked back into his eyes and saw the demon looking back at me. It had to know that I had recognised it. I had only seconds to act. There was no choice.

'I want my freedom. I want a normal life. I want to have a family and grow old with someone who I love and who loves me.' I smiled with regret and sadness. Antonio nodded solemnly.

'I want that for you too, my love.' The demon grinned at me. If it had a chance to make me another offer, I might not have the resolve to turn it down. Antonio closed his eyes and when he opened them again they were shining with unshed tears. I didn't even think he could cry. 'Eve...' When he spoke again his voice was strained, fighting against resistance. Could he be fighting the demon for control? One of his hands moved towards my forehead but he held it back. His teeth were clenched tight in a pained grimace as he wrestled with himself. 'Do it. Please. Before it makes me hurt you. Free us both.'

His whole face stiffened and his neck tensed, a tendon bulging as he strained against the demon's efforts to control him. I pushed away from him, reached for the stake and spun back to face him. With one last glance into his eyes, I flung up a hand and swiped hard so that the curtains and blackout blinds were ripped from the window beside the bed. He began to smoke instantly as the dazzling sunlight fell upon his bare back. He reflexively writhed against the burning, his face contorted, and a cry rose in his throat. With a terrible ache in my chest, I plunged the stake hard into the centre of his chest with a deafening cry. Shock appeared on his face for a split second before his whole body began to turn grey. I scrambled away from him across the floor, staring in horror as he rapidly aged right in front of my eyes, like some sick time-lapse video of a body decaying. His flesh receded away from the bones and he crumpled to the floor before turning into dust and vanishing.

I sat, frozen, staring at the lingering specks of dust swirling in the shaft of sunlight. My fingers rose to my mouth; my breath was hot on them. My shoulders shook and I closed my eyes. Pain and regret surged through me, but before I could break down completely the room grew suddenly darker, as if the blind had been restored to the window and the lamp extinguished. Thick, dark smoke filled the room and I dragged myself across the floor towards the door, my heart pounding so high up in my throat that I felt sure I was about to be sick. I leapt to my feet, yanked the door open and rushed out onto the landing, slamming the door behind me. I held it closed, panting. I fished in my pocket for my talisman but it wasn't there. I closed my eyes and held back a scream. I'd dropped it in the catacombs and not picked it up.

'Miss Eve?' Frederick's voice called from the end of the hall where Antonio's sunlight-proof staircase was. My gaze darted to him, and a sinking sensation pulled my stomach down several inches. 'Is everything all right?' He walked calmly towards me. 'I didn't know you were here.'

'I—' I looked at the door and grudgingly released the handle. I glanced down at the floor and the shadow creeping out from under it. I backed away quickly and flattened myself against the opposite wall, pointing at the tendrils of black oozing out from under the door. A flicker of alarm crossed Frederick's face.

'Is Mr Vitale in there?'

I shook my head.

'No. We have to get out of here, now. Is Dante here?' I ran over to him and grabbed him by his bony shoulders.

'Yes, I believe so, and Mr Laguardia. But it's broad

daylight. Where is Mr Vitale?'

'He's gone. Lost.' My voice was barely audible. There would be time for the full truth later. 'The demon had him. It's loose now. We have to get out and let the shifters do what they do. The demon might be looking for a new host, someone else to tether to. It can't be either of us. Come on.' I took his arm and pulled him towards the grand staircase.

'I don't understand,' Frederick said, scurrying along with me. I suddenly realised it was possible that he somehow lived in complete ignorance of the supernatural, but he had just expressed concern over the sunlight, so I had to believe that he at least knew what Antonio and Dante were. There was no time to explain anything. I hurried around the landing to the other wing of the house.

'Dante!' I called. I banged on the first door and ran to the next, banging on that one too. 'Dante! We need you!'

'It's this one,' Frederick said. Shaking slightly, he pointed to the second door on the other side of the corridor.

'Dante?!' I called, banging hard on the door with the edge of my fist. The door flew open and the tall, black vampire stared down at me with a deep frown on his brow. He was wearing silk pyjama trousers and nothing else.

'What's happening?' he signed, his hands flicking through the gestures almost too fast for me to follow.

'Antonio's gone. The demon is loose,' I replied.

'Gone?' Dante signed.

'The final death. Dust.' I glanced at Frederick. His face had gone completely grey and his sharp eyes fixed onto mine. Movement behind him caught my attention and I looked past him to see the thick, dark smoke flowing into the corridor and moving towards us. Dante disappeared in a flash back into his pitch-black room. He reappeared a moment later tugging a shirt over his head, a pair of boots in his hand. He scooped me up and I let out a squeal. He raced with me over his shoulder down the corridor away from the sunlit foyer. Laguardia burst from another room on the corridor. He looked from me over Dante's shoulder, to the black smoke billowing through the house, and bolted past us to the end of the hall. Dante ran at lightning speed after him, down a narrow staircase just like the one at the other end of the house. My feet touched the floor at the foot of the stairs, where Dante placed me. He disappeared back up them and reappeared with Frederick, who he placed carefully beside me and patted on the shoulder. The old man nodded shakily and caught my eye. We both knew we would need to have a serious conversation later.

Dante took my hand and set off at a run along the narrow passage that ran behind the kitchen, with Frederick and Laguardia hurrying in our wake. We turned the corner at the end of the corridor, and Dante darted for the door to the basement and rushed through it. We filed swiftly down the stairs into the dark and I bumped right into Dante at the foot of them where he had come to a halt.

His head was cocked on one side. He turned slowly to look at me. I had left the basement with the door to the catacombs ajar and the crate that had been covering it shoved to one side.

'I came in this way,' I whispered, trying to keep guilt out of my voice. Dante merely nodded and took my hand again to lead me into the tunnel. I glanced over my shoulder, unsure if Frederick would follow. 'What about Nicholas?' I asked, pulling Dante to a halt. 'He's up there, isn't he?'

'He was in the garage,' Frederick said.

'We can't just leave him.'

'If the shifters deal with the demon, then he won't be in any danger. Will he?' Frederick asked, acidly.

'I suppose.'

Dante tugged my arm and we filed into the tunnel. Frederick pulled the door closed behind us. I could barely see and Frederick had to be struggling as much, if not more, but I scurried after Dante, his hand still clutching mine. Laguardia brought up the rear, muttering to himself. Our feet pounded against the stone and my knuckles occasionally grazed the rough wall as I ran. Finally we burst out into the big cavern and Dante skidded to a halt. Flames lit the space from the torches on the walls. Peter and his pack stood frozen in front of us, every eye on our odd party. I pulled free of Dante's grip and ran into Peter's arms.

'What happened?'

'Antonio's dead. The demon's—' Before I could finish the sentence there was a low rumbling and thick, black smoke billowed out into the cavern from the passage we had run down. It rushed out and filled the space, engulfing Dante, Laguardia, and Frederick. 'No!' I lurched forward, but Peter held me back.

'Open the veil.' Kirk barked the order over his shoulder at Crystal as he strode forward to meet the demon. 'Spectre-of-Maleficence, you are not welcome in this realm! We demand you withdraw!' Kirk's usually calm demeanour was entirely absent. His eyes blazed and his nostrils flared. He squared up to the demon, puffing out his chest. Peter released me and looked earnestly into my eyes.

'Are you all right?' All I could do was nod. 'Can you help Crystal?' I nodded again and hurried over to where she was quickly pulling ritual tools from her little bag. Peter moved over to his father, and Strikes Twice joined them.

The demon rippled like the surface of a vast, black lake, and Dante burst out from the heart of it, Frederick in his strong arms and Laguardia just behind him. He ran towards the shifters in a blur and gently deposited the elderly man at the shifters' feet. Kirk stooped to check him over, but I couldn't make out what his conclusion was.

'Here,' Crystal said, snapping my attention back to her

as she thrust a large piece of clear quartz into my hand. She stepped back and held up her knife, drawing a large circle in the air with it. Blue light burst from the tip of the knife and left a trail behind it so that a bright, sparkling circle hung in the air between us and the others. 'Lift it!' She snapped her fingers at me and I quickly hoisted the quartz over my head. The light reflected in it and the centre of the circle lit up. Beyond it the demon was swirling and writhing, swelling in size and creeping closer to the others.

'How are they going to fight this?' I asked, looking desperately at the shifters, who stood gazing up at the vast demon. It was like something in-between liquid and gas, and it kept on expanding so that it brushed the ceiling of the huge cave and blacked out the lights of several of the torches.

'They aren't,' Crystal said, her voice straining with the effort of opening the hole in the veil. 'You are!'

My head whipped around to face her, my eyes wide. 'What?'

'You have to. It's been controlling you too, Eve. You have to fight it to get it all out of you.'

I was about to ask how I was supposed to do that when a surge of rage flooded up through my veins and I felt the demon's presence inside me. An icy darkness seeped into my skin. I looked up to see a fine tendril of shadow coming down from the demon above me like a string tied to the head of a marionette. The muscles of my arms tensed and my grip on the piece of quartz tightened. *Crush it!* screamed a voice in my head, but I was used to hearing voices that didn't belong to me. I pushed back against it, resisting the compulsion to keep squeezing the crystal, and held it lightly in my hands instead.

'We cast you out!' Kirk cried above the rushing sound of the demon as it continued to grow and fill the cavern. Its inky blackness reached the other shifters and began to swallow them. Poor Frederick still lay in a heap at Dante's feet. The vampire braced himself, tensing his shoulders against the smoke as it billowed around him. Laguardia, the coward, had done a runner.

'Return to your own realm!' yelled Peter.

'The veil parts for you,' Strikes Twice added. He was mostly invisible but his hand thrust out towards me and the shimmering blue circle in the air between us. I visualised the demon being sucked into the hole in reality, starting with the thin tendril that was attached to me. I mentally plucked it from the top of my head and funnelled it into the portal. The icy sensation in my veins turned suddenly white hot and I winced, doubling over.

A massive roar ripped through the torch-lit cavern and the demon shimmered. Darts of red light shot through the mass. I forced myself upright, despite the burning in my veins, and resumed forcing the demon into the hole. The quartz in my hands glowed white and grew hot against my skin. I looked up at it and focused my energy on the light. I drew it out and a great beam erupted from it, shining on the demon above and in front of me. Spectre-of-Maleficence screamed and writhed away from the light. I closed my eyes and imagined the light expanding like a glorious sunrise. When I opened my eyes the light burst out and shone in bright rays all around the cavern. It was a light the demon couldn't swallow.

'I see you! You can't hide from this light, demon!' My voice rang out clear and bright, echoing off the cavern walls beyond the demon. Flickers of torchlight peeked through small gaps in the mass of swirling smoke. The shifters, Dante, and Frederick emerged from the darkness as it receded. I looked up again and the tendrils were syphoning off the large mass and flowing into the gap in the veil, disappearing in the centre of the circle.

Crystal approached me and placed a hand on my shoulder. She grinned at me and nodded encouragingly. Energy flowed from her hand into my shoulder and through my aching muscles. I nodded in thanks and returned my attention to the demon. There was so much of it; its influence reached far out of the cave, but slowly it began to shrink as more and more of it was dragged across the veil. The shifters gathered around me, leaving Dante to attend to Frederick, who still seemed to be unconscious.

'You've got this, Eve,' Peter said, placing his hand on my other shoulder. I drew strength from all of them gathered there, even though my arms and legs were shaking with the effort. Flashes of memories passed through my mind. Some of them belonged to Peter and Crystal, but other fragments came from De Luca, Isabel, Antonio and god knows who else. Hot tears flowed down my cheeks. My whole body ached and shook. I couldn't hold it much longer.

Stop now, Eve, that voice inside my head said, soft and calm. *Release me now and I'll give you everything you ever wanted. I'll take your curse away and you can go and be with Blade and live in peace.*

I wanted to say yes with every fibre of my being. A great cry bubbled up in my chest and burst out of my mouth. Peter and Crystal's hands tightened on my shoulders and Peter pressed himself right against me, propping me up.

'Keep going, Eve, nearly there,' he said softly in my ear, his face almost touching mine.

I can give you the perfect life, Eve. If you spare mine.

I hung there on the cusp of accepting the demon's offer. My veins were throbbing with white heat. The cavern was almost back to normal, with just the last wisps of the demon's smokey body remaining. It was desperate. It was nearly done.

'NO!' I roared. I pushed myself away from Peter's support and stood strong on my own two feet. I dragged the last of the demon out of the air and out of myself, funnelling it into the light from the quartz. A piercing shriek filled the air and the flames of the torches flickered ominously. My body ran cold again and the taste of ash filled my mouth. I coughed and a wisp of black smoke puffed out of my mouth. It hung in the air in front of me for a moment and then whipped up as if caught on an eddy. It whooshed up into the beam of light from the crystal and vanished through the hole in the veil.

Crystal promptly took the quartz from my hand and dropped it to the ground. She stomped on it with one heavy-booted foot and it smashed to dust. The circle zipped closed and the blue light flickered out. I collapsed and Peter caught me.

'You okay?' he asked softly. I nodded meekly. 'Did it try to tempt you again?'

'Yeah, but I told it where to go.'

'Straight to hell?'

'That's the one.' I smiled weakly and Peter chuckled gruffly.

I peered past him in the gloom through bleary eyes and saw Kirk and Strikes Twice grinning down at me.

'We did it,' I said, still smiling that sleepy, lopsided smile.

'You did it. We can't thank you enough, Eve,' Kirk replied.

Strikes Twice added something, but I couldn't hear him. A rushing sound in my ears like a wave racing up a beach swallowed everything. My eyes flickered closed and I was plunged into darkness.

374

CHAPTER THIRTY-SIX

I WAS LYING IN ANTONIO'S BED beneath his black, silk sheets, bathed in moonlight. His smooth chest gleamed silver and his glossy hair hung down from his smiling face. I hummed appreciatively at this sight to greet me on waking. He leaned down and pressed his cool lips to mine. My fingers entwined with his hair and I pressed my body against his. This was perfection. All of our arguments were forgotten; there was brightness and depth in his eyes, rather than cold darkness. We were in love and nothing could interfere with that.

I peeled back from the intoxicating kiss and blinked up at him. The light was a touch too bright. There was a fuzziness to things. I could hear music playing in the distance. It was his piano in the ballroom, the same piece of music he had been playing the first time I visited his mansion. But it couldn't be him playing if he was in bed with me. A frown inched its way onto my brow. I gently ran my fingertips over his face, and his skin was warm. Breath left his lips.

'This isn't real,' I murmured. 'You died.'

'I'm right here,' he said. His voice sounded as though it was on the other side of a thick door.

'No,' I said, rolling away from him. 'You're not.'

I opened my eyes for real, though I could hardly tell as it was so dark. The bed beneath me was firm and familiar. It was my own. I rolled onto my side and reached for the bedside lamp. Light filled the room and I blinked against it. Voices murmured up from downstairs and I caught the words, 'I think she's awake.' Damn those shifters and their super-hearing.

I swung my feet to the floor and looked down at my pale skin against the dark carpet. I was dressed but for my bare feet. Someone had thoughtfully removed my boots before putting me into bed. Probably Peter. I got wearily to my feet and made my way slowly downstairs, the voices growing louder with each step.

There was a light on in the kitchen and I gingerly opened the door to find Peter, Kirk, and Crystal sitting around my kitchen table.

'How long was I out?' There was a painful rasp to my throat and before I could finish asking, Peter was passing me a mug of tea. 'Thanks.'

'A few hours. How do you feel?'

'Like the dead.'

'That's understandable. You channelled a lot of energy,' Crystal said, smiling reassuringly. 'It's bound to take it out of you.'

'Not to mention having the demon right inside you,' Kirk said. He wasn't smiling. I swallowed an uncomfortable gulp of tea and made my way into a chair opposite him and next to Peter.

'I knew about that, Dad.'

'I wish I'd been told. Never mind. It's done and it's gone now.'

'Are you sure? We got all of it, right?' I asked, searching their faces.

'As far as we can tell, yes. It certainly seemed that way down there in the cavern,' Crystal said, nodding enthusiastically. 'You did amazingly well, Eve. Thank you. Again.'

'It was the least I could do.' I was bracing myself. One of them had to ask about Antonio soon. 'Was Frederick all right?'

'Yes, Dante took him home.' Kirk nodded and rubbed his palms over his stubbly jaw.

'What'll happen to the mansion now?' I asked in an attempt to confront the inevitable.

'It'll depend on what Vitale had in place,' Kirk replied. Our eyes met. His were watery and pink. There were dark circles under them. It looked as though he hadn't slept in days.

'Right. Don't you know that?' I asked. Kirk had been doing Antonio's books for years.

'I only dealt with the money, Eve. I don't know if he had a will or anything like that. I'm not really sure what the legal implications are for a man who should have died centuries ago. I'm sorry. I suspect Dante will keep living there and take on ownership. Unless you want to make a claim for it.' He arched an eyebrow at me. I spluttered my tea.

'God, no! I'm not interested in anything like that.'

'What happened, Eve?' Peter asked, his gaze fixed on the table.

'The demon tried to control me again and I decided I had to act right away in case it succeeded. So I went there to kill Antonio. And I did it.' I couldn't meet anyone's eye. My cheeks trembled and I held back the tears. 'The demon got mad and we ran. That's it.'

'That couldn't have been easy,' Kirk said solemnly.

'No,' I replied, still not looking at him. 'He realised the truth at the end, though, and asked me to go through with it. He knew what had to be done.' I finally looked up at Kirk. He was looking at me and nodding with a regretful half smile on his lips.

Over the next few days we found out that De Luca had been arrested for Isabel's murder and implicated in Michelle's death too. I knew Antonio was better at hiding bodies than that, and a little part of me hoped he had been deliberately careless so De Luca would get his comeuppance in the end. Maybe he had some idea of how things were going to pan out.

Dante didn't stay at the mansion. He and Laguardia disappeared. I never got to thank him. Frederick came to see me and we had a frank conversation about Antonio's final death.

'I am sorry, Frederick,' I said, not able to meet his gaze. We sat with tea in front of us, but neither of us drank. 'I wish there had been another way.'

'It is what it is,' he said, bristling with resentment. 'There is the matter of his estate.' He slid an envelope across the kitchen table towards me.

'What's this?'

'It was Mr Vitale's wish that you have the mansion, the cars, the money. Everything. Aside from generous settlements for myself and Nicholas. He set everything up for you at Christmas and hadn't changed anything, despite your relationship ending.'

'I can't take it.' I slid the envelope, unopened, back to him. He got to his feet without picking it up.

'Do what you want with it. It's yours now, whether you want it or not.'

I wish I could say that we parted cordially, but he was angry with me and we went our separate ways without resolving those feelings. I regretted that. He was a loyal servant and he deserved better, but there wasn't much I could do about it after the fact. The envelope contained a will, the deeds to the house, and everything I needed to take on his wealth. I ignored it for days, unable to face it. Finally, I gave it all to Kirk.

'Have the house. You and Peter deserve to live somewhere beautiful and free of the memories of Lucia's attack on your family. The shifters can use it if you like. You can all live there together.'

'Eve, this isn't right.'

'I'm leaving Oris. I don't need a great big mansion. Do something worthwhile with the money. I don't want it.'

'Are you sure?' His kind eyes crinkled and tears formed there.

'I am.'

'Thank you.' He drew me into his arms and filled me with his calm warmth.

Even though I wasn't going to resume my degree until September, I got everything ready to head back to Caerton sooner. I couldn't stand the ghosts everywhere in Oris. Every day that I stayed felt a little bit heavier. I packed up more of my things and made arrangements with Kirk to rent out my house once I left.

Peter drove me to the station in silence and helped me with my bags to the ticket barrier.

'I'll see you in a few days when I bring the rest of your stuff down in the van,' he said with too much cheer in his voice.

'Yeah, I suppose you will.'

'Weaver's meeting you at the other end, right?'

'She is.'

'Text me anyway, won't you?'

'Every day if you like. At least at first.'

'Deal.' He pulled me into a hug and squeezed me tight. I tried to smile but it was too painful. I was going to miss him so much, but I had to go and live my life. I pulled away from him and picked up all of my things. I didn't want to say the words and neither did he.

'See you soon.' I backed away from him until I got to the barrier. I turned and made my way through it without looking back.

I took my seat on the train and unlocked my phone. I typed the message and hit send with a small smile.

"Good news, Blade, I'm coming home today."

It was time for a new chapter to begin.

PLEASE LEAVE A REVIEW

I hope you enjoyed *The Power of Blood*. I would really appreciate it if you could take a few minutes now to review the book on your favourite retailer.

Independent authors rely heavily on reader reviews, they really are like oxygen. Reviews help other readers decide whether a book is a good fit for them or not. Much as I want everyone to love my books, I also know that it's important to find the right readers, so just a few words from you could help me to do that and reach other readers who will enjoy my dark and twisted tales!

Thank you!

Join My Tribe

If you enjoyed this book and would like to check out more of my world, you can get short story collection *Little Lies the Dead Tell* for free when you subscribe to my reader Tribe. I'll also email you regularly with news and offers.

Get your copy here: https://BookHip.com/NCMACX

ABOUT THE AUTHOR

H.B. Lyne is an urban fantasy author, podcaster and bullet journal enthusiast with a knack for organisation and getting stuff done.

She lives in Yorkshire with her husbeast, two children and midwife cat. When not juggling family commitments, she writes dark urban fantasy novels, purging her imagination of its demons. Inspired by the King of Horror himself, Holly aspires to be at least half as prolific and successful and promises to limit herself to only one tome of The Stand-like proportions in her career.

For More Information

hblyne.com

Follow me on Instagram: @hblyne

And on Facebook: facebook.com/authorhblyne

ALSO BY H.B. LYNE

In the Shifters of Caerton series:

Fate of the Blue Moon

Ghosts of Winter

Demons of the Past

Rise of the Furies

Dark Echoes: Tales from the Shadows

From Ashes to Echoes

In the Jones & Maxwell Casefiles series:

The Hidden City

www.ingramcontent.com/pod-product-compliance
Lightning Source LLC
Chambersburg PA
CBHW031000190726
48285CB00004BB/1396